The Miles

The Miles

Robert Lennon

KENSINGTON BOOKS
www.kensingtonbooks.com

KENSINGTON BOOKS are published by

Kensington Publishing Corp.
119 West 40th Street
New York, NY 10018

All Kensington titles, imprints, and distributed lines are available at
special quantity discounts for bulk purchases for sales promotion, pre-
miums, fund-raising, educational, or institutional use.

Special book excerpts or customized printings can also be created to fit
specific needs. For details, write or phone the office of the Kensington
Special Sales Manager: Attn. Special Sales Department. Kensington
Publishing Corp., 119 West 40th Street, New York, NY 10018. Phone:
1-800-221-2647.

Kensington and the K logo Reg. U.S. Pat. & TM Off.

ISBN-13: 978-0-7582-7173-0
ISBN-10: 0-7582-7173-5

First Kensington Trade Paperback Printing: June 2012
10 9 8 7 6 5 4 3 2 1

Printed in the United States of America

For my father, Daniel Lennon,
who taught me anything is possible.

Acknowledgments

Writing is too often a solitary process, but I have been very lucky at every stage of the journey to have great people in my life to make it less lonely. First and foremost, I have to thank my agent, Mitchell Waters, of Curtis Brown, and my editor, John Scognamiglio, at Kensington, for never leaving me in the dark or losing faith in me. Their endless patience and their honest insights helped make my prose much tighter and this book much more readable. My partner, Mark Gilrain, has made every single aspect of my life richer and has, more than anyone else, helped me find the time and the belief in myself to write and to focus on what matters most. I would also like to thank my father, to whom I dedicated this book, for encouraging me to play with letters and make words; as a child, I never knew what a powerful gift that would end up being. As a father now, I hope to share that secret, always, with my sons Ephraim and Dash. My mother and all five of my siblings have also provided a tremendous support system for me and have helped me define myself as a person and as a writer and have added a lot of (much needed) color to my life along the way.

Lastly, this book belongs to a very special running club—Front Runners New York—that found me at an unforgiving and vulnerable stage of life as a twenty-something and made me realize how much I could learn about myself and about others through running. In particular, Dennis Giza, Kelsey Louie, Jeff Werner, Michael Orzechowski, and Michael Benjamin helped form a narrative thread that was sometimes knotted or frayed but always rich, vibrant, and true. My thanks and gratitude always!

MILE 1

The morning could not make up its mind. The strong sun yielded, more and more, to the army of clouds taking hostage of the fall sky. Icy winds gusted around the fields of Van Cortlandt Park trumpeting the coming of winter, but then let up as the sun winked through the heavy sky. It was the middle of November, and the seasons were duking it out over New York City.

Like many of the runners, Liam waited by the baggage check, wearing his warm-up pants and gloves. He hopped up and down and ran in place to stay warm. The moment would come, and shortly, when the officials corralled everyone to the starting line, and Liam would need to strip his pants off and exchange the fleece pullover that warmed his upper body with his skimpy racing singlet. Having just joined the running club, he felt it was important to don the team uniform today.

The megaphone honked some indiscernible instruction and the throng of long-limbed runners jogged toward the far end of the narrow playing field. The grass already browned and much of the normally soft dirt had hardened with the recent cold fronts. Liam felt the uneven turf through the thin soles of his racing flats. No matter how many races he ran, stretching back to grammar school, Liam always savored and dreaded this starting-line moment. There, standing among a sea of determined athletes, he understood that the race was still a font of possibility, the result dormant in the fast-twitch fibers of everyone on the starting line. This beautiful and cruel fact of running connected Liam with all of the other gangly runners out on this 45-degree Sunday morning at just a shade past dawn.

A wizened man, who looked to be in his early seventies, whistled to command the runners' attention. The wind shot down from the hills just north of the field, lassoing the man's thin wisps of white hair into a makeshift Mohawk. Nervous laughter rustled through the crowd as the man furiously batted down the errant hairs. Bristling from the unwanted attention, he picked up the megaphone to hasten the start of the race. "On your mark!" the old man shouted. Liam canvassed the start one last time to get a sense of the competition. After doing just a smattering of local races, Liam already recognized a few familiar faces among the anxious masses. After deciding to get back into running following a long post-college hiatus due to burnout, Liam had participated in about a half dozen races solo before being approached to join the Fast Trackers. Apparently club leaders used their gaydar to scout for potential new members at the start and finish lines of local events. Having viewed running as a solitary endeavor for so much of his life, Liam looked forward to the camaraderie of being part of a gay running team. But right now, Liam enjoyed the eye candy offered by the super-fit runners from the other teams present at this race. One, a hollow-cheeked guy whose chocolate eyes and full red lips bestowed a vaguely French look upon his underfed face, had inched past him at the finish of the last 5K. Runners tend to remember moments like that and plot careful revenge. The gaunt man's eyes twinkled as he acknowledged Liam's stare. And the gun went off.

After jostling through the first hundred meters of the field, Liam began to feel comfortable and well positioned. He kept telling himself to control his breathing; the adrenaline could ruin a fine race with too fast a start. His high school coach, Daryl Humphries, an almost-member of the 1984 Olympic distance team who lived vicariously through whomever he was currently coaching, had always warned that a road race could not be won in the first mile, though it could easily be lost, "if you go out like a fool with something to prove."

As he rounded the turn toward the backstretch of the field, Liam caught sight of the three lead runners. They had already picked up a sizable lead after only five minutes of racing. There was something enviably effortless and offensively unobtainable in the way their lithe bodies moved. The pale November light emphasized the architectural beauty of their sinewy arms and legs. The thin straps of their singlets moved up and down on the knobs of their shoulders where the collarbone protruded. Liam tried to control his breathing and focused on his gait as those more naturally fleet of foot charged up the hills and into the woods, where the race course truly began.

Autumn had come late this year, and mounds of recently fallen leaves coated the middle section of the running trail. Knowing how uneven and rocky this winding path was, Liam looked for the open spaces between the leaves throughout the race. He played a game where he tried to find leafless patches large enough for his entire foot, and used that challenge to keep his mind off the pain that now funneled through his body. You weren't running your hardest if you didn't feel these slight twinges of pain. That was another one of Daryl's famous running credos. Liam's lungs were always fine while racing, but his stomach heaved whenever he ran at top speed for more than a mile. He knew that if he ignored the awful sensation, then nothing bad would happen to him. The body can withstand amazing stress.

The first set of rolling hills proved to be easier than Liam remembered. He had hit his stride and was neither being passed nor passing other runners. A good omen. The course took a sharp downhill and then hooked left before climbing into a monstrous uphill. Even though Liam had readied his body, the steep rise began to take its toll. He shortened his stride and focused on quickening the turnover of his feet to maintain his pace with slightly less effort. So much of running well was about physics and mechanics. Liam didn't realize that his breathing had become grossly audible until the Parisian runner strode up alongside him and asked if he was okay. Understanding this as a psych-out technique, Liam nodded and choked down his abbreviated breaths. He knew that if he just stayed in step with this runner through the crest of the hill, he would be completely fine. While not the greatest uphill runner, Liam had complete faith in his ability to tear down hills with unmatched speed. As they moved above the peak of the trail, Liam imagined all the tension in his spine uncoiling as he worked his arms and let gravity catapult him down the hill. He knew that he had to step confidently and allow the momentum he generated to glide him through the next series of rolling hills, which would deposit him near the finish line of this 5K loop.

As soon as he passed his newfound nemesis, Liam wondered how far back he was and found himself listening for his competitor's breathing and for the fall of his feet along the cross-country trail. Remembering a cardinal rule of running, Liam refused to look over his shoulder and instead concentrated on the runner ahead of him. The tall figure was just a smudge in Liam's field of vision, too far ahead right now to be passable. Liam moved his arms with more force and determination, so that his legs might not slow from the exhaustion.

Bearing right at the final fork of the cross-country course, Liam could see the bright yellow banner that hung above the finish line. He directed all his attention toward his legs and leaned into his stride. He reminded himself that pushing through the end of the race, speeding toward the finish despite exhaustion, is what separates the extraordinary runner from the average one. Anyone can run fast when they're fresh; it takes desire and determination to run fast when tired.

In a matter of seconds, Liam realized he was closing ground on the runner in front of him. Was he truly running faster or had this other runner slowed down? The orange star on the blue microfiber tank top soon became clear. This was a team member whose head now bobbled and whose arms flailed as he attempted to finish the race. A squadron of spectators screamed and hooted, and Liam could feel his legs lighten. It was possible. He could run at any speed now; he would accelerate and accelerate and accelerate. As he passed the Fast Tracker, Liam shouted, "Come on, man! Suck it up and count to ten. We're there!" And with that wake-up call, the sluggish guy was roused and attempted to match Liam stride for stride. Liam could not hold back, though he knew that finishing on the line together would be a pleasant gesture of camaraderie, a way for the new guy to show that he was a team player. And Liam *did* think of himself as a team player. But he had to be true to the instincts that overtook him during races. What was the point of training to the brink of exhaustion during workouts and then pushing your physical limits on race day to suddenly rein it all in? Liam flew through the finishing chute, practically crashing into the man recording the times and places of the racers.

"Good job!" Liam felt the sweaty touch and knew it was the Fast Tracker he'd just bested. As he lifted his head to offer congratulations, Liam saw the emaciated Frenchman cross the finishing line.

"That course kicked my ass!" It was the truth, but Liam felt embarrassed to have offered up the least original thing one runner had ever said to another.

"Yeah, right!" The sallow-faced man struggled to catch his breath. "Your ass seemed just fine to me." Now he brushed some sweat from his brow before extending his hand for an introduction. "I'm Gene . . . You must be new to the team."

"Excuse me! Excuse me! Could you take the small talk somewhere else? People need to walk through this chute to get out of here."

The Frenchman scissored by in a huff, but Liam couldn't help admiring the angles of his face and the self-important manner with which he moved.

"Maybe he's sore that I got the best of him out there." Liam chuckled.

"You'll get to know that one," Gene said. "Didier Vallois. He's a real peach. All the Urban Bobcats take themselves way too seriously. They're the fastest guys in town so they expect a parting of the seas worthy of Moses."

"At least he's cute."

"Best part of running is the scenery. I've been saying it for years."

Mischief darted through Gene's eyes. Liam had seen the act before. Gay men couldn't help but flirt, and nine times out of ten Liam reciprocated the advances. Dozens of clever lines sprang to his mind, but he resisted the temptation. This Gene person seemed perfectly nice but completely sexless, with a soft face and hairless arms and legs. Liam preferred men whose sexuality howled through their pores. Plus, for the time being, he wanted Fast Trackers to be an outlet for making new friends and running buddies, not an avenue for sexual liaisons or romantic dalliances. He had enough of that combing the bar scene in New York City since graduating college. Liam decided to take a cordial approach here; after all, it never hurt to be polite.

"You know I should probably be doing a quick cooldown around the field before heading back to the subway station. I need to get home soon."

Liam was exaggerating slightly, but he did have brunch plans in a couple of hours and showering beforehand would be nice.

"With this colder weather, I should be doing the same. How 'bout I keep you company?"

Liam sensed that Gene had an adhesive quality that was amiable for only the very briefest period of time. As they jogged around the perimeter of the field, Liam actively avoided engaging Gene in small talk by studying the steely tufts of sky. It now looked like a winter's day. Liam cherished the first days of winter, when the novelty of the new season offered some fresh perspective on life and the possibility of change. There was something noble and definitive about the start of winter.

Despite Liam's stony silence, Gene wore on about his own personal training regimen throughout the cooldown. Liam heard the words *ladder* and *interval* and *hill repeats* over and over again but zoned out on the details. The lack of encouragement did not dampen Gene's march through running tales—a trio of PRs (the abbreviation road racers loved to use to indicate their "personal records" or best times) at various distances parachuted into the story line as complete non sequiturs. Liam wondered what Gene's "personal record" for longest hiatus from talking about himself might be.

Rounding out their half-mile loop, Liam patted Gene on the shoulder to signal his good-bye. A group of runners in blue and orange who had been clustered near the finish line trotted toward Gene and Liam.

Making his way up the hill that led away from the cross-country course, Liam looked over his left shoulder to get a better impression of the group. Heads dangled and turned in conversation, then one pair of eyes caught Liam's and suddenly a few hands waved nervously.

Liam decided to jog toward the downtown train. The damp chill of the November morning had sunk its teeth into his bones, and he began to crave the lure of home, the press of a hot shower, and the worn comfort of his couch.

MILE 2

"It said the Daniel Webster Statue, Liam. Why do you insist on questioning me? I knew I shouldn't have let you drag me along with you. *Your* honor doesn't need any protecting, babe."

Whenever Monroe turned sassy like this, Liam would tease him by simply answering "Yes, Miss Marilyn" to whatever complaint he voiced. Today Liam resisted the temptation because Monroe was going above and beyond friendship's call of duty by agreeing to tag along on a 9:30 A.M. Saturday morning fun run.

"I believe you. But are you sure this is the right transverse? We've been up and down it twice and I don't see any statue. Maybe we should jog up to 102nd Street."

"Liam, which do you think is more likely? Really? On the one hand, you have Seventy-second Street, the center of residential life on the Upper East and Upper West Sides, and on the other, 102nd Street, which is simply too far uptown for a bunch of Chelsea queens."

To distance himself from the story lines that Monroe was spinning, Liam had begun to pick up his pace and was now practically out of earshot. The light, wet snowflakes that had drifted aimlessly through the park all morning finally found their destination. The bark of the bare trees that lined the park roads was becoming mottled with snow. Liam watched his feet press wide and flat against the newly dusted asphalt.

"Over there!" He finally heard Monroe's winded scream from behind him. Liam turned to see his friend clutching his side with his right arm and pointing due west with his left. "That group of queens in the tights and funny hats . . . those are for sure your boys."

"Good eyes! Sorry I doubted you for a second, *Norma Jean.*"

"It's still too early in the morning for me to be amused by your antics, so be careful."

They made their way into the semicircle that had formed on the edge of the large loop that cuts through the entire park—all the way from Fifty-ninth Street up to Harlem Hill at 110th Street. Liam had never noticed this particular intersection before and was still searching for the statue that had been designated as the meeting spot. As he met Monroe's gaze again, Liam caught sight of a rotund figure looming behind the pack of runners, enshrouded in the skeletal embrace of some old, leafless elms. Now he wondered, *Daniel Webster?* The statesman was large and bronze and imposing, just a few feet from the transverse. Why was Daniel Webster here watching over the pageantry of Central Park? The assemblage of monuments and tributes and honoraria throughout Manhattan had puzzled Liam ever since he was a little kid and his father pointed out the Garibaldi statue in the then grimy paths of Washington Square Park.

"Okay, okay, everyone! Let's get this party started." The voice boomed from a swizzle stick of a man with thick graying hair. "Everyone introduce yourself. Let us know if you're a first-timer or visitor from another city, and we'll hook you up with a buddy who runs your pace."

Liam could feel Monroe's eyes on him. After scanning the club's website, Liam assured his friend that things would be incredibly casual and that Monroe wouldn't even have to run with anyone if he didn't want to. This should not be the end of the world. Monroe had always talked about how he ran on the treadmill three times a week. Surely he would be able to keep up with some of the roly-poly guys gathered here.

"And you there! Yoo-hoo! I know you might have been out at Therapy until the wee hours, but wake up and tell us your name!"

"Sorry. I'm Liam. Sorry."

"You're too cute to apologize, hon. Now tell me, is this your first time?"

"Sort of . . . I have been racing here and there, but this is my first fun run with the group."

"Gary, this is the dude I was bragging about. Zoomed right past me at Van Cortlandt during the 5K Championships."

Without this pronouncement, Liam would have never pegged the pale face under the moss-colored hoodie as Gene's. After giving Gene an acknowledgment so cursory it bordered on rudeness, Liam looked over at Monroe. No words needed to be exchanged. That's what Liam loved about their friendship. Monroe just had a sense of things, a wisdom of situations.

"Well, Gene. You've had an opportunity to meet Liam. Let's have Marvin run with him this morning. Marvin can give him a nice fast run."

The wiry man leading the announcements pointed toward a red-haired man with a splash of freckles across his nose. His legs were short but their muscle-thick definition popped through the black tights he wore.

"Okay, last and I hope not least."

"It's Monroe."

"Love the name! Now what pace, hon?"

"Oh, I don't know. How fast is real damn slow?"

"Don't you worry, Monroe. We leave no runners behind here. Horace will run with you."

A lanky man in neon-blue warm-up pants and a violet Windbreaker waved over toward Monroe. Clutched in both hands, Horace had bronze weights that looked to be a few pounds each. His thick seventies mustache had yellowed with age or bad habits.

"God, do you owe me," Monroe muttered through clenched teeth. "Start saving your lunch money, bitch." He then dashed off without looking at Liam.

Marvin could not have been more different from Gene. During their run, he offered almost nothing in the way of small talk and answered Liam's questions in a manner suggesting that he wasn't looking to make a new best friend. Liam did learn that Marvin taught astronomy at a fancy Upper East Side school for boys and had raced seriously since competing as an All-American for his college cross-country team. As they finished their five-mile run, Marvin asked Liam if he planned on going back to the church for brunch. While Liam had read about the Saturday ritual online, he had not been sure what to make of the whole affair and told Monroe that they would play each step of the morning by ear. Despite his being quiet during their run, Marvin now enthusiastically insisted that Liam go to brunch. It was apparently what made the whole morning, the whole run in the park, worthwhile. And when Liam suggested waiting for Monroe to return with Horace, Marvin snickered and claimed that they would both freeze to death by the time those slowpokes got back.

"Everyone heads back to the church," Marvin repeated. "Horace hasn't skipped bagels since the Pointer Sisters started burning doing the Neutron Dance."

It all sounded logical enough. Surely Monroe would want some food after running out in the cold. Even as he supplied himself with this cast-iron logic, Liam could imagine his friend's pursed lips and could hear Monroe's curt reassurances that he had managed to fend for himself just fine despite being abandoned. There would be snide innuendo and passive-aggressive back-and-forth, but nothing that Liam had not encountered—and successfully handled—before. After six years of friendship, replete with dramatic fights, Liam had learned how to maneuver the minefield of Monroe's sensitivities but still often chose to live dangerously.

When Monroe rescued Liam from an aggressively drunk hanger-on at Starlight Club on Avenue A back in the early 2000s, Liam sensed it to be a more than auspicious start to their relationship. Not having had a lot of gay friends at Amherst College, Liam had to learn how gay friendships differed from straight ones. He chose to ignore the undercurrent of sexual tension at play in his encounters with Monroe and believe there was a tacit understanding that theirs was a platonic connection—nothing more, nothing less. It sometimes saddened Liam that gay men seemed to place a much lower premium on relationships of this ilk in favor of those centered around the ephemeral pleasures of the flesh. Over the years, Liam and Monroe had strengthened their bond, despite the entrance of petty jealousies here and there.

"Looks like we're the first runners back today. Bravo to us," Marvin said, patting Liam firmly on the shoulder. Liam puzzled over the wide chasm between mid-run Marvin and post-run Marvin.

There were about a dozen men assembled in the gym-like basement area of the church that they had just entered off of Broadway. The bright primary colors of the mats that lined the walls and part of the floor imbued the room with the childlike simplicity of a third-grade PE class. Two men in matching sweater vests split bagels in half while a cluster of chatty men in street clothing assembled chairs in a half moon on the gymnasium floor.

"That's the judging circle. You'll learn all about them in due time. There are volumes for you to learn. You're in for a trip if you stick around. And it is worth the price of admission. Ah, to be a newbie again!"

As Marvin reeled off club factoids and fodder, Liam eyed the men who were so methodically setting the stage for breakfast. One gentleman in suspenders and a maroon and green plaid dress shirt spread a plastic tablecloth over a long rectangular card table and then placed jars of cream cheese, peanut butter, and jams and jellies at equal measure along its periphery. The man would place a jar on the table and then step away to see how it looked before positioning something new on the surface. Watching the slow Balanchine-like precision of each man's moves, Liam stopped to think about whether anyone young would be at the breakfast. Sure, there was Monroe. Liam liked to think of Monroe as his own age, even though the twelve-year gap made him more like a much older brother. But the non-runners working in the room right now had to be fifteen years Monroe's senior. Of course, there were also Marvin and Gene. But their age was difficult to decipher; they had the boyish style and affectation that keeps gay men looking young until one day, out of the clear blue nowhere, they look silly and sad—and old.

"So I'm going to rinse this run off me." Marvin had gathered up a towel, Dopp kit, pair of jeans, and a crewneck sweater. "Beat all those smelly bastards to the showers."

"I had just planned on running home." Liam offered the words like an apology that came too late and did nothing other than fill in an awkward silence.

"Please, lots of runners skip the showers. If you want to use the bathroom or wash your hands—whatever!—just come this way."

The hot water from the faucet hurt Liam's numb hands, but he turned the yellow hunk of soap over and over, letting it slip faster and faster through his fingers to cast his mind away from the pain. He noticed a ridge of salt across his forehead leading down through his sideburns and tossed a handful of the scalding water over his face. As he turned around to dry off with some paper towels, Liam saw that Marvin had stripped down for his shower. Marvin now stood naked, fumbling through his Dopp kit, just two feet away from Liam. Finding it impossible not to stare at the long arc of Marvin's penis as it swung back and forth, Liam dried his face with his shirt and darted out of the bathroom.

Outside, the gymnasium floor had filled with new constellations of people, some who had been in the park for the run and others who had clearly foregone exercise this morning. Liam scanned the room for Monroe. A quick apology and they could both leave. Horace in his electric blue and purple ensemble was nowhere to be found. Neither was Miss Norma Jean.

"Come, come. First-timers eat for free." The voice had approached from behind but by the time Liam turned, Gene's sweaty hoodie was bunched up in his face. The bear hug made Liam cringe.

"I'm just going to wait." Liam didn't know how to finish the sentence. "My friend's going to get back here in a few minutes."

"And what? He's going to begrudge you starting without him?"

The way Gene framed the question caused Liam to blush, like he was an adolescent tethered to his best friend. Liam often resented the way Monroe got stuck on the details and could never let anything go, and he hated the predictability of the diatribe that would be delivered now that the morning had diverged from their original plan. But Liam also loathed the juvenile lure that Gene now coaxed him with, particularly since it was working.

As he spooned some fruit salad into a bowl and took a quick sip from his coffee, Liam noticed Horace and Monroe entering the room. Horace pumped the little weights in his hands belligerently, as though he could wring out some torment they were causing him. Monroe nodded to fend off the barrage of Horace's words. A skinny man with a wicked Boston accent approached, and Liam indulged the man's banal questions to avoid the probing glances that Monroe now shot at him.

In no time flat, this beefy man in the Boston College T-shirt managed to bolt through all the standard questions that everyone in the running club seemed determined to find answers to. While Liam did not mind sharing his favorite distances to race and his best times at different events, he did wonder whether people in the club had anything more to offer. As Joey, who had moved to New York just three months ago from the Beacon Hill section of Boston, finished telling of his hamstring injury from the fall, a young guy dressed in black pants and a purple V-neck barreled into the room in a flurry of hellos. Those gathered around the floor looked up eagerly with changed expressions, delighting in this young man's arrival. Liam decided this must be a surprise cameo from someone who had moved away.

"Zany Zane . . . that boy definitely knows how to make an entrance."

"Zane?" Watching the manic display of jumping up and down, the frantic meeting and greeting, Liam felt overcome by a sense of déjà vu. *Was it last year's Gay Pride? The Phoenix Bar? The pier in Provincetown last summer?*

"Oh, I've only been around the club for a little bit," said Joey, "but Zane is kind of everywhere—even when he's not. It's impossible to know Fast Trackers without knowing Zane Tyro. You should meet him."

Before Liam had a chance to object politely and note that he needed to reconnect with his friend, he was double-whammied with Monroe intersecting right as Joey yanked Zane into what was now an odd quartet. Liam could feel his heart flutter and prayed that he might escape an embarrassing recrimination from Monroe. Liam attempted a look of entreaty with his friend, only to find that Monroe was trans-fixed by Zane.

"So, Zane," started Joey, "this is a new runner. His name is Liam."

"Oh, I know you! You're a celebrity in the making! I saw you pass Gene at that race up in Van Cortlandt." *Yes! No wonder he was so familiar.* Liam nodded, feeling as though an itch inside his head had just been scratched. "You've been the talk of the club ever since—and a veritable mystery man at that. And now here you are."

"Zane, this is my good friend Monroe. It's his first time too."

"Don't we all wish we could say that!" Zane punctuated his joke by reaching out and tousling Liam's hair. "Well, it's always great to have new people come to the club," he added as an afterthought.

"So, Zane, do you have an official role here?" Monroe asked. "You flitted in here like a little queen bee buzzing around her little worker bees."

Monroe's biting sense of humor had always bordered on rudeness. Even good friends often became offended by his combative brand of sarcasm. Behind the focus of his hazel eyes, Zane appeared to examine Monroe's statement like a trinket that he noticed glittering at a bazaar, something that captivated him for a second but proved valueless upon closer inspection.

"Are you only focused on short-distance running, Liam?" Zane gazed again at Liam. "Actually, scratch that thought. It doesn't matter. Even if you're interested in longer distances, you'll benefit from our indoor training program. We're starting up at the track just next week in fact. You can get the whole winter season in. You'll be a huge addition for us."

"Indoor training? What, like the ordeal of high school track practice? Once in a lifetime was more than enough on that front."

"Believe me," Zane said, rubbing his hand along Liam's bicep to emphasize his trustworthiness. "It's a good group of guys who meet up two nights a week—work hard, play hard, and a lot of camaraderie."

"And people of all speeds can join, right?" As the words came out of Liam's mouth, his eyes moved toward Monroe, and he knew he had made an error in judgment.

"I just showed up to keep Liam company," Monroe said, diverting his eyes toward the floor. "Don't worry, I'm not interested in the track. It was lovely to meet you, though, Zane."

Questions about the track program immediately surfaced. *How much did it cost? Where were the facilities? Were the runners at the track younger (cuter) than the ones who showed up to jog in the park?* But was Liam expected to disengage from Zane? Would a good friend join Monroe at the buffet station where he currently lathered an onion bagel with cream cheese and jelly? It was a catch-22. If he showed solidarity against the slight suffered by his friend, Liam would be accused of pandering and of mortifying Monroe by reducing him to a charity case. On the other hand, continuing to enjoy conversation with the perpetrators would smack of disloyalty, a trait that Monroe abhorred. Finding it impossible to make his friend happy, Liam served his own needs and drilled down his list of questions.

"Don't worry about the specifics," Zane implored. "Just show up this Tuesday night at seven thirty, and we'll figure everything out."

Zane took Liam's palm into his own and scribbled the address on his hand. Beneath it, he included a phone number.

"Just in case you need anything before then," he said.

After the long meet-and-greet social with the Fast Trackers, Liam thanked Monroe profusely for joining him that morning and providing the requisite support throughout the event. Monroe demurred and said that he had not really done anything praiseworthy, and Liam could sense that his best friend still needed some tender loving care to feel that everything was truly right in the world—or at least in their friendship.

"We're going to Barneys Co-Op," Liam insisted as they strode into the winter glare of a bustling Broadway.

"You think you own the key to my heart, handsome," Monroe said, averting Liam's glance. "But don't overestimate the powers of your persuasion."

"Please," countered Liam. "You cannot feign indifference here. I know you love getting your designer labels for less. Now, the store is only a block and a half away, so let's quit this faux fighting and get on with our day."

The beautiful fur-trimmed jackets and ski pants provided the perfect antidote to the bickering that had marred their morning. Luxury goods have a tendency to make one feel that there is no need to sweat the small stuff. Everything is going to be right as rain. Monroe tried on a lumberjack vest and strutted through the store as though he were the Jolly Green Giant. Liam donned an extravagant, multi-zippered parka and pranced around as though he were in the new James Bond flick. And suddenly all the tension dissipated. They were two friends whose only interest was making it through another day in the big city. Each knew the other was there for them through anything that truly mattered—boy problems, financial snafus, work issues, and family drama—and everything else was just a diversion. Background noise.

Liam picked out a cashmere skull cap in the most vibrant shades of hot pink and fuchsia he had ever seen.

"I am buying this for you!" he said to Monroe, triumphantly. "I need to be able to spot you in crowds."

He handed the surly cashier a fifty-dollar bill and told him to keep the change. (The gesture was worth more than the $1.48 he was about to get back.)

"I do look fierce, don't I?" said Monroe, sashaying out of the store, sporting the new gift proudly on his bald head.

"Don't ask the obvious, sweetie. I am not here to bolster your already huge ego."

"The hell you're not!" screeched Monroe. "Why do you think old shrews like me keep young lovelies like yourself around, Liam? Don't open that pretty little mouth of yours and guess . . . Let me just tell you that it ain't the witty repartee!"

With that flourish, Monroe pivoted around to hail a taxi across town, while Liam headed swiftly in the opposite direction to get the subway downtown.

MILE 3

Leaning against the bathroom stall, Liam rushed to re-move his dress pants. It was already a shade past 7:30, and the prospect of being late worsened his nerves. Why had he decided to come to the track anyway? His nerves had got-ten the best of him during the week since Zane had success-fully persuaded him to augment his participation in Fast Trackers with these speed workouts. The sweat had built up during the forty-five minutes of subway time spent stuck be-tween a militant preacher rambling about hell on earth and two teenage girls cracking gum and hyena-laughing, and now his undershirt was glued to his back. Peeling it off, Liam lost his balance and tripped away from the bathroom stall with his bare foot landing in a pool of liquid that had formed as a nasty result of the overflowing urinal and a poor drainage sys-tem. Liam had not complained when the attendant in the lobby barked that there were no locker rooms and insisted that everyone change in the bathrooms. Normally, he would have asked where his $350 in membership dues went, but getting ready in a timely fashion trumped exacting pointless revenge on the hourly-wage Armory employees.

The mint-green cotton shorts that were free with his gym membership renewal and the old Amherst T-shirt he had crammed into his bag as he left the office were now a wad of wrinkles. He compared himself to the three runners lined up at the urinals, the slit of their racing shorts and the light tech-fiber of their tank tops lending a clean line to their long, lean bodies. (They were what his mother would have called *tall drinks of water.*) Liam felt like a dilettante. The people in the club had definitely done their part to make him feel wanted and at home, but he still questioned the wisdom of enlisting in their training program. He hoped that more attractive men who were capable of talking about things other than running might show up to these workouts. Zane had alluded to that possibility during the follow-up call Liam made the day after the fun run, reasserting all the benefits of running intervals on an indoor track and also hinting that "recreational" oppor-tunities existed. After ponying up more money than he could afford—almost half a month's rent—to join the program, Liam knew he had to follow through even if it meant pissing off the other fact-checkers at the magazine with his early de-partures twice a week.

Liam also sensed that pushing himself out of his shell through attending these workouts would be good for facing the insecurities he had about his body, his talent, and his wardrobe. Though he had run in high school and college, Liam had always felt as though he were going through the motions, flying under the radar. In high school, he ran so that he would have a solid extracurricular for his college applica-tions—and he kept it up in college out of habit more than a burning desire to compete. But now after a few years off, Liam felt he was rediscovering something special about the sport, the therapeutic feeling of mental clarity that could be achieved on a run. Liam knew now that this would be the time to push himself.

Liam made it to the team's meeting area on the side of the track about ten minutes late but was relieved to see that the evening's roll call had only just begun. A short black man in impeccably tailored pants and a lavish turtleneck read off a list of names. About twenty Fast Trackers had signed up for the program, and it sounded as though everyone had arrived for the debut session. As the man with the clipboard, whom Liam soon reasoned was the coach, spelled out a series of safety procedures and explained his theories about improving racing performance, Liam's mind drifted off into the surroundings. Thick-legged sprinters pounded down the banked curves of the track as a female coach with a stopwatch shouted out times. Names of local colleges—Hunter, Fordham, C.W. Post—breezed across the chests of skinny athletes who ran in huddled packs. The seating around the track was limited and everything inside the amphitheater was utilitarian. There were the large digital displays of time ticking by and the storage rooms for the javelin, high jump, and shot put equipment. Each field event had its own little station on the interior of the elliptical track, but Liam couldn't believe that collisions between runners and field athletes didn't happen regularly given the confined space. The track itself looked teeny and manageable, which Liam found comforting. He had overheard the coach noting that eight rotations around the track equaled one mile.

"So what did I say to convince you?" Zane whispered to Liam as the coach said something about easing everyone into the 200-meter track with forty-five minutes of "hut-hut" running.

"I think I just needed a change of pace," Liam answered. "And, no pun intended there."

Liam had not been able to distill the reason when mulling over the decision in recent days and surprised himself now with such an apt response. Nothing had changed in his life in the past five years—same job, same apartment, same body. The only thing he cycled through was boyfriends. And even that was a tired, old pattern that he wished he could change. Or at least he wanted to believe that he did. His entire sexual life lately involved going out with Monroe and other friends to the bars until last call and seeing who wanted to sleep with him. At times, it could amusingly bolster his self-esteem to see a parade of guys scope him out from the corners of the bar. Occasionally, he'd even find someone who provided a hot night and a satisfying release but no one that Liam ever wanted to latch on to, or build something with. Mixing things up definitely couldn't hurt.

"Well, good. We need a change of pace here in the club too, and something tells me that you're going to move us in that direction."

"Okay now, boys. Save some of that energy for the hut-huts." The coach pointed directly at Zane as he spoke and then ushered everyone into the interior of the track to start the workout.

"So what's with this hut-hut business?" Liam sensed Zane taking him under his wing and decided that someone as well connected and central to the club as Zane would be beneficial as an ally.

"It's politically correct speak for Indian relays. We all run single file and when the leader raises his hand the person in the back has to sprint to the front and then set the pace for the run until he lifts his arm and then the person in the back flies up and on and on. It sounds easy but after doing it for a few miles, it can be a real bitch. You're lucky in that you'll be one of the fastest guys. The slowpokes suck major wind— choke on our exhaust—in this type of group workout."

A little dismayed by the fact that his one strong finish in a 5K led to such great expectations, Liam nervously bundled himself into the middle of the pack and hoped for the best. The track was a-rumble with fast runners. As the group of Fast Trackers strode around at a pace faster than Liam had ever run on his own, sinewy men from other teams pressed by without showing the slightest bit of effort. After a half mile, Liam realized he was the last in line, and when the guy in front waved his arm up high, it would be his turn to sprint. He felt both severe anxiety and a nascent swell of pride. And when the hand went up, Liam focused on making his body as efficient as possible, on looking only at the person at the head of the line and propelling himself toward that position—and beyond—to capture the lead spot. It took all of about twelve seconds, but the force and power lit Liam with a thrill and left him with the deep desire for more.

About fifteen minutes into the workout, six of the ten runners in Liam's group had quit in hunched-over dry heaves and spells of light-headedness. With only three other runners battling it out, the sprint portion of this exercise came around with increasing frequency. Liam knew he could complete the second half of the workout; he embraced the pain that now tested him over and over again. Gene suddenly raised his hand—for the only other runners left were Gene, Zane, and Marvin, whose thick calves were rife with batches of bright red hair—and Liam edged into the outer lane and revved up his leg turnover. He straightened his back and leaned forward just slightly, mimicking the suggested running form that all the magazines touted for optimal performance. As he passed Marvin and Zane, Liam noticed that Gene only grew farther ahead in the distance. The coach had specifically stated that everyone should run at a consistently hard pace throughout the workout and should only pick up speed when sprinting to the front of the line. Liam turned his head to silently question Gene's motives with Zane, but Zane had trained his gaze toward the track. And so Liam strained to increase the rate of his foot turnover until he was shoulder to shoulder with Gene, who had begun to squint with pain and wheeze as he thrust his arms faster and faster. Despite the silliness of this battle of wills, Liam had to see this test to the end. He imagined the tips of his toes just barely touching the track before they kicked back in more forceful and definitive strides. As he passed Gene, Liam made sure to glide rather than gallop, unequivocally asserting his dominance. And when he slid into the lead position, he only ratcheted the speed down slightly to continue to tax Gene as he struggled behind. It felt like the least he could do to return the favor. By the time that Liam decided to pull a new runner into pole position, he saw, off in the corner of his field of vision, near the bleachers, Gene leaning by a trash can with his hands cupped over his mouth.

Now that the group was whittled down to three, the rotations went more smoothly, with Zane, Liam, and Marvin running efficiently and respectfully. But in the final minutes of the workout, Liam heard the pounding of a new set of footsteps come up on his right shoulder out of nowhere. There was no breathing audible—just the pounce of a sprinter. Liam looked quickly to his right and saw the angular jawbone and those unmistakable brown eyes, steeped in concentration and loaded with determination. The workout had been going so well that Liam did not want to cave in now and ruin his last set due to silly competition. He kept his pace strong but consistent and Didier followed suit. While the gamesmanship exhibited by certain Fast Trackers that evening had intrigued Liam and stoked his competitive fire, he preferred working out for himself and not others.

In the final lap of the workout, Didier ran stride for stride with Liam, and Liam never looked over his shoulder. Instead he focused all his mental reserves, which were now running low, on maintaining perfect form. As they crossed through the finish line, Didier thrust his bony chest out as though he were trying to edge out Liam in the photo finish of some race. With a solid forty-five minutes of hard running behind him, Liam crouched over on the side of the track and collected his breath. Didier swiped his hand quickly over the curve of Liam's spine and thanked him for the hard aerobic run. His teammates from the Urban Bobcats had apparently left for the night already and he needed a reliable fast pacer for his last mile. Liam lifted his head in a gesture meant to connote "not a problem," but Didier had already begun to jog out of the facility. Liam stared longingly at the lithe outline of Didier's shoulders as he faded out of view.

As Liam changed out of his sweat-heavy T-shirt, Marvin came over to thank him for a good and steady workout. Liam had noticed Marvin's strong and prominent legs when they ran in the park but still could not stop looking at his calves. They were not the massive, bulbous calves of gym mavens who bench pressed hundreds of pounds. Not at all. They were taut and tapered down to his vein-strewn ankles, which somehow supported his overly large feet. Liam pegged them as a size 14. But his eyes lingered over all the wild and prickly hair that sprouted from Marvin's legs, in all manner and direction. The beauty of his legs made up for the more workaday aspects of his face and his forgettable upper body.

"It's always this bullshit warfare out on the track with Fast Trackers," Marvin said and patted Liam consolingly on the shoulder. "Don't let it bring you down. You've got a much better running instinct than all these queens who can't help but shoot their loads prematurely."

Liam looked more closely at Marvin and imagined he might be slightly attractive if his eyes were a little larger and set a bit farther apart. They were a strange dark blue, but their beauty was lost to their smallness, to the compact economy that guided every feature of his face.

"It was a bit intense for a first day. And yet it's always like this, you say?"

"Please, don't let it scare you off," Marvin said. "In time, you'll find it amusing. You'll be able to predict which ego will get crushed on the track first. There's a lot of . . . well . . . a lot of *personality* in this club. I swear if it hasn't driven you away yet, you'll be good to go around here for quite some time."

"My heart hasn't raced like that in quite some time." Liam realized he batted his eyelashes in a flirtatious reflex.

He thought of the arc of Marvin's engorged shaft from the shower the other week. "And I guess that's a good thing."

"So come to the restaurant with us now. It's just around the corner. You'll get a bigger peek into the club psyche."

Liam smiled in acquiescence. He *did* have to eat dinner after all.

A badly conceived cocktail of Washington Heights locals and post-workout runners, the restaurant wore the unsavory scent of cheap musk and drying sweat. As the group entered the pub, a jovial black man greeted Zane with a televangelist's hallelujah smile and an immense hug. He waved the Fast Trackers toward a back room that was somewhat shielded from the off-key wails of the bar's karaoke Tuesday. As he sat down at the table of twelve, Liam could hear the reverberation of the screaming chorus: "I only WANNA see you, baby, in the purple rain!"

Some of the faces around the table looked familiar. Directly across from him sat Zane and next to him Gary, the leader in the park whom Liam learned was lovingly called G-Lo by the team, a moniker that apparently substituted for the clumsier Gary Loblonicki. A few cute young guys dotted the perimeter of the oblong table, and Gene and Marvin were there too. In fact, Marvin plunked down right next to Liam and began nervously tapping his foot so that his hairy leg brushed up against Liam ever so slightly. Marvin had mentioned his partner when they first met, but Liam had met enough couples with special "arrangements" to know that did not guarantee exclusivity or fidelity. As Liam leaned into conversation with Zane to avoid Marvin's coy advance, Liam felt the press of his penis against the threadbare cotton of his boxer shorts.

On the train ride downtown after dinner, Liam sat purposefully alone, choosing a spot across the train car and several feet from the bench that the other Fast Trackers had occupied. A young guy (he had to be around Liam's age) with features that were round, though not quite fat, stood up and scooted down the car to sit next to Liam. Feeling burdened by the prospect of small talk, Liam avoided eye contact and handed the fellow a section of *The New York Times*.

"Come on, you can do better than that. You're new. It's *your* duty to endear yourself to people like me." The guy threaded each syllable with just enough comic edge to disable Liam from both acting put out and from taking him seriously. But it was also far too late at night for Liam to manufacture any biting repartee.

"I'll try to improve on that next time," he said and returned to the paper.

"I get it. I get it. The whole cultivating an air of mystery." The guy, who still hadn't volunteered his name, now slid his Elvis Costello eyeglasses down and then up his nose. "A sense of the forbidden unknown . . . the loner mystique."

"Just reading the newspaper—nothing mysterious or forbidden about that." Immediately after he spoke, Liam regretted the *now-go-shoo!* tone of his statement, although he still wanted more than anything to be left alone.

"Look, do me a favor and just chat with me already. I'm tired as anything of all their talk about mile splits from the results from the last 10K or which half marathon they plan to race next. I have a rule that you can't talk about a race for longer than it took to run it. And forget about that Gene; he's the worst offender. He has talked about his 2:59 New York City marathon to the point where homicide would be justifiable. You'd think that no one ever broke three hours in a marathon before. About a thousand other runners also did it this year in New York City alone. Unfortunately, no one else on our team did—with the notable exception of Marvin. Thank God that Marvin is racing under the Fast Tracker name. Now here I go blathering on about running. I guess it's contagious. Ugh, I feel like I need to take a shower—I feel oily just being within earshot of that Gene."

"Okay, do me a favor, because it seems I have no choice but to converse with you now." A smile began to inch up Liam's face. "Tell me what your name is. That circle of introductions at the track just whirred on by me."

"You tell me your name first." He took off his thick eyeglasses and cleaned the lenses on his shirt.

"You don't know my name?" Liam did not care if his vexation was showing.

"You don't know mine. Don't be so self-involved!"

"Fine, it's Liam . . . Liam Walker."

"Pleasure to meet you, Liam." Pause. "Liam Walker. Funny name for a fast runner."

Unimpressed by the lack of originality, Liam looked down again at his newspaper.

"I'm Ben. Ben Cargenstein. And don't forget my name again. That isn't allowed. Pay attention to me, kid, and I'll give you the lowdown on all these bozos. You'd better pack some prophylactics and a tube of fungicide, it's going to be a filthy ride."

MILE 4

The same guy as always took Liam's name and cockily announced a thirty-minute wait. Liam was tempted to reach out and snap his little bow tie off, but he knew he had to suffer the wait and attitude for the reward of the burgers. It was Monroe's neighborhood, but Liam had chosen the spot for dinner.

While he waited at the edge of the bar sipping an Anchor Steam draft, Liam admired the impossibly cute families and ensembles of friends gathered around the tables enjoying their suppers. They were borrowed from country clubs and J.Crew catalogs, all crisp cotton and wide-wale corduroy. At the bar a freckled guy in a sports coat ran his hand through waves and waves of chocolate hair, as he gabbed with a pair of drinking buddies. He did a double take when he noticed Liam. Once face-to-face, Liam recognized A. J. Ashbery. The editor of Amherst's literary magazine *Pin-Striped Prose*, A. J. considered every conversation a piece of performance art, a stage on which he could dazzle the listener with some new interpretation of reality. In these close quarters, Liam knew he had no choice but to acknowledge his former classmate but wondered why the fuck Monroe couldn't be on time for once.

Liam listened to A. J. pontificate about his internship helping edit the "Talk of the Town" section at *The New Yorker* and managed a smile as A. J. insincerely praised the job at *Entertainment Weekly* that Liam felt truly blessed to have snagged. As A. J. turned the conversation into a discussion of his future plans, including at what age he would step into Graydon Carter's role as editor-in-chief of *Vanity Fair*, Liam let his eyes range over the dark walls that were crammed, everywhere, with images of melons. There was the pastel painting of an orange honeydew sliced-open and readied for breakfast, the flat wooden likeness of a slab of watermelon, and the drawing of cantaloupes fresh off the tree. Liam did not like to admit how much he loved the homogeneity of all this privilege and perfection; being around the rich made him feel tranquil, as though there were a sense of order to the world.

"Oops, I hate to interrupt your plotline, A. J., but I think I see the friend I'm meeting for dinner. I'd better jet."

"Who, that shriveled old prune who just walked in? God, Liam, if you're going to do this gay thing, you've really got to live large. You're too hot for these old trolls; you ought to be cavorting with some heroin addict from a Calvin Klein ad."

"I'll take that under advisement. Best of luck making your way through the fray. Loved your piece on the lost art of the ascot—tons of facts and history of which I was totally unaware."

As Liam slalomed through the tweed to get to the door where Monroe stood expectantly, he managed to signal the bartender to pour two more mugs of Anchor Steam. He pulled Monroe over to the periphery of the bar and faced away from A. J. and his posse. While Monroe had an uncanny knack for being overly sensitive and inconveniently temperamental, he read body language better than anyone Liam had ever known, a trait that came in surprisingly handy when trying to avoid people in Manhattan. Liam took two long swallows of his beer, savoring its bitter fullness, before he addressed Monroe. It occurred to him that he was happy to have squeezed in his friend between his niece's birthday party in the early afternoon and the Fast Trackers boys' night out that started at ten. After they had attended the Fast Tracker Saturday fun run together, Monroe distanced himself from the club, saying that only the young, fast, cute boys were embraced. Liam had tried to convince him otherwise, without being too emphatic or condescending. Monroe had his own definite viewpoints and prided himself on being stubborn. And so when Liam suggested Monroe join him for the latter part of the evening, he knew not to give too much push back once his friend demurred. Not wanting to indulge his good friend's unwarranted insecurities, Liam promised himself that he would not bring the topic up at dinner tonight.

"So you saved me from a pretty monstrous peacock parade back there. I thought A. J. was hot the one time he accidentally dropped his towel in the dorm showers freshman year—shocking dick for his frame—but, man, his mouth could turn a rock-hard erection soft inside of one *wry* rejoinder."

"You're bound to run into those types when you choose to dine at the corner of 'Preppie Boulevard' and 'Country Club Lane.'"

"I know, but it's soooo worth it for the burgers. Anyway, tell me about your day."

"Usual B-cubed shopping protocol—hit the sales at Barneys, Bergdorf, and Bloomingdale's. Didn't buy anything but spent half an hour eyeing a cute little twink in the Michael Kors section. Yum."

Liam knew that his facial expression would give away signs of disapproval, so he quickly took a drink of beer.

"What, I can't foolishly flirt now? Don't get holier than thou with me, Liam. I'll be forced to drudge up your past."

"Please. Flirtatiousness is next to godliness in my book.

It's not that. I just hate the thought of you spending $785 on *another* denim jacket."

Liam could never honestly assess Monroe's wardrobe— friends like to think that they can perform that type of frank analysis when it's really just a lie to foster closeness—but hoped that Monroe would stop buying expensive designer clothing in the false belief that it would transform him, like stardust, into a prince. If truth really were the currency of friendship, Liam would tell Monroe that all the hundreds of dollars spent on labels did nothing to disguise his gut and failed to make his squat frame any longer or leaner. While supplying that unwanted advice, Liam could add that Monroe would be better off funneling $100 per month into a local sports club membership. Six-pack abs and expansive shoulders could make passersby drool over a five-dollar tank top. Instead of that dose of honesty, Liam resorted to gay gal-pal speak.

The queenie little man with the bow tie came over to collect Liam and Monroe, escorting them to the best table in the back room, far away from the bathrooms and the bustle of the dinner crowd. A stack of menus awaited them on the table, but Liam had no idea why anyone would ever order anything but the signature J.G. Melon burger that had been heralded by *The New York Times* as "too sublime a piece of meat to have once walked the earth." The only question was rare versus medium rare. Within five minutes the waitress, whose look befitted the sanitized affluence of the institution in her prim tartan skirt, appeared at their table. They both ordered the medium rare burger with a bucket of fries to split.

"Surprised you're splurging on a calorie fest before your night out with the boys," Monroe quipped. "What will they say if your midriff isn't rock hard and vein-y?"

"We're going to Splash, smart-ass," Liam replied. "No one takes his shirt off in Splash. There's probably going to be some tragic stage show and a busload of gay tourists from Germany. So how come you're not going to come and protect me? I could use someone with your brand of subtle bitchiness to get through this evening."

"It's very sweet of you to include me in things, Liam. I get it. You are being considerate and doing the right thing, but I just can't be your tagalong guy. No matter what the context is, you're the star and I'm the underling making sure you stay in flattering light and that no one photographs your bad side."

"First of all, I don't have a bad side." Liam laughed as the waitress brought over their food. She raised an eyebrow at him, moving the salt and pepper shakers and their mugs of beer to fit the plates of food on the teensy tabletop. "And second, you need to stop that whole thing. It's not even funny to joke about that. You get a ton of play and boys like you just fine, so I don't know why you keep pulling this shy act around Fast Trackers."

"You're so naïve. But then again you've never really been part of a gay organization. They're all runways with teeth— metaphorically speaking. People who were passed over in straight society their whole lives trying to claw their way into the inner circle of some club they have erected for their own vanity."

"Whoa, that's quite an indictment against a club you spent one solid morning with."

"I've been gay a long time, Liam. But learn this all for yourself. It's better that way. I can't wait to hear all the dirt, the stories, the backstabbing. Just be careful. Gay men have a million ways to measure each other. . . . Fast Trackers can make it a million and one by adding in all this shit about who ran a faster time than whom in the Wall Street 5K."

Liam dabbed some mayonnaise on his burger and sunk his teeth into the sandwich. Some blood colored the bun. He shook the burger approvingly at Monroe in a show of affection and celebration of something they could both agree upon, the perfection of this meal.

"It's just a group of guys who like to run together, Monroe. I haven't been brainwashed. My body has not been snatched."

"I know, babe. I never said as much . . . tonight you're going for your first *splash* in the club's pool. Promise me you won't sleep with any of them. No good could come of that before you get the four-one-one on everyone."

Liam rolled his eyes and nodded his head in response.

Monroe took a huge bite of his burger and smiled as he raised the sandwich in reciprocation.

"I've got to admit. It's a pretty fucking good burger."

MILE 5

Riding the Number 6 train downtown after dinner, Liam felt momentarily sluggish, as though every drop of blood in his body had been corralled to absorb the hefty meal he had just eaten. The thought of bypassing Chelsea and heading home for a solid night's sleep tempted him, but he knew all the Fast Trackers would be waiting for him. Liam decided to get out of the train early, at Twenty-eighth Street, and walk for a while so that the crisp night air might jolt him awake. He also looked forward to the prospect of cutting across Madison Square Park, his favorite public space in Manhattan. Unlike the parks at Union and Washington and even Tompkins squares, the patch of land that spread out east from the Flatiron remained eerily quiet at night. No teenagers gathered around the jungle gyms and only a homeless person or two might be getting shut-eye on the wooden benches. Liam imagined the park would be even more desolate than usual since it was the Saturday before New Year's Eve and many people would be out of town with relatives or stowing away energy for "big night" celebrations. Liam never understood the emphasis that people placed on the first day of the year; he opted to stay in and read passages of Proust every year as a way to detox from the holidays.

He walked alone south along Madison Avenue with the frosty winds buffeting him at each intersection, as the streets howled a lonely cry. Coming up on the park, Liam took the entrance that led diagonally toward the Flatiron, the most majestic way of experiencing the landscape. He stopped briefly at the squat, fat evergreen—rotund enough to be deemed a bush rather than a tree—that was clumsily adorned with large colored lightbulbs. The way the thick wire connecting the bulbs bulged out from the branches reminded Liam of the hastiness with which his father used to tend to the Christmas decorations. He wished he had gone home for longer than just one evening for the holiday this year but always felt awkward once he was at home with his family. While they accepted him for who he was, Liam always felt himself criticizing his family for not being as educated or as urbane as him—and he hated himself for having those judgmental thoughts. He always ended up disengaging and heading back to the city, where the anonymity and the ceaseless energy could erase all his anxieties. With the splendor of the season now all around him, Liam surprisingly craved the feeling of being on the couch in his parents' living room watching the lights on the tree reflected in the shiny glass ornaments.

Looking at his watch, Liam noticed that it was almost ten thirty, and he was moving beyond fashionably late toward inconsiderate and rude. As he hit the center of the park, Liam saw the Flatiron Building and was immediately reminded of Stieglitz's famous photographs. The beautifully fenestrated triangle simply grew out of the far end of the park like one of the leafless trees that rocked in the wind tonight. Only a handful of the windows were lit up; it was, after all, a Saturday night near the end of the year. He knew he needed to work himself into a more social mood now that he had let himself get pensive. Quickening his pace, Liam left the park and strode into a light jog down Fifth Avenue toward Seventeenth Street.

"Where's the fire?" The scream came from behind him as he turned west on Seventeenth. Already accustomed to the trademark whine, Liam didn't have to turn around to know that Gene was rapidly approaching. Everyone complained about Gene *ad nauseam*, but the in crowd seemed to invite him out even when not required by club protocol.

"Just trying to stay warm by jogging."

Forced to wait outside and enter the bar with Gene, Liam worried whether the joint entrance would get people talking. Monroe's warnings about the club must have affected him more than he realized. He knew it was silly and did not want to give in to his high school impulses to be a slave to the popularity gods, but he still felt his skin crawl when he thought about the looks he would get coming in on the heels of Gene.

The velvet rope and body-builder bouncer outside the door lent a bridge-and-tunnel seediness to the establishment, reminding Liam why he never included this bar in his regular weekend rounds.

"That'll be five bucks each." The man made a concerted effort to look straight ahead and not make eye contact with Liam and Gene.

"Crap, I didn't realize there would be a cover." Gene flipped through his empty wallet as though he might find a bill hidden somewhere. "Would you mind, Liam? I'll pay you back after I use the ATM inside."

In his latest effort to live squarely within his means, Liam had brought only $100 out with him, and he had already spent $35 at dinner. But even with blowing another $10, he would be fine for the evening. He knew better than to expect a payback after the night of drinking got underway.

"Yeah, of course," Liam said, handing the bouncer a $10 bill and scurrying into the bar quickly, so that it might look as though they had actually arrived in tandem instead of near synchronicity.

"Oh good! You guys got here just in time for the start of

the show! It's amateur night. Come, come . . . we've marked
our territory in the center of the bar to watch." Gary didn't
walk, he hopped, over to where the Fast Trackers had congregated. A familiar set of faces rounded a fairly big area right
in front of the makeshift stage. Zane, Ben, Marvin, and some
other participants in the speed training sessions stood around
with a couple of cute guys whom Liam hadn't met before.
Liam definitely began to sense that there was an inner circle
to the club, and that he might, in fact, be gaining entrée into
it. *Damn that Monroe,* he thought, *for making me question everyone's motives.*

"Please, tell me he didn't trap you in his lair. When I saw
the two of you stroll in together, I nearly fainted." Zane dramatically clutched Liam's arm as he whispered orders in his
ear. "Don't let him glom onto you—trust me. It sounds cruel,
but you need to completely disengage. He won't understand
anything different."

"We just bumped into each other on the street. Come on,
Zane, give the new guy a break here!"

"Let's move on," Zane said. "The whole club talks about
him too much as it is. I agree."

The bartender brought over a long silver tray of green
shots and began to split them up among the Fast Trackers.

"Which one of you putzes had the virgin shot?"

Zane scooped up the shot and smiled smugly at the waiter.

"Really, a virgin shot? I guess I've heard everything now,"
said Ben. "I'm assuming it's gonna be mighty sweet—what
with it being straight candy apple mixer."

"I don't have to explain myself to *any*body." Zane shook
his head in an exaggerated fashion as though he were extending the sentiment to a gathered congregation. "I'm one
hundred percent pure."

"Pure?" Ben raised his index finger as he spoke. "Pure
trash, maybe."

As the lights dimmed, everyone quickly raised their shots

and downed them in unison, even Zane, though he choked a little on the thick green syrup that needed some liquor to cut its intensity. Rising out of a trapdoor in the stage floor, a tall black drag queen in a blue sequin gown with a cone of flaming red hair commanded the crowd to attention with an a cappella rendition of "Gypsies, Tramps, and Thieves." By the time she finished, the waiter had brought over another round, and the Fast Trackers enthusiastically obliged. Liam played along to be a good sport, but the hard alcohol amplified the slight beer buzz he had from the restaurant.

The drag queen, whose name was Miss Apple Brown Betty, jumped up and down knocking an invisible tambourine against her hip to rouse the crowd into a froth of excitement. She then went to great pains to shush everyone down so that she could have complete silence while she explained the contest rules. Once on the stage, contestants had to do whatever she demanded or else they were disqualified and had to return to their seats immediately. Anyone who flashed his penis would not only be asked to leave the stage but would also be kicked out of, and potentially banned from, the bar. Crowd applause, as judged by Miss Apple Brown Betty, would dictate the winner. And the winner would go home with $250 in prize money.

After a moment of silence, she asked for a show of hands as to who wanted to participate. Throughout the bar, which had about three hundred customers at this point, there were clusters of arms raised. Friends pointed frantically toward their friends, who reddened and shrank behind the shoulders of yet other friends. Miss Apple Brown Betty left the stage cautiously to inspect the crowd, her heels sticking in the sequin train of her dress. She chose some of the people whose hands were raised and then forced a few of the people trying feverishly to avoid her glance to head up to the stage. When she got to the Fast Tracker circle, she declared that they still needed two more contestants. Gene jumped up and down and unbuttoned his shirt to reveal his nipples. Finally, she rolled her eyes and tapped him on the shoulder. And then she paused and grabbed Liam by the waist.

"You're caaaah-yuuuuute! You're standing right next to me on stage while we rock this joint."

As he looked out over the crowd from the stage, Liam had to squint to make out the smirks and chuckles of the Fast Tracker clan. Gene rubbed Liam along the leg and then mouthed the words "good luck" to him. Liam started to feel the thrill of competition rise as the warmth of the alcohol coursed through him.

Miss Apple Brown Betty stood next to each contestant, showcasing him like a piece of furniture that might be offered up as a game show prize, while the audience yelped and hooted. There were ten men up on stage and after her first walk-through, she eliminated two contestants. She then instructed the remaining eight to take off their shirts. The two men in the center who had both their nipples pierced with thick, Flintstone-like bones of silver received roars from the crowd that guaranteed them entry into the next round. When she got to Gene, she poked his middle and wryly muttered into the microphone: "Skinny-fat." Laughter peeled through Splash, but a few Fast Trackers proved themselves good friends by shouting: "Gene, Gene, the lean machine!" Liam stood as straight as possible when the drag queen ran her fingers down his chest, her long fake nails plucking at his nipple and then skimming down the faint hairs that ran from his navel toward his groin. The applause was considerable. As if to show symmetry of standards, the drag queen knocked one short guy and one sequoia of a man off the stage, sparing both Liam and Gene. Only six contestants remained on stage.

The next command hardly surprised Liam. The game moved in the fairly obvious direction of everyone on stage wearing less clothing. When Miss Apple Brown Betty declared that pants had to go, a few guys paused momentarily, but Gene unzipped his Lee jeans and threw them at the circle of Fast Trackers inside of five seconds. Liam slowly undid his pants, feeling thankful that he had actually worn underwear tonight.

With only six men standing, the drag queen summoned all her histrionics in presenting each and every specimen to the crowd for examination. The two men with pierced nipples had thick thighs and strong calves that garnered hefty approval from those watching from the floor—and the eyes of absolutely every soul in the bar were glued to the stage by this time. Of the other two guys, one had a swimmer's build with hairy legs and the other had the lithe body of a prepubescent boy. Different factions supported each of the six contestants. When it was Gene's turn, the drag queen yanked his boxer briefs and drawled into the microphone, "Boy, you better get rowdy tonight!"

Liam stood expectantly when his turn came. He posed like Michelangelo's *David*, bowing his head slightly in a gesture of feigned modesty. Miss Apple Brown Betty kissed the rear of his powder-blue-and-white-striped briefs and moaned long and slow to the crowd. She then collected herself and said, "Now, you can be my superhero any day of the week."

The crowd looked extremely anxious to see who would remain. After the audience applauded in turn for each contestant, the drag queen, who now guzzled from a chain of martini glasses, kicked Gene and the hairless boy-man off the stage. Liam and the swimmer stood demurely next to each other like two guys avoiding eye contact in the locker room while the two muscle-bound men flexed and flaunted before the admiring masses.

"Okay, shut it, people!" The drag queen let her ladylike voice lapse into a raspy baritone. "Hold tight. Things are going to get freaky."

With that, Miss Apple Brown Betty made one more trip

across the stage, stopping and fondling each man as she passed. She rolled her eyes and licked her lips to whip the men, who now filled Splash to capacity, into a frenzy. She then instructed Liam to bend down on his knees in front of Mister Swimmer while the shorter of the two beefcakes had to do the same before his ripped friend. It was then ordered that they simulate blow jobs through their clothing. Miss Apple Brown Betty reiterated in a domineering shriek that anyone who actually exposed himself, or caused someone else to be exposed, would be banned from the bar.

"Now, have at it!"

She scooted to the edge of the stage so that all the spectators could see the simulated sex acts. For a few seconds, Liam stared at the thin cotton briefs that clung suggestively to this lean man, and he pressed his face against the guy's leg to feel the steel of his leg hairs against his face. Liam immediately felt turned on and rubbed his nose slavishly into the man's briefs, playing with the cock head through the fabric. It didn't take long for the guy's shaft to stiffen. Then Liam licked along the outline, tracing the arc of his penis. The crowd erupted, but Liam had no idea if the noise was for him or for the fellatio simulators a few feet away. To cap off his performance, Liam bit into the fabric right by the swimmer's penis and pulled it away, with a bark like a dog. Liam kept repeating the motion until he finally fit his mouth over the entire swollen cock head and grabbed the swimmer's butt cheeks as he bobbed his head up and down over the fabric.

The drag queen stopped the show but needed a solid five minutes to calm the place down so that she could conduct the voting. Two more would fall, she announced. Liam received thunderous ovations, and his partner in crime met with a few scattered hoots. Liam had trouble discerning which of the other guys had scored better with the now very drunk and disorderly crowd. Glancing at his watch, Liam realized that almost half an hour had passed since they had ascended the stage. All the Fast Trackers still stood with their attention fixed on the stage, but many were now woozy-eyed and slurring.

Miss Apple Brown Betty declared it no contest—Liam and the muscleman who had been on the receiving end of fellatio were the final two standing. The big man flashed his biceps at the audience and then scooped Liam up in a King Kong–like embrace. Liam nudged the guy gently in the ribs so that he could stand again on his own two feet.

"I hope you two boys are sweet for each other. You better be! You're going to make out like teenagers in the back of a Seven-Eleven. We want to see desperate, sexy steam come off this stage. Now get to work!"

Liam found the guy's overly red face and thick meatiness a turnoff, but he played along and leaned in to softly caress the man's lips. The prelude to intimacy was the most irresistible sex act. Nothing could top that. As Liam's lips touched his partner's mouth, the man shoved his tongue down Liam's throat with a brute force that caused Liam to stumble back two steps. Feeling Liam slip away, the man grabbed him at the waist and drew him tight against his heaving chest. The man then ripped his mouth off Liam's lips and focused hard and fast on Liam's nipples, pulling them through his teeth as he pumped his fists and flexed his muscles at the audience.

After about two minutes, the drag queen pulled them apart as a referee might yank a steroid-fueled boxer off his pummeled competition. Liam could still feel the guy's heavy tongue scratching his esophagus. His nipples were hot and raw. No decibel register was needed to gauge who the winner was. The crowd had thoroughly appreciated the sheer force and determination of the brawny contender whose veins popped as he cheered for Liam's runner-up status. The five free-drink passes that Miss Apple Brown Betty presented as the second-place prize seemed a poor substitute for $250, but such is life, thought Liam.

As he slipped back into his jeans and pulled on his shirt,

he could hear wisecracks from the crowd—"Take me home!" and "*You're* the one that *I* want!" and "I'd treat you real gentle." Oddly, Liam felt like he was under the microscope for the first time all evening and walked with his head down to the circle where his friends (was it too soon to think of them as friends?) enthusiastically supported him.

Ben took his glasses off to wipe away the condensation that had formed while he had watched the event. Without the heavy frames of his Elvis Costello glasses, Ben looked like a little boy with a round, Mr. Magoo nose and a circular mouth that was small for his face but alluring with its overly plump lips.

"You did good up there," he said to Liam in a tone that made Liam believe that he may have actually been proud.

Liam could feel his face become warm with self-consciousness.

"It wasn't higher math," he said, finally.

"Can I kiss you?" Ben asked, so low that Liam had to scoot closer and ask him to repeat the request. "Can I kiss you? I have always wanted to be able to say that I kissed the prettiest boy in the bar."

Liam stood stunned as Ben moved in and lightly pressed his lips against Liam's.

MILE 6

After passing the last in a long series of stoplights on the West Side Highway, the taxi driver impatiently thumped on the gas, and Liam fell back in his seat from the shock of speed. The lights across the river in New Jersey raced by in streaks of yellow and green as the cab accelerated. Liam's eyelids struggled against the weight of his exhaustion. Ben traced infinity signs on Liam's leg, moving slowly from the top of his knee to the interior of his upper thigh.

"No, no, no!" Ben screamed suddenly. "You need to get off at 125th Street."

As the taxi veered across three lanes of traffic, Liam slid down the fake leather seat and landed on the floor of the car. Ben helped drag Liam back onto the seat and used the opportunity to move his hand right under Liam's groin. Ben's fingers were now positioned around Liam's balls. Broadway blurred by and Liam nodded off in the backseat of the cab, feeling vaguely indifferent as Ben undid the buttons on Liam's pants and worked his fingers inside, reaching and feeling for his cock head. Liam's beer buzz had faded into a dull headache, but the warm sensation on his penis still caused him to stiffen with anticipation.

Just as Liam was about to ask where in the hell they were

heading, Ben instructed the cab driver to pull up on the right at the next streetlight. Liam re-buttoned the fly on his jeans as he exited the car; Ben stayed in the cab to settle up with the driver. No one was on the street, and all of the brownstones on the block were completely dark. The shine of bare branches against the old-fashioned streetlamps lent the surroundings the pristine and slightly artificial look of a Hollywood movie set. The street was so quiet that Liam could hear the idle of the taxi cab and the flicker and hum from the dying bulb in a nearby streetlamp. The signs on the corner read: 139TH AND DOUGLASS BOULEVARD. Liam could never correctly map out all the streets that were named after historical figures—"Adam Clayton Powell" and "Malcolm X Boulevard"—within the grid of Upper Manhattan. At the moment, he had no true sense of where he was.

"I love coming home in the middle of the night," Ben exclaimed as he staggered out of the taxi. "The best part of living in this neighborhood is the desolation."

Ben grabbed Liam by both hands and walked a few paces so that they were standing directly under a streetlight. A bed of ivy and a gnarled cherry tree were to their right, and a large black Bentley gleamed beside the curb. In the harsh, incandescent light, the blemishes and discolorations in Ben's skin showed prominently but only increased the charming goofiness of his round features and his chunky, black glasses. Liam leaned over and kissed Ben. The move must have surprised Ben; his thick lips stayed closed for a second before opening up to the press of Liam's tongue. Ben's self-consciousness at the idea of kissing in public turned Liam on. He forced Ben's body against his own and slipped his cold, damp hands into the back of Ben's jacket and under his wool sweater. Liam ran his fingers over the soft fuzz of Ben's back hair and tilted his head to draw his tongue further into Ben's mouth. A hard gust of wind tunneled down through the empty street, and Liam could feel his mouth sting and his eyes water from the bitter cold.

"Okay, my balls are somewhere up inside my large intestines. We have got to go inside!"

With that pronouncement, Ben yanked Liam up the stairs of a brownstone only a few yards from where they were standing. Stacks of books, some old marble busts, and a few antique mirrors cluttered the narrow hallway that led into Ben's living room. Once inside, Liam reclined on the long green sofa that faced a wood-burning fireplace as Ben prepared a plate of cheese and poured glasses of Cab Franc in the kitchen. The room looked to have been decorated by somebody's eccentric great-uncle, with three globes on tall bronze stands anchoring one corner of the room and books of collectible postcards lying open on the mahogany coffee table.

"Wanderlust?" Liam asked as he made space on the coffee table for the tray of food and drink Ben carried in.

"I don't know . . . ever since I was a kid I always wanted to know where else I could be."

"That's funny. I always assumed city kids had the world at their fingertips. Isn't New York City where everyone wants to be?"

"People who don't live here," Ben said with a deep belly laugh. "But that's the way it is with everything. I moved up to this neighborhood to get away from the city. This is still Manhattan, I know, but it's not the city of my youth—Madison Avenue boutiques and pretentious neighbors and the established protocols of affluence. It was so fucking claustrophobic. For eighteen years, I saw the same kids at the museums, at tennis lessons . . . the same parents hosting fund-raisers at the Boathouse, having cocktails at Island. It was a sea of gingham and plaid. So, yes, I dreamed of far-off places."

Liam picked up his glass of wine and walked across the room. The warped floorboards creaked under his feet. When he got to the corner, Liam took a big swallow of the Cab Franc and felt the tart tingle of cherries along the back of his tongue. He ran his fingers across the faded landscape of the largest of the globes; the outdated names of countries like British Guiana and the Belgian Congo placed the antique somewhere in the earlier part of the twentieth century.

"My father owns an old store of collectibles on the Upper East Side," Ben offered. "He supplies me with all these relics you see around here."

Ben walked over toward the globes, and Liam downed the rest of the glass of wine in a fit of nerves.

"Hey, that bottle of wine goes for about sixty dollars. It's to be sipped, not guzzled!"

Ben had cozied up behind Liam and pressed his tongue to Liam's ear. All of Monroe's warnings now flooded over Liam. If he slept with Ben, Liam knew that his relationship to the club would have to change in some fashion. Maybe he would be touted as a good lay. Maybe he would be criticized as a slut. Maybe he would enjoy the experience and fall for Ben. Or perhaps he would hate it and feel awkward enough to avoid the club forever. As Ben roped his arms around Liam's rib cage and padded his lips down his neck, Liam knew he was going to have sex. To change his mind now would be impolite.

"Can I get a refill?" Liam asked as he disentangled himself from Ben. "I promise to savor it."

Ben brought the bottle over to Liam and poured some more into his own glass before refilling Liam's.

"Let me show you the rest of the place."

Ben took Liam by the hand and led him through the oversized French doors at the opposite side of the living room. They walked into a large kitchen where two tall stools flanked a tile breakfast bar. Liam quickly thumbed through the stack of magazines by the blender; working in the industry, he had a sharply honed ability to judge people by what they chose to read. Ben blushed as Liam nosed through the most recent issue of *Entertainment Weekly*.

"Let's get on with the tour," Ben said. "This isn't a lending library."

Liam noticed the notes and scribbles next to a short article he had written about the Olsen twins.

"I like to bone up on pulp and gossip," Ben said with a hurried and nervous laugh.

Liam had pursued journalism as a career so that his thoughts and opinions would be read by thousands of people he didn't know and bandied about over countertops just like this—but he felt embarrassed that five years into his professional life he was still writing about celebrity nonsense.

As they walked toward the back of the apartment, Ben changed the topic unexpectedly, explaining how he had converted the walk-in closet in the hall into a study. There was no door at the end of the long corridor; the space opened up directly into Ben's bedroom.

"What do you like?" Ben asked as he turned on a small lamp on the nightstand next to the bed, one of the only pieces of furniture in the large, square room.

"What do you mean?" Liam felt his eyes turn away as he spoke.

"Are you going to play that game? You know. Top or bottom. Fast or slow. Naughty or nice. All those big, important philosophical questions."

Ben's mocking tone annoyed Liam. He had always hated the pigeonholes that gay men boxed themselves into and didn't want to get into a long conversation about what they were and were not going to do. If they were going to have sex, Liam wanted to have sex—not talk about having sex.

"Stand right there and take your clothes off, Ben."

Ben obeyed, pulling his sweater off quickly and undoing his belt. He unbuttoned his fly and his jeans fell to the floor. The cone of the lampshade cast a wide, swerving shadow over the bedroom walls. The uneven light lent the scene the forbidden sense of call girls in rented rooms, and Liam felt his penis move down his leg. With just a threadbare T-shirt, black boxers, and a thick pair of woolen socks on, Ben turned in a circle to model a little bit before continuing the strip show. Liam sat on the corner of the king-sized bed to enjoy the spectacle. Ben's thick, hairy thighs and meaty butt surprised Liam with the possibility of hot, thrusting sex. Leaning down slowly, Ben peeled off one sock and then the other. Liam laughed as Ben hopped around dramatically to demonstrate the cold chill of the bare wood floors. Liam wanted to reach over and run his fingers up and down Ben's muscular thighs but decided it would feel better to let the anticipation linger. Ben pulled his shirt off and assumed the vein-popping pose of a body builder in competition. His chest was in need of some muscle and his stomach some tightening, but Liam found something sexy about Ben's casually athletic physique. Ben skimmed his fingers along the elastic waistband of his boxers before stepping out of them and tossing the underwear toward the hamper on the other side of the bedroom. Liam lay down and stretched himself across the heavy duvet. The linens smelled of vanilla.

"Now do me."

"Oh, I intend to," Ben said with a growl.

"Ha ha. Now, take *my* clothes off. Slowly please."

Ben shook his head quickly and emphatically.

"Nope—my turn to make the rules," he said, tugging Liam's pants off and rushing to remove his sweater and T-shirt.

Within seconds, Liam was lying naked on the bed, and Ben had begun to rub the shaft of his cock.

"Could you turn the light off?" Liam asked.

"But I want to see every inch of your hot body."

"Sorry, Ben. It's just a habit. But not to worry, in Manhattan there's always enough light to see."

Liam wanted to imagine Ben's strong, hard legs pressing down on him without having the reality of his love handles and his chicken chest jiggling above him and ruining the fantasy. There could be no light. As Ben walked over to the nightstand, Liam took stock again of his solid ass and tree trunk legs and jumped off the bed and grabbed Ben from behind. Liam turned the light switch off and then tackled Ben onto the bed. Once he had pinned Ben down on his stomach, Liam ran his tongue along Ben's backside, starting at the center of his spine and working all the way down one leg and then starting over again and moving down the opposite leg. Ben's skin smelled of sweat and tasted of salt. Liam could feel pre-cum trickle from the head of his cock as he spread open Ben's butt cheeks and worked his tongue inside. Ben relaxed his sphincter as Liam probed farther inside his hole.

After a few minutes, Liam turned Ben over and repositioned himself so that he could stick his cock in Ben's mouth while he sucked on Ben's penis. Feeling enlivened and sexy, Liam began to do push-ups over Ben's body. Each time he dropped down to start a push-up, his cock went down Ben's throat, and Ben's dick rammed down his own throat. As Liam moved, their cocks slid back into the front of their mouths. Liam's arms started to tire after the first ten push-ups, and he dropped more heavily into position, with the force of his penis into Ben's throat causing Ben to gag in pain. Liam immediately rolled off to the side so that Ben's mouth and entire body would be free from any contact.

"Do you want me to get you a glass of water?"

Ben continued to gasp and to choke, dry heaving like someone in the throes of the stomach flu. He ran out to the bathroom and spat up into the sink.

"Sorry, I bet that just about killed your erection, didn't it?" Ben gargled with some water from the faucet as he spoke.

"Not at all," Liam said. "I still want to get off. Is that okay with you?"

They returned to the bedroom and moved against each other's bodies more cautiously. Liam stroked Ben off while licking his balls. After Ben shot a small but thick load of cum,

Liam scooped it up in his fingers and rubbed it over his own nipples. He then knelt over Ben and took Ben's fingers and placed them on his chest. Having Ben spread his seed on his hardening nipples was making Liam's cock thick and fat. More pre-cum dangled from his head, and Ben raised his head so that his tongue could catch the long gooey strands. When he couldn't take the pressure any longer, Liam moved Ben's right hand from his nipple and had him caress the shaft of his penis.

"Get it wet with some spit," Liam said as he could feel the skin of his penis getting raw. Ben had already warned that he did not have a drop of lubricant in the apartment. Ben stuck Liam's dick back into his mouth and sucked it until it was completely wet. He tried again to jerk Liam off.

"Faster, you've got to go faster." Liam had seen this happen too many times before. Once a guy came, it was nearly impossible to get him to pay any attention to the other half of the sex act. All they ever wanted to do was fall asleep. Liam knew that he himself was no different.

After about a minute, Liam gave up on Ben and began to masturbate. Each time he moved his hand up and down, he let the cup of his fingers inch farther along the head of his cock. The sensation caused Liam to goosepimple all over his butt and his legs. He arched his back and watched as the cum sprayed out onto Ben in long, clear ropes. Liam had closed his eyes while ejaculating and when he looked down again, he noticed that Ben had fallen fast asleep. The cum was dripping down his face and onto his neck.

MILE 7

"Wake up." Liam pushed each word through his tightly clenched teeth. He nudged Monroe in the rib cage to further call him to attention. "We have to receive communion in a minute. Our pew is next."

Monroe bristled as he fidgeted awake. Liam saw one of his aunts a few feet away turn to inspect the scene, and he looked at his friend intently so that there would be no misinterpretation as to what would happen next. They had not taken the long, winding bus ride out to Rockland on a frigid January day to make spectacles of themselves at this family event. Everyone in the Walker family received communion at mass. It didn't matter how hung over or burdened by sin you were; Liam's family prided themselves on the rigor and ritual of their religious observance. Liam had spoon-fed Monroe the rules as they roped their way through the local roads of New Jersey on the way to St. Margaret's Church. By the time they got off in the center of Pearl River, near the intersection where the King Kone and old Fotomat used to be, Monroe had reminded Liam that this was not his first trip to a church. As they walked the half mile from the bus stop to the church (Liam knew that a relative would have picked them up but imagined they would have more than their fill of family time by day's end), Liam tried to focus on being calm and on appreciating Monroe's generosity. Monroe certainly had more exciting ways to spend his Sunday but understood that Liam needed the moral support to make it through another family christening—the fourth in less than two years. A sizable number even by Roman Catholic standards.

Liam inched across the narrow pew and headed into the aisle. Monroe followed suit. The walk toward the altar always stretched on forever, each step its own act of penance for the sacrament about to be received. Liam looked straight ahead and marched forward, feeling scanned by the eyes of those who knelt in prayer at either side of him. He opened his mouth slowly and stuck out his tongue as the priest made the sign of the cross and spoke the words—*the Body of Christ.* The image of Ben moaning as Liam took his cock into his mouth flashed fresh in his mind. Liam knew that he had not done anything in the last week to purify himself. He left that morning before Ben awoke and hadn't spoken to him since. Every time that Liam had thought about Ben, he felt ashamed. He knew Ben wanted something from him—his time, his company, his body—and that fact made him retreat. The people he'd been with in the past had called Liam "careless" or "narcissistic" for withdrawing after moments of intimacy, but he could not handle the thought of someone expecting something from him. He would only disappoint them the way that he disappointed himself. But no one ever wanted to hear the woes and the complaints of the aesthetically and intellectually blessed. *Yes, please, tell me more about everyone wanting you and your never being able to make up your mind because there are so many possibilities at your doorstep, and you never know what better prospect might be coming along down the road.* The guilt burned through his hyperactive conscience like a forest fire.

When he was a teenager, he would squelch that conflagration with his weekly trips to the confessional. No matter what he had done, each week he could start anew. But Liam had not been to see a priest in almost a decade; he had gone to weekly mass with his parents steadfastly while he was living at home but dropped the ritual almost instantaneously upon starting college. It was as though he had awakened from a dream and found himself sleepwalking near the edge of the roof; he no longer felt the need to put himself under a microscope and have others judge his imperfections. But eighteen years of Catholicism proved difficult to shake. As a gay guy, he still—to this very day—wondered if his sexuality would banish him to hell. He did not know whether the sins would pile up or absolve themselves over time. Even though he had forsaken the church (at least to some degree), Liam could not help but feel unworthy—dirty even—as the priest pressed the wafer onto his tongue at his niece's christening. Liam bowed his head and blessed himself before returning to his pew.

As they shuffled out of the church, Monroe muttered something to Liam and then walked over to a bench by some barren bushes—a spot where newlyweds might sit for photos in a warmer season. The wind picked up audibly, and Liam turned up the collar on his new Burberry coat. His sister Rachel clutched her newborn daughter close to her breast and hustled over to the crowded parking lot. It was decided that the requisite array of family photos would be taken indoors once they arrived at the party. As Liam discussed the arrangements with his mother, he noticed a plume of smoke rise from Monroe's silhouette and craved the immediate rush that came with the first drag of a cigarette.

Liam had hoped against hope that his sister might have chosen a new venue for the party but was told that they would all be heading to the local Elk's Lodge. Looking at his watch, Liam wondered if it would be unseemly to down a beer at a quarter past twelve in the afternoon. As everyone dashed to their cars, Liam's mother explained that she had cleaned out the back of her station wagon to make room for "her youngest son and his *friend*." Though Liam had mentioned Monroe to his parents by name on several different occasions, they invariably referred to him by the generalized "friend." While they had begrudgingly accepted his being gay when he came out to them, his parents still seemed so inexplicably awkward as they grappled, tongue-tied, over the actual terms of his sexuality. And so the word *friend* now stung Liam, but he tried to write it off to the tension of the moment or the chaos of keeping track of the sensitivities of five grown children or the lack of modernity that comes with being from a completely different generation.

The uncomfortable silence in the ten-minute drive to the party provided ample time for Liam to think about the next three hours and to question introducing Monroe to his whole extended mess of a family. He took some solace in knowing that the sheer number of people—four siblings, four siblings-in-law, sixteen nieces, at least a dozen aunts and uncles, and twice that number of cousins—would create a barrier against any real or probing conversation. If history were any guide, his immediate family members would spend their time pushing the six-foot American subs and buckets of macaroni salad onto the guests while his more distant relatives would ask a question only to springboard into a vignette about their own lives, wrapped in some thinly veiled judgment about Liam's.

"Oh, do you still live off Bleecker Street? Did I ever tell you that I had a construction job one summer right there by the corner of MacDougal? We would go for beers at this bar on West Fourth— Boxers, I think it was. Liam, you ever go to Boxers? . . . Let me tell you, loud and dirty but there would sure be some snatch in there, bridge-and-tunnel girls all dolled up for a night in the big city. It was a great gig. Nothing like the city for a night out, but I don't know how you live there with all the filth and noise."

Liam had spent his whole college and post-college life trying to distance himself from this middle-class and middling existence that had been the crucible of his youth. He knew that his teeny apartment and modest salary at a magazine did not grant him any real reason to feel superior to his family, but he still felt pangs of inadequacy and self-doubt seeing himself through the suburban lens of their lives. He knew they tried their hardest, but the more they tried, the more contempt he felt; Liam hated that his family represented all that he had tried to change about himself by moving to the city and becoming cosmopolitan and urbane. He had tried to run away—but all roads seemed, always, to lead back home.

As they pulled into the parking lot of the squat Elk's Lodge, a broad woman dressed in a long brown leather coat with a leopard print scarf scurried through the entrance balancing a small child on her left hip and a big bowl of fruit salad on her right. From a distance, Liam could not say for certain whether the woman was one of his aunts or the wife of one of his cousins. Lately all the women at these family gatherings wore their hair the same ersatz shade of yellow with loose clothing to hide the extra twenty pounds they still carried from their last pregnancy. The men were all graying early and paired creased Lee jeans with the white tube socks and tennis shoes their wives purchased for them at Sears. Liam eyed Monroe's patchwork Commes des Garçons cashmere sweater and tweed pants and knew he was headed for a culture clash.

"Monroe Fields—suburbia! Suburbia—Monroe Fields!" Liam used the sweep of his hand to present the landscape to his party companion. He realized that despite any butterflies he was glad to have someone with whom to navigate the melee.

Liam's mother stayed in the parking lot to fish a platter of food out of the trunk but insisted that Liam hurry in with his *friend* before they both caught their death from the cold. The din of Rolling Stones music and the stench of stale smoke hit

Liam before he reached the back entrance of the lodge that led into the recreational room. A baby wailed in the distance. Liam remembered the layout of the room from the last family function, although now he couldn't recall if that was his niece Theresa's communion or his nephew Kevin's fourth birthday party. Monroe smoothed out the pleat of his trousers as they walked through the room. Liam stopped himself from telling his friend that his appearance was utterly unimportant. He knew he had already bossed around Monroe enough for one day.

"Hey there, little brother!" The boom of the greeting came from somewhere to the left, and before Liam had the chance to fully turn, his older brother had him in a bear hug. "And who do we have here?"

Liam's mind went blank. Standing before him in oversized khakis and a Notre Dame sweatshirt, his brother looked in sad disrepair, a house with solid foundation and a fine frame in need of some love and attention. The extra pounds had robbed his face of its angular qualities, but his clear green eyes, which were even lighter than Liam's, still held a childlike belief that everything was good with the world. Liam wished he could reciprocate the enthusiasm by saying something, showing some honest interest in his brother, but he found himself utterly mute.

"Hi, Patrick." Liam avoided looking his brother directly in the eye or answering his rather simple question. If given the chance, Liam knew he would start to judge Patrick, judge him for taking the simple path and never leaving their hometown, judge him for letting himself go, judge him for not wanting something more out of his life. So instead of meeting his brother's eye, Liam took a quick survey of the room. A long card table at the far end, next to the fire exit, housed all the food. Smoke billowed out of four sterno-lit aluminum trays, which Liam assumed contained stuffed shells and ziti, and condensation formed on the bowls of bread and iceberg lettuce that sat directly next to them. The huge sheet cake anchored a fleet of helium balloons, each a different shade of pink and decorated with storks and babies. The blank white walls were dotted, here and there, with streamers and accordion letters spelling out HERE SHE IS and BLESSINGS FROM GOD. And to the right of where Liam's brother was standing hung the only other wall decoration—a framed poster of an eagle set against the flag of the United States of America. The warning LOVE IT OR LEAVE IT was emblazoned across the bottom edge.

"Patrick, this is my friend from the city—Monroe."

"It's a pleasure." Patrick gripped Monroe's hand firmly in his own and shook it three times as if processing some important piece of information.

"So you live in the city too, Monroe? Do you live in a shoe box like my brother here? You know, I am always telling him that for what he pays in rent each year, he could put a down payment on a nice little house here in the country. Sure, there isn't all the hubbub and action, but you can have more than one room to move around in, a yard, build some equity . . . a life. I guess it's a tradeoff, right? You guys have a better commute, access to culture."

Monroe's mouth had opened as though he were prepared to answer each of Patrick's questions, but Patrick quickly excused himself to run after his two-year-old son, who had made his way into the sheet cake. Before Liam had the chance to ask Monroe how he was acclimating, he felt sets of small hands grabbing at his legs.

"Uncle Liam! Uncle Liam! Look at the new toys we got for Christmas!"

The trio of toddlers clamoring for attention brandished "Super Soaker" water guns that were half their size. The children belonged to his sister Kathleen.

"Those things aren't loaded, are they?" Liam stepped away as he spoke. "You realize those are outdoor toys and this is an indoor party, kids."

"You talk funny," said Harry, the oldest, and Caitlyn and

Roger erupted in unison. And then the three scampered away to accost someone new with the weapons Santa had brought them.

Embracing a laissez-faire style of parenting that bordered on willful neglect, Kathleen tended to view parties as a heavenly form of day care. They were free and with so many adults around someone would surely be minding her kids at all times, plus she got to eat and drink all day long. The family joked that the only reason Kathleen married her husband, Richard, a recovering alcoholic, was to have a designated driver for life. Kathleen had moved out of the house by the time Liam started middle school, so most of what Liam had gleaned about her came from old stories of her misspent adolescence and wild early adulthood. Motorcycles and misdemeanors.

As they inspected the rest of the room, Liam whispered the words, "I warned you it would be a madhouse," to Monroe, which he deflected with a forgiving laugh.

After settling in at a table, Liam rummaged through the cooler looking for a beverage. Surprised to see a Brooklyn Lager amongst the cans of Bud and bottles of Bartles & Jaymes, he grabbed one for himself and asked Monroe what he would like to drink.

"I'd love a glass of Chardonnay," he said as though he had been thirsting for one since they'd left Manhattan. "But if they don't have that then anything wine will do."

"Unless you want a Zinfandel, I would maybe suggest a wine cooler. Lots of flavors here!"

"Surprise me."

"Ayyyyy! You're making me so happy. I'm loving this." Liam turned and acknowledged his sister Evelyn, who had appointed herself chief party planner for this event given that Rachel would be taking care of her new baby. "When Liam told me he was bringing his *friend*, I bought these fancy beverages for the city folk. Feel free to get drunk, guys. That's one of the benefits of bus travel—no DUI worries!"

Liam quickly drank one Brooklyn Lager and opened another. He hated to admit that the stress did dissipate with each beer that he drank. Monroe had opted for a pomegranate-raspberry wine cooler, which he sipped responsibly between forkfuls of potato salad. Rachel had arrived and now visited from table to table with her newborn baby, who slept soundly in her arms.

"I always forget how small they are at this age," Liam said as his sister leaned in for a kiss from her baby brother. "She looks just like Dad."

"That's what everyone is saying," Rachel began, "I'm hoping it's not just the bald head and scrunched forehead."

"She's beautiful!" Monroe interjected. "You should be very proud."

"That's so sweet of you. I'm Rachel and this little sack of sugar is Elyse. You must be Liam's friend from the city."

"Yes, sirree. Monroe." He leaned down and kissed her hand.

"You're a good friend to travel in from the city. I know that my brother hates the bus ride, so I am sure that the company was a real treat for him."

"It was an hour . . . Honestly, no skin off my nose."

"Still, this is a LOT even when you're related to the motley crew here." Rachel smiled at Liam as she handed Elyse to Monroe.

Liam had always had a stronger connection to Rachel than to his other siblings, having someone with whom to joke over the crazy dynamics and silly antics of big-family life had helped Liam survive the mayhem of family gatherings. Rachel and Liam were the youngest of the Walker clan and both tended to be more measured and circumspect in their views on life, which had helped to cement their relationship from an early age.

Monroe held the baby very still at a safe distance from his body, as though the tiny bundle might explode if handled improperly.

"It would take an earthquake to wake her up, Monroe. You don't need to hold her so carefully." Rachel threw back her head and laughed. Liam had never seen her so loose and whimsical.

"It's been about a million years since I held one of these," Monroe cautioned. "From everything I've heard, they are high on the fragility scale."

"Please." Rachel picked up Monroe's wine cooler and took a quick swig of it. "Humans have survived for tens of thousands of years. We can't be that delicate."

Monroe laughed and leaned back in the chair, nestling the baby closer to his shoulder.

"So tell me what's going on in my little brother's life, Monroe. He couldn't be stingier lately when it comes to sharing the details with his darling family. We used to be so close when he was living at home, but since he fled to the city, he is like a safe deposit box. We need to mine for precious details every chance we get. And now you are here. B-I-N-G-O! So dish the dirt please. You've got my undivided attention."

Monroe glanced at Liam helplessly.

"Ooooh, there must be some interesting gossip to spread around if you're looking to him for clearance!"

"Monroe." Liam stood and picked up the baby and rocked her in his arms. "Don't let the wicked Walker sense of humor derail you. My sister is just trying to goad you for fun. Is life so dull here in the sticks that you're resorting to these games, sis?"

Rachel raised her eyebrow and took back another gulp from Monroe's bottle.

"Here you go, Rachel." Monroe handed Rachel a fresh wine cooler from the ice chest. "I don't want you to have to suffer through my backwash."

"You've landed yourself quite the catch here, Liam." Rachel eyed her brother as she finished the statement.

"I didn't *land* anything, Rach," Liam sniped back. "We're friends."

"Sor—ry! You see, he leaves a girl to draw her own conclusions, Monroe—being so mysterious and all."

"Oh, shut up already, Rachel! There isn't anything to tell. Sad but true."

"I doubt that, a strapping buck like you living in the big city. Right, Monroe?"

"Sorry not to have any good dirt on him, Rachel. All his time has been spent with the running club these past few months."

"Running club?"

"You know, Fast Trackers—the famous lesbian and gay running club."

"I had no idea! Is that how you're staying so lean and mean, Liam?"

Liam turned bright red and swiftly slugged the rest of his beer.

"Why, it's nothing to be ashamed of, little brother. I should join you guys to help shed some of this baby lard. Do you guys accept straight people?"

"Monroe, we should get some more food while it's still hot. Rachel, I am sure you have to make the rounds. You've given us more than enough of your time."

Rachel collected her little girl and moved along to the next table. Liam skipped the buffet table and went for another bottle of lager, his third within the hour. He knew that drinking on an empty stomach would make the alcohol hit his system harder and faster, which he felt would be essential over the next two hours at the party. All he wanted was to numb himself to the experience.

Monroe flitted around from table to table as though he were a long-lost member of the Walker clan while Liam talked to his parents about the status of his job at *Entertainment Weekly*. They still had not wrapped their brains around the fact that he could be well respected among the top editors and on an upward career trajectory in journalism while only earning $37,500 a year. The discussions—and today's would prove no exception—invariably led to them slipping him a hundred dollar bill, which he pocketed guiltily.

After Monroe finished his second piece of yellow cake with chocolate frosting, Liam told his friend that they would need to grab a ride over to the bus stop to make the five o'clock back to Manhattan. The family insisted on some quick snapshots in various combinations around Elyse before Patrick drove Liam and Monroe over to the bus kiosk on Main Street. The fog of inebriation helped shield Liam from the babble of the car ride. To his credit, Patrick tried to further convince Monroe and Liam of the merits of suburban life. Maybe they could even go in together on a down payment? True to form, Patrick answered any suggestion that he put forth, so Liam just let his head rest against the cold glass of the front passenger window.

The bus was directly behind them as Patrick pulled onto Main Street so their good-byes were very rushed. Patrick said something about hoping to make it into the city soon, perhaps for the St. Patrick's Day Parade, and Liam patted his brother on the shoulder as he climbed out of the front seat and motioned for the bus to wait.

"Your family was very gracious, Liam," Monroe shared as they found a seat together near the back of the bus. Liam looked out the window and noticed the magenta of the winter sunset through a long procession of split-level homes. He could already sense the days getting longer and felt hopeful about the spring.

"Are we not speaking to each other on this bus ride home, Liam? Please let me know now, and I'll recline this seat and nap."

"Family time always exhausts me. Thanks for coming."

"They clearly love and adore you. But you must know all that."

Liam turned toward Monroe to gauge the seriousness with which his friend offered this observation. There did not appear to be any irony in Monroe's tone or expression.

"Of course, I know my family loves me. They just don't have the ability to understand me. They don't have the capacity to listen."

"You don't know how lucky you have it, my friend." Monroe appeared to be on the verge of tears. "They stretch themselves as far as they can to try to reach inside your world. Take your sister Evelyn. She may not be well versed in beer and wine, but she went out of her way to think about what we might want to drink. And you certainly didn't have any problems drinking it. I'll take you home to a Fields' family gathering sometime if you want to see dysfunction and disinterest on parade."

"I wasn't trying to have a pity party for myself, Monroe. Do you really need to make me feel *privileged?* I do the best I can."

"Forget I said anything." Monroe rested his head on Liam's shoulder. "I appreciate your letting me get a little closer."

Before he had an opportunity to respond, Liam heard the soft tone of Monroe snoring lightly beside him.

The bus flew along through the back roads of the country and before Liam knew it, the skyline of Manhattan popped up across the icy expanse of the Hudson River. Liam took in the long, lean view of the city, which for his whole suburban childhood had lured him with the promise of something unattainable. As a teenager, Liam had sought out the vibe and the energy of the city to jolt him out of his ho-hum existence. The verticality of the city, the lights of the buildings, it all held such allure and was all so tantalizingly near. But as a kid in the suburbs, Liam knew the fifteen miles to the city may as well have been 1,500. It was all too distant and impenetrable. Now Liam watched the lights glitter in the black water and wished the city would not go by so fast. But in just a few minutes they would be through the Lincoln Tunnel and into the thick of Manhattan. Liam thought about how heartbreaking it must be for the residents in these Fort Lee high-rises to look at that lovely sight every night and then have to face their New Jersey lives.

Monroe awoke as the bus turned down the ramp into the tunnel.

"Hey, it's only six o'clock," Liam said. "Let's head down to Chelsea for some cocktails to eke all we can out of the weekend."

"I'm too old to start my workweek with a hangover, young fella."

"C'mon," Liam insisted. "Just one more—it will be my treat. You have to give a guy the chance to pay you back."

MILE 8

Liam hadn't been to the Upper East Side since his first year out of college, when he roomed with a high school friend in one of the nondescript high-rises on First Avenue that functioned as a dormitory for recent graduates. After coming out, he despised the expensive cab rides to the hot gay bars downtown and cajoled his way into a teeny railroad apartment in a sixth-floor walk-up on Grove Street. This gorgeous stretch of town houses at the western edge of the Village provided Liam with a literary oasis. By living the life of an artist in a little room by himself, Liam felt removed from the commerce and the pace of the city. But now here he was again at the Eighty-sixth Street subway terminal, looking up at the big box stores of Lexington Avenue. Only today he was headed toward, not away from, the park.

Liam had heard of the specific building address before. His parents were Kennedy family devotees, and his mother, in particular, was enamored of Jackie O. (*She transformed the White House. We did our Christmas tree in the tasteful gingerbread and white lights the First Lady brought to vogue.*) Yes, Liam thought, his mother's eyes would fill with longing to think of her son walking into 1040 Fifth Avenue, the building in which the former First Lady had spent her final years.

As he turned onto Fifth Avenue, Liam marveled at how he could not see another pedestrian for the entire stretch of road downtown from Eighty-sixth Street. It was as though the top-hat men standing guard outside the limestone buildings had scared away any potential passersby. The façades of most of the regal, old apartment buildings were dark, with only a few lamplights spotting a window here and there. The canopy of 1040 flapped suggestively in the wind.

Having forgotten Gary's last name as soon as the attendant opened the heavy glass door, Liam mumbled the embarrassing sobriquet "G-Lo," before quickly correcting himself and asking for Gary.

"I know." The doorman smiled dismissively. "He's the only one in the building right now. And he's expecting guests so please go right up. It's the penthouse."

A small paisley settee graced the dark wood cabin of the elevator. Liam wondered if anyone ever sat on it during the thirty or forty seconds it would take to reach their apartment. The heavy formality of the space made him feel claustrophobic, and sweat began to bead along his forehead. How on earth would he explain the sequins of perspiration on an evening at the end of January? Just then as his heart raced, the doors of the elevator opened into a vestibule with a little square rug on the floor, a thick brass mirror with fish-eye convexity in the middle of the wall, and a porcelain column overstuffed with umbrellas in the corner. A chandelier of frosted glass hung overhead, casting just enough ambient light to bestow a level of adult seriousness on the small waiting area. Two doors presented themselves, one to Liam's right and one to his left. No number or name adorned either entrance. More sweat trickled down his temples. After knocking unsuccessfully on both doors, Liam decided to be bold and simply open the one on his left.

"Hello! It's Liam. Gary, are you home?" Liam tried to

scream but he had never mastered the ability to raise his voice above conversational tone.

Liam could hear the distant garble of heated discussion as he stood in a long hallway with a procession of doors to his right. He turned around and noticed another set of doorways behind him. Walking slowly, he saw the noble expanse of Central Park through each room that he walked by. The voices grew louder as Liam turned and saw all the Fast Trackers—five assembled so far—gathered in a library wall-papered in the rose and silver stripe of expensive gift wrap. The room was a square on the corner of the building, with one window looking out across the blackness of the reservoir and the skein of naked trees toward the shiny spires and tow-ers of Central Park West and the other affording a long view of the glass and concrete of midtown Manhattan. The room was easily twice the size of Liam's apartment.

"Sit, sit, sit," Gary pleaded, putting his whiskey glass down on the ledge between the two armchairs in the corner of the room. "I didn't even hear Harold ring from downstairs. I had no idea you had arrived."

"You really need to prepare people for this, Gary. With a nickname like G-Lo, I fully expected you would work in an inner-city high school or for the Department of Sanitation or . . . well, anything other than a titan of industry."

"Please." Ben stood up from a curious ottoman of tan and white pony skin that completely clashed with the Louis XV motif of the overstylized room. "G-Lo, a titan? I've heard him called a lot of things before, but never a titan. A titan of trash talk, maybe. Is that what you had in mind?"

Ben shot a penetrating glance at Liam as he spoke, and Liam gazed out the window again to avoid his scrutiny. There had only been two unreturned voice mails in the past few weeks, but Liam knew that Ben was smart enough to read the writing on the wall. In moments like this, Liam wished he was a bigger person, the type of guy who broke awkward silences with truthful confessions, a man who would risk being hated to embrace the opportunity to be honest, someone who would simply return a phone call from someone he had just slept with.

As soon as they had had sex, Liam knew that he would disappoint Ben. Every time the thought of Ben popped into his head, Liam knocked the images further down the recesses of his mind. On paper, Liam could only come up with positives—Ben had a sharp wit, was well educated, held down a stable job, owned a lovely home, and treated Liam as though he were the sun, moon, and every brightest constellation in his solar system. Maybe that was the problem. Liam had gotten so accustomed to the chase, to the games of decoys and deception. Lately, he could only truly feel that he desired someone else if they withdrew their affection or suddenly became unavailable, unattainable. Or maybe New York City had made him jaded—lulling him into the belief that there would always be some shinier object just around the corner, waiting for him like a quarter on the sidewalk. Liam did not want to string Ben along if he knew that, in the end, he would only discard him for some hotter asshole who would likely treat him badly and cause a whole cycle of overindulgent self-analysis, guilt, and despair. For now Liam would simply have to suffer Ben's accusatory stares.

But strangely, Ben's posture and body language did not exude the self-consciousness of someone who had been ignored and disregarded. In fact, as he stood in the magnificent sitting room, Ben spoke with the bravado of one trying to hold court. Liam couldn't help but think that each pair of eyes in the room was sizing him up and imagining him having sex with Ben. If he had felt scorned or jilted, would Ben have possibly told someone? He had explicitly promised not to, but then again, how much could that promise be worth now? The paranoia caused Liam's stomach to clench.

"Here, sit in this armchair, love." Gary took Liam by the

shoulders and placed him into the chair. "Now, don't you listen to that bitter bottom, Liam. Ben's talking nonsense. We're not going to bore you with stories of me tonight. Let me get you a whiskey. Everyone is drinking from this bottle that I got in Scotland over the holidays."

"It's nothing to be ashamed of, G." Ben stood with his hands apart, ready to dole out the details of wealth accumulation that Gary seemed determined to shelve.

"Gary has an agenda for the evening, Ben. All this nonsense isn't on it. You're old enough to know that money talk is gauche and uncomfortable." Zane spoke definitively so that Ben would not feel emboldened to challenge him. Gary paced back and forth with his back to the group.

Ben turned his head away from Zane and rolled his eyes. The situation had deflated Gary of his youthful buoyancy, and he looked hard and tired when he turned back around. He walked over and picked up his drink, holding it at eye level for a minute and turning it into the light the way that a young fiancé might inspect a diamond, straining his vision to find a flaw.

"You'd think it would look different at $400 a bottle," he said cryptically. "But it's all the same. Just a higher price tag."

"Good job, Ben. You've really livened up this party. Are you trying to push Gary to the brink here?" Zane straightened up in his seat as he commandeered the room in an effort to set matters right. "Now, Gary, how many more are we expecting? I hope we're having at least twelve members tonight?"

"Ten aside from myself. It's just Ferdinand, Mitch, Marvin, Riser, and Matthew who are still to arrive. We should give everyone a few minutes, though. People inevitably think this address is closer to the subway than it actually is."

"Do you have anything to eat other than these nuts, G?" Gene winced as he fingered the mix of filberts and cashews.

"Gene, this isn't a dinner party. It's nine o'clock. Didn't you eat before you came?"

"But, G! Come on, G-Lo, you always have the yummiest of yummies here. Maybe just some goat cheese and crackers?"

Reluctant footsteps once again tested the hallway outside, and Gary threw his hands up in the air, exclaiming the worthlessness of the fancy building's doormen.

"It doesn't matter if you pay $10,000 a month in maintenance or $500. Just like the fucking whiskey, it's the same damn thing."

The last five guests to arrive now creaked in concert, walking toward the library as though they might trip some elaborate alarm system. The men were definitely familiar from the Armory and each one looked distinct from the others, but Liam would have had to blindly guess at their names.

Given the intimate size of the gathering, Liam did not imagine a roll call would be in the cards, so he made the bold move of announcing his embarrassment at not knowing everyone's name and requesting a round of introductions. Even as he heard the names, Liam realized that he was failing to put them all into his permanent memory. He could not focus. The names just floated out of mouths interchangeably. He knew the main cast of characters—Gary's bitchy style was inimitable; he had had sex with Ben; Gene had creepily hit on him; Zane had been solicitous but friendly; and Marvin had those beautiful calves and oversized feet. It would take some effort to place the others in context. For the time being, Liam decided to refrain from using first names in addressing anyone. Eye contact would have to do.

After pouring the new arrivals each a whiskey on the rocks, Gary topped off everyone else's glasses and then declared that it was time to get down to business—before the party, or at least before he got blotto. Gary assigned everyone a proper seat, but Liam decided to abandon his armchair for the perch of the windowsill overlooking midtown Manhattan. It looked like winter outside even though the holiday decorations had long left all the buildings in the city and there was no snow or ice on the ground. The light just looked different. The air had created a frosty halo around the buildings as though its glow could keep the tall structures warm.

"I have big news for you guys." Gary drew out the words *big* and *guys* and then paused dramatically. A few confused looks were passed around the room, but no one said anything, and a look of disappointment fell over Gary. "Well, since no one is going to bite, here it is! We are being propositioned by the Urban Bobcats. They approached Fabio after one of the recent workouts at the Armory with a proposal. They want to pit the top five finishers on our team against their sixth through tenth finishers."

Gary stopped again and surveyed the room.

"I know, I know. It confused me at first too. Basically, their second string does not feel challenged because they are in the shadow of their own teammates, who are some of the fastest runners in the city. And we'll never be able to compete head-to-head with the top runners on a team of their caliber, so this levels the playing field. We designate one race a month and compete against the Urban Bobcats. At the end of the year, the winner gets some sort of dinner out on the town and, more important, bragging rights! Fabio thinks this is an absolute no-brainer. Our club must accept this challenge."

Continuing to punctuate his speech with purposeful moments of reflection, Gary stopped and walked over to the end table where his drink sat and took a long, slow sip.

"I agree with Fabio," he said with gravity. "This is just what we need to restore our racing focus. As president of the club, I've called you all here tonight because I think that as the fastest guys on the team, it's all of you who need to accept or reject this challenge. If you accept, then you're committing to racing seriously this whole year. I am not going to vote on the proposal because I am not one of the runners who will be toeing the line in the ice of February and in the humid grip of August, so it wouldn't be fair of me. But you all know how I feel about this team and our racing potential, so I'll just open the floor."

When Gary stopped for yet another pregnant pause in which all of the runners were supposed to ruminate on the immenseness of the situation, Liam found himself puzzling as to whether or not he had realized that Gary was the club president. In some ways, Zane appeared to be at the helm of the club. Gary did, however, lead the Saturday run, which the club referred to as the centerpiece of Fast Tracker tradition. It occurred to Liam just how little he understood about the relationships, the protocol, and the members of the Fast Trackers. So far everything he had gathered had been by innuendo or by the triangulation of shoddy clues from sources of unknown reliability.

After about thirty seconds, a Greek chorus voicing doubt, skepticism, and some unbridled enthusiasm sounded through the room. Zane rose first to say that the team's pride as runners and as gay men rested on taking up the gauntlet. With a smirk of irritation, Gene reduced the idea of the challenge to an effort by a dominant team to belittle the city's "squadron of queer-footed athletes." It would be a revival of the neighborhood bully strong-arming the pansies on the playground. What laughs the Urban Bobcats would have after their second string runners annihilated the best possible team that the gays could assemble. Gary looked fearfully among the men who sat and stood speechless while Gene orated. It was clear that the prospect of unmitigated failure weighed heavily on at least two or three of the members gathered around.

Ben then offered his two cents, seizing the chance to pillory Gene. "Don't you think we'll look like a bunch of pansies," Ben spoke without looking up from the hat that he had begun to knit, "if we're afraid to take them up on this challenge, Einstein?"

In a sharp and sudden whirl of gesticulation, Marvin bolted from his armchair to speak about competition and what it means to be a runner. The only person whom you should be in a neck-and-neck or foot-to-foot race with, he implored, was the man inside your head. The beauty of running and what completely separates it from almost any other sport, Marvin went on, is the ability to compete with *yourself*. What did it even matter, he asked in disgust, if you beat someone else on a day when you didn't run your best? Everything outside of the self-test was arbitrary, meaningless, and juvenile.

A look of defeat settled into Gary's face, as he seemed determined to stay quiet and let the runners duke this out themselves. As he finished his drink and walked across the room for a refill, Gary eyed Liam imploringly. Liam had no idea if he could even race competitively for a whole year and decided he was far too new to the club to be leading the charge in either direction. The only thought that crept through his mind was that Fast Trackers had a schizoid identity—the club constantly underscored the importance of remaining a casual and social outlet for all runners, but then this powerful cabal of the, by and large, cuter, younger, and faster runners made decisions in private that would dictate the club's reputation among the city's racing community.

"Does anyone else have anything to add before we vote on this?" Gary asked.

Zane, Gene, and Marvin scanned the room to see if any other brave souls would stake a claim of support or refutation. Ben cavalierly angled his knitting needles as loops of yarn took the form of a gray skullcap. Riser stared out the square window that faced the blackness of Central Park, and others just examined their drinks in the large silence that followed Gary's question.

"Okay, then . . . " Gary readied slips of paper for everyone to write their vote on, creating the false semblance of anonymity.

"No, wait a second, G." It was Mitch who spoke in a reluctant tone that anticipated dismissal by others.

"I just wanted to say that I really love racing and anything that brings the team out there, all together and supportin' each other at the races," Mitch said. He then paused to collect his conclusion. "Well, I just think that's a good thing . . . who cares about the Bobcats? It'll be good for us. I remember watching Liam here go head-to-head with Gene at Van Cortlandt and it made me mighty proud to see Fast Tracker jerseys out there racing well."

Liam's face reddened from the attention as everyone in the room eyed him to measure or to confirm some fact about his speed.

"I just like to race, but it's all new to me," Liam started. "I have no idea what type of commitment it will take to race well at all these different distances in different seasons, month after month for the whole year. I just don't have the experience."

"C'mon, Liam." Mitch leaned over to nudge Liam's arm in encouragement. "None of us knows. We'll find out together."

Gary drifted off into Mitch's eyes in a look of quiet admiration and longing that did not snap until Ben cleared his throat three times, in loud and rapid succession. This action prompted Gary to instruct everyone to write their decision on a slip of paper. If it ended up 5-5, Gary noted that he would flip a coin to decide.

Liam stared at the blankness of the white paper and thought about how easy life can be when you do not commit to anything. Every Saturday night can be a new adventure, a new trick. But, on the flip side, Liam could feel his twenties slipping away and he secretly did yearn for something to show for the decade. He realized that he could really use a mission—a sense of purpose. When you don't push your own boundaries, you may never disappoint anyone but you also take the risk that life will just happen to you. Liam witnessed that routine complacency every time he visited his family back in the suburbs, and he knew he did not want that fate for himself. The prospect terrified him.

Just two months ago this club did not exist for him and now somehow he was in its undertow, and he didn't know why but he was letting himself be pulled along. He realized that he felt part of something. He considered too what it might be like to have to spar head-to-head with Didier all year long—the stress, the intensity, the thrill. He wrote the word "yes" on the paper and then folded it quickly into halves and quarters and eighths and circulated the scrap toward Gary.

Instead of teasing the crowd by reading each vote one by one, Gary impatiently pulled apart all of the pieces of paper and counted quickly and quietly to himself before exclaiming the 7-3 decision to take on the challenge. The club would need to discuss the racing calendar for the entire year with the Urban Bobcats and get ready for a possible race in the next few weeks. Now the work would begin.

MILE 9

The weather had worsened, even in the forty-five minutes since Liam left his apartment, and pockets of wind now skirted the edge of the park in little tornadoes of snow. What a day! It was the type of miserable dead-of-winter morning that could inspire someone to camp out in bed all day with a remote control and a bag of Cheetos. Liam wished he had done just that as the morning unfolded in a series of minor calamities. The alarm clock did not go off (Liam realized later that he had set it for P.M., not A.M.); his entire cup of coffee spilled in the mad dash toward the only cab he found patrolling Hudson Street at this early hour; and a hidden puddle of slush greeted him at the corner of Fifth Avenue as he jogged toward Central Park.

And as he now approached Engineers' Gate, Liam realized he was totally unaware of where the race started. He had assumed he would see packs of joggers by the entrance to the park, but he seemed to have missed the crowds. Perhaps other runners had abandoned the idea of racing in the cold slush of a January morning. With only ten minutes to spare, Liam picked a direction and jogged off to investigate, heading north along the east side of the park. As he nearly slid down the hill that ran along the side of the reservoir, Liam saw a small row of snow-dusted Portosan toilets and a roped-off circle that functioned as the baggage drop for the race. An older gentleman with a stern and ashen face told Liam to hurry along and get to the starting line; the race would begin precisely at 8:30 A.M. When Liam asked him where the pickup tent for his race number and timing chip were, the man eyed him with malevolent satisfaction, as though crushing a young runner's spirit was the unexpected present he had received for braving the elements all morning in Central Park.

"The number pickup is at the New York Road Runners headquarters on Eighty-ninth Street, just east of Fifth Avenue," he explained with a smirk edging his lips. "You really better hustle if you expect to make it all the way there and still hit the starting line on time."

Just as the man finished breaking the bad news, Liam heard the hurried splatter of footsteps and turned to see Gary and Mitch motioning frantically as they advanced. A little black plastic bag dangled from Gary's hand; he took a moment to collect his breath before launching into his tirade.

"The father, son, and holy ghost! Where in the hell have you been, Liam? We've been circling the area for the last half hour trying to hunt you down. Now, pin your number to your shirt and lace that racing chip to your sneaker so that your time gets properly recorded. We need to make sure everything goes smoothly this morning . . . And trust me, we're going to need all the help we can get to best the Bobcats."

Liam fished these items out of the plastic bag and readied himself for racing. Mitch threw some warm-up clothing into his duffel bag and the three teammates jogged to the start of the race together. It was 8:28 according to Liam's watch, but they only needed to turn onto the 102nd Street transverse, where the race was scheduled to begin.

The announcer had just finished explaining the five-mile race course, which consisted of the lower loop in Central

Park, as Liam and Mitch angled their way through the scores of runners corralled according to their expected race paces. Gary had opted to cheer along the course rather than run. He claimed he would be doing a greater service to the team in that capacity. As Liam tried to thread through two rotund men in sweatpants and parkas, somewhere in the heart of the eight-minute-mile section, the gun went off.

The first fifteen seconds after the gun sounded were maddening in their stillness. Liam finally made his way to the edge of the course, and he ran along the dirt path to bypass the serpentine crawl of the recreational runners making their way slowly across the transverse to the west side of the park. Once on the west side loop, Liam lengthened his stride and began to work his arms. Zane had reminded him earlier in the week that one should never feel totally comfortable during a race. Comfort equaled death. A racer always needed to be drawing on mental and physical strength, whether that strength be readily available or held in reserve.

Due to his inauspicious start, Liam spent the first mile of the race passing runners who were considerably slower than he was. It lifted his ego. Even though the clock read a disappointing 6:15 as he crossed through the one-mile mark, Liam knew that he still had the energy and focus to pass his competitors. Approaching the two-mile point by Tavern on the Green, Liam felt himself gasp for a little air and decided to focus not on the quickness of his foot turnover but rather on the smoothness of his breathing. Within a minute of relaxing into the run, Liam found the tension in his back and the burning in his lungs had dissipated.

To focus on something external, Liam ran toward the table where volunteers were handing out Dixie cups filled with water. As Liam hurried the cup toward his mouth, he felt a thin sheet of ice break against his lip and the entire contents of the cup gushed forward, falling down the sides of his face and flooding the microfiber of his long-sleeved T-shirt with brisk water.

Rounding the southern edge of the park's outer loop, Liam could not make out any of the objects in front of him. The wind, which had been at his back on the west side of the park, now pelted him mercilessly. Running north along the east side, which comprised the final two-and-a-half miles of this five-miler, was going to be a bear. Liam had passed several runners in the last few minutes but the swirling weather had turned people into indiscernible smudges along the white horizon, and Liam chose to relax and see what happened. To save his eyes from the burn of the wind, he peered down at the ground. At the four-mile mark, just as he came upon the southern edge of the reservoir, Liam saw the frosted blur of the race clock. It read 24:00 even. He had managed to average a six-minute-per-mile pace despite all the setbacks from the morning.

Liam looked over his shoulder and saw no one at his back, but he knew that to help the team now he needed to speed up and pass the invisible racers who must be out ahead, and he chased the last mile of this race with a heightened sense of purpose. The Urban Bobcats would surely be taking this challenge seriously despite the horrific weather. Bolting down the hill that led from the northern edge of the reservoir toward the finish line, Liam spotted the yellow and black singlet several yards ahead. The slender arms and knobby shoulders gave the runner away instantly, even under the veil of passing snow drifts. Liam noticed the gloved hands of his competitor pumping hard to work his arms faster and speed up toward the finish line, now less than half a mile away. This morning Liam took no chances. Waiting for the final feet of the race was too risky. Liam closed his eyes and sprinted past Didier. The slight uphill by the park's baseball fields was slick, and Liam worried he might lose control and skid toward the ground. His chest burned and his lips had chapped from the icy air.

Liam ignored the quaver in his stomach and told himself that his legs would continue—they simply *had* to—despite the numbing that tingled through them. The wind whipped harder, blowing around the snow that had coated the branches of the trees. Liam flew around the final turn at 102nd Street, striding commandingly onto the transverse where the finish line was just within sight. He looked straight ahead toward the festive banner of red and blue floating under a tapestry of snow and ice.

Once past the line, Liam decelerated to a stop and no longer had the strength to hold his back upright. He crouched down with his two hands pressed hard against his knees and gagged on the foul taste that now resided at the back of his tongue. The wind continued to pummel him and without the concentration of the race, Liam began to feel the rawness of his lips and the damp chill of his chest.

"You can't stop here! We have other runners coming through!" It was the woman whose job it was to clip off the timing chips. She was also in charge of clearing out the area. Liam hobbled over to have his chip removed and then stumbled off into the margin of road where a cluster of bushes listed under the weight of the snow.

As he walked over to the baggage check to reclaim his belongings and throw on some warmer clothes, he saw Didier hunched over in an embankment by the side of the transverse, puking into the snow. Liam knew that if another Fast Tracker saw him giving aid to the enemy, he would be lectured on the seriousness of the competition, but he could not stand to see a fellow runner in distress. Didier pushed Liam away when he approached, clearly humbled and embarrassed. Didier looked lean and severe, and Liam was drawn to him even more in this compromised state.

"Don't mind me," Didier said. "Bad races take more out of you than good ones." He paused a second and then took Liam in with a long and studied stare. "I'm Didier. It's about time we were formally introduced."

"Liam. It's Liam."

With nothing clever at the ready, Liam excused himself. Didier rested his hand in the crook of Liam's neck and rubbed it gently as he nodded good-bye.

Wanting nothing more than to return the sensation of touch to his fingertips, Liam decided to jog out of the park toward the subway. In order to be on time for his shopping safari through the West Village with Monroe, he needed a little bit of luck and a good deal of foot speed. He knew he was cutting it close by double-booking his morning plans but also knew that there would be hell to pay if he blew off Monroe. The complaints about his spending too much time with Fast Trackers had already been filed and re-filed.

As he turned onto Fifth Avenue, Liam's cell phone rang from inside his backpack. Barely retrieving the phone before the call had gone into his voice mail, Liam did not have time to look at the number of the incoming call, and the voice was unfamiliar and abrupt.

"Where are you, guy? Come meet us at Metro Diner—101st and Broadway."

"Who is this?"

"Babe—it's Zane."

"I'm running late. Can I call you back later?"

"No! You can come meet us now. We're going to look up the team results online."

"I am late to meet a friend. . . ."

"Come meet us. It's a diner right off the park. Breakfast in under an hour—easy. Pretty please. Just sprint over here. You're a speed demon."

Liam's slight pause was quickly interpreted as a yes, and Zane hung up the phone. As a teammate committed to the competition against Urban Bobcats, Liam *really* wanted to hear more about what had happened at the race and to be a part of things. He wanted to fit in. Surely Monroe wouldn't mind moving their plans an hour; Liam would call him and make something up about train delays. Quick and easy.

"I almost didn't recognize the number when it popped up on my phone—it's been something like a century since you've actually dialed me." Monroe's sarcasm traveled very well over the phone lines. "I worried my baby's finger had broken."

"And conversation starters like this one are going to engender many more phone calls from me, babe. Look, I have had a helluva morning running around and doing errands and the New York City transit system has had it in for me. I need an extra hour to prep for our shopping extravaganza. I can't go into Marc Jacobs looking like a bedraggled panhandler. You understand, right?"

"If they are out of the cashmere hoodies that I have been coveting all month, I will snap that toothpick frame of yours in two. *Ca-piche!*"

"You're a doll. See you at two—on the dot."

Click. It was so easy that Liam wondered why he didn't concoct little white lies more often. And then he felt a slight rumble in his stomach. The lying clearly did not fit his constitution and had already left its mark on him. But it was just an hour. Monroe probably could use the extra time to primp for their outing. Liam heard himself justifying it all and felt even guiltier. Sometimes he wished he could just shut off his brain for an hour or two and enjoy life.

Liam began to jog west across the park and noticed the day was growing prettier. The temperatures still huddled in the midtwenties, but the winds had slowed and the sun seeped through the once lowery skies. The gorgeous landscape of the park rolled out before him like still shots from a movie scene. In about an hour, parents would descend on the park with children and sleds streaming along behind them. Knowing the mayhem down the bend, Liam appreciated, even more, the complete absence of anything as his feet crunched through the winter setting.

Even Broadway had been more or less deserted, except for

the few homeless people who dotted the median of the avenue. The diner glowed on the corner in the most inviting way. Its chrome countertops and checkerboard tiles created the feel of another time. The Fast Trackers—there appeared to be six or seven in total—were a study of hi-tech gear. The window of the diner showcased a mosaic of Spandex tights, multilayered Windbreakers, and aerodynamic hats and headbands. Liam paused at the door for a minute and admired the colorful group enjoying one another while waiting for a table in the busy restaurant. Everyone bellowed his name as Liam entered.

MILE 10

"Hey, hey, hey! You can't just sit there." Zane swatted Gene off the chair he was about to lounge into. "I prepared a seating chart."

Gene rolled his eyes and stepped away to the bar where the bartender poured bottomless pitchers of margaritas and daiquiris for the Fast Tracker crowd. Zane may have kept dry, but he was not begrudging anyone else a good time. Liam downed three icy drinks and had begun to flirt with the Brazilian guy tending the bar. He would have preferred a longer happy hour to the dread of a tedious dinner where he didn't even get to choose his own seat. Assigned seating seemed overdone for a Mexican restaurant.

"Don't worry," Zane whispered. "I have you seated right next to me at the center of the table. Gene will be quarantined to the far end—that chair right next to the entrance."

Liam looked at the area in which they would be eating and thought Zane grandiose for referring to it as one long table, as though the group were a big family who had put all the leaves in the dining room set so that service for sixteen could take place around the Danish modern furniture. The restaurant staff had, in fact, pushed together a series of ill-fitting two-person tables to accommodate the oversized party.

"I don't know why Gene has to ruin every event by attending. Just once it would be nice to have an evening free of his ickiness."

"It's *your* birthday party, Zane. Why did you include him on the guest list?"

"Don't be stupid, Liam. Not inviting him wasn't a choice. Be real, please. Oh! Oh! Oh! Let's try to guess what cheap, inappropriate stunt he's going to pull tonight. That's always fun."

Liam understood the need for groups of friends to have an enemy within. Human nature and the evils of collusion forced cliques to align against an outsider, someone about whom gossip and bad will could be generated. And it helped to fuel the fire when the outsider was actually an insider. It would be pointless if the pariah were someone whom no one knew, some person foreign to the scene. How could anyone become appropriately invested in a stranger? What would be the fun? By inviting the maligned one in and making sure he is at every event, the clique assures itself a constant arsenal of vinegary anecdote. While Liam knew that a more mature person might not cave to the group pressures, he had to quench his own very real thirst to fit in. And he seemed to be doing just that quite beautifully with the Fast Trackers these days. Every once in a while Liam was, however, saddled by a nagging thought—what if the winds shifted and he himself blew into the crosshairs of the group's scrutiny and displeasure? He was all too aware of the vagaries of gay men's tastes and predilections. There were no guarantees in these types of petty games.

"Fine." Zane pushed Liam away coyly. "Don't play the game. See if I care. You go refill your drink. I'm going to do a rotation before telling people to take their seats."

As he ordered another frozen margarita with salt, Liam noticed Riser sulking on a bar stool, massaging his face between his hands and moaning quietly. While Liam had not yet developed a one-on-one rapport with Riser or Matthew or Ferdinand (the three seemed to travel as a trio), he felt moved to make the effort now that one of his teammates appeared glum.

"Everything good?" Riser lifted his head at the question. Upon closer inspection, Riser appeared more angry or sullen than sad.

"Good? Sure." He shook his head in disgust as he spoke. Liam had no sense of where this conversation might go. "I'm so completely nauseated with myself. I already ate about half a bowl of guacamole, and we haven't even sat down to dinner yet. I'm going to look like a bloated buffoon dancing tonight."

"Dancing?" Liam realized that he hadn't responded to the part of the statement that Riser was angling for.

"Yup, anytime we go out in Williamsburg on a weekend night, you can count on a trek over to Sugarland for dancing."

"But Zane didn't put anything about dancing in the invitation. It only mentioned dinner."

"You're cute. Here's what will happen. After dinner—it will be around ten thirty or eleven o'clock—Zane will cry that he doesn't want to go home yet. He'll shout that he needs to be around his friends come midnight—or something like that. Then someone will have to suggest the trip to Sugarland, as though it has never been suggested before, as though it isn't suggested every time we go out to eat in Williamsburg. It's like a fucking script."

Liam nodded as Riser dug deeper into the diatribe. For some reason, Liam placed his hand against Riser's cheek and caressed it gently, in a way that was meant to be comforting. Riser pulled away quickly.

"I'm not a charity case. I'm just fat," he retorted.

"You look fantastic. You're incredibly lean." Liam was not mollifying Riser. In fact, Riser probably had less body fat than Liam.

Riser pulled the tight sweater he wore up a few inches to reveal his concave stomach.

"See, these rolls just drip off my sides."

"That's just because you're sitting. That happens to everyone."

"Sure, you'll see later at the club just how much fat everyone has dripping off their six-packs. I appreciate the sentiment, but you don't know what you're talking about. You'll see for yourself soon enough."

"I think that the boys will be buzzing around you like bees to the hive, my friend." Liam smiled as broadly as possible and made sure that he looked Riser right in the eye as he spoke. Riser attempted a grin of recognition back and then excused himself, trotting over to the restroom.

While Liam understood that runners had an often single-minded focus on enhanced performance and the never-ending quest for "perfection," he sometimes wanted to shake some sense and perspective into his new group of friends and let them know that they might not want to miss the forest for the trees. After all, sometimes, it can be really fun to just enjoy the guacamole and still have dinner and even take your shirt off on the dark dance floor. Sometimes just going on a run and not clocking the time can be a boatload of fun. Liam sensed a deep sadness in Riser and hoped that he would come back from the bathroom and enjoy his good friends and a good meal.

Just then Zane pulled everyone from the bar to the dining table. He sat each person individually according to the cards he had propped up on the place settings. As he had intimated, Zane placed Liam directly to his left, with the rest of the guests situated in proximity to Zane based on his taste, or distaste, for them. Gary dined to the right of Zane, and Ben was directly across from the birthday boy, flanked by Mitch and Riser. Some non-club members were strewn about, including a heavily tattooed black man who trained Zane at his gym on Astor Place, as well as the Laotian woman who ministered to his massage needs twice per month. Gene huddled for warmth by the restaurant door that kept brushing in gusts of winter.

Liam found himself eating around the heavy lip of melted cheese that oozed from his burrito. He touched the area of his abdomen between his waist and his navel and it felt soft and untoned; he needed a good tempo run to jump-start his metabolism. Never one to shy away from the spotlight when shirts started to fly off, Liam knew that if they did go dancing, he would want to have as empty and taut a stomach as possible.

"Looks like we have another light eater on our hands," Gary said through a series of boyish giggles. He quickly lifted his icy margarita glass. "I'm with you, Liam. Save the calories for the liquids!"

"You'd lose more weight if you cut out the alcohol." Marvin had craned his head and projected his voice loudly enough so that everyone could hear the wisdom he meted out from his perch next to Gene. "Not only is that concoction riddled with calories, but it also slows your metabolism."

"Well, Liam and I don't need to lose weight." Gary winked at Liam, and they clinked glasses in an alliance against Marvin's attempts to kill their buzz.

"The clocks don't lie," Marvin said, waving his hand directly at Gary and Liam. "Look at those guys who came in ahead of Liam in the five-mile points race. I can tell you for certain that they were almost all thinner than he is. I'm not talking twenty pounds, but if Liam dropped four or five pounds, he'd be a much greater asset to the team."

"No one named you coach, Marvin," Zane spoke emphatically, looking at Liam instead of the subject of his censure. "When that happens, you can put us all on diets. But for now let's enjoy my birthday."

"Liam, next time you go for a jog, carry a five-pound weight with you and let me know if it slows you down." With a snicker, Marvin returned to his chair and shared what appeared to be a final rejoinder with Gene, who then patted him on the back.

While Liam appreciated the intensity of elite runners—that discipline that hollowed their cheekbones and drew every millimeter of fat from their sunken bellies—he also loved the fact that he got attention for his biceps and chest. He never considered the gym a mecca and only lifted three or four times a week, for tone more than bulk, and did not want to give that up to run faster. Had it been any other Fast Tracker at the table, with the exception of Zane, and Liam would have swung back with a reminder that his five-mile time had been faster.

When Gary pulled out his laptop at the diner after the last race, Liam's jaw dropped to learn that he had managed to finish the run with a 5:30 mile. He clocked 29:30, breaking 6-minute pace for entry into what Zane referred to as the "high-five club." Only a few members of the team had ever managed to race at sub-6-minute pace and the only others to have achieved that feat at the last 5-miler were Marvin and Zane. Both had beaten Liam handily. Marvin had clocked 28:25, which was astounding for a forty-one-year-old, and Zane placed first for the team with a 27:55. It was a tight race for the fourth and fifth Fast Tracker spots, with Gene coming through fourth in 30:18 and Riser crossing the line in 30:21. Ferdinand, Mitch, Ben, and Matthew followed in 30:29, 31:09, 31:20, and 32:06, respectively. Every runner had come close to his personal best, but Zane still failed to edge out the tenth-place runner from the Urban Bobcats, and so the Fast Trackers team had not only failed to best the Bobcats, it had failed to even make them sweat. A pep talk ensued at the next track workout, with Fabio insisting that the team had only scratched the surface of its potential. By May, those who stuck to the program would be lopping off minutes from their five-mile time. Nothing but the boundaries of their imagination and their spirit could contain them.

"Don't pay any attention to him," Zane whispered into

Liam's ear as he began to open his presents. "You have more natural speed than Marvin—no matter what the scale says."

"I want to beat him." The words surprised Liam as he heard them trail from his mouth. The internecine competition with Fast Trackers had turned him off at workouts. But he smarted over Marvin's smug tone.

"Are you willing to do anything it takes to beat him?" Zane asked, barely suppressing a Cheshire grin.

Liam nodded, curious to hear what was coming next. The question had been asked with a gravity of tone, making Liam imagine the handing over of a firstborn son or the sacrifice of his most favored possessions.

"Good." Zane paused for effect. "You will be my protégé. I can slice your race times down. I believe that if you believe in yourself, you can take him."

"Okay."

"So you promise to do whatever I say?"

"Yes. Okay."

"It's a deal. I'll call you tomorrow. I have to finish opening the gifts. Otherwise, the crowd gets bored!"

After unveiling seven different combinations of running shorts and tank tops and three different gift certificates to athletic stores throughout the city, Zane cleared all the presents off the table and tearfully thanked those who had taken the time to shop for him.

"It's all over." Zane sighed. "Nothing left to open, but I can't bear to see the night end. You all can't let me go home yet!"

It was as though a script *had* been prepared, and now the audience waited for someone who had forgotten a line. Finally, Mitch piped up that given that it was still only eleven o'clock on a weekend night, they should all go dancing at Sugarland. The suggestion came out so innocently that Liam almost doubted that Mitch had witnessed this scene play out a dozen times prior.

A small line greeted the pack of Fast Trackers as they approached the outside of the club on Ninth Street. The man monitoring the door glanced in a wide, swooping *S* over the group and waved everyone inside without saying a word. An orange-haired man in a striped polo shirt and his mousy female companion shot an accusatory look at each and every Fast Tracker who waltzed by them and through the club's velvet rope.

Liam had never been inside Sugarland. As the gay scene crept across the river into Brooklyn's Williamsburg in recent years, Liam still preferred to frequent the East Village hot spots along the corridor of Avenue A between Houston Street and Fourteenth Street that housed Detox and The Phoenix and Eastern Bloc. But this gritty wonderland where the club owners blasted patrons with classics from Madonna along with the best remixes of songs by Lady Gaga and eighties gems like the soundtrack to *The Breakfast Club* had flown under his radar. The interior of Sugarland matched the desolation and grime of the street outside, with the main bar recalling the seediness of Times Square's heyday. A few hundred meters from the club's entrance, music blared and two or three groups of two or three people danced halfheartedly.

"It's still the warm-up music," shouted Zane, motioning for everyone to settle along some stools that flanked the dank bar. A trio of emaciated hipsters still sporting remnants of adolescent patches of acne self-consciously rolled and unrolled the sleeves of their flannel shirts. They twirled the skinny straws in their mixed drinks while discussing the distinctions between Verlaine and Rimbaud. The bartender flipped through the copy of *Honcho* he had resting on the knicked and worn surface of the long bar.

"Tequila shots for everyone!" screamed Mitch, throwing down a hundred-dollar bill on the bar before anyone had the chance to protest.

The bartender jolted awake from the centerfold of a furry

farmhand pitching hay while stroking himself off, and he quickly lined up more than a dozen shot glasses. Liam despised tequila shots. All the sane people he knew felt the exact same way when sober, and yet it seemed to be the rallying cry of drunk people everywhere—the first and last resort in barroom camaraderie.

"To victory!" Mitch yelled as he raised his glass up high. His voice echoed through the mostly empty bar.

With the exception of Zane, everyone downed their shot quickly and quietly. Mitch snatched the shot out of Zane's hand and gulped it down while the others still cringed from the repulsive burn of their first shot.

"It'd be a shame to see four bucks go to waste," Mitch said, wiping a dollop of drool from his lip.

Gary threw his arms around Mitch and Liam and yelled at Zane to come over for a group huddle.

"Let's always remember the way the four of us are right now," Gary said. "The Four Musketeers! We can do anything if we band together."

Liam wanted to drink in the syrupy sweetness of Gary's words but felt that he had not paid the dues of friendship that such a sentiment required. As they all emerged from the stranglehold of the group hug, Zane announced that they needed to hit the dance floor. Mist from a dry ice machine snaked through the room, roping the shirtless torsos on the dance floor. "Kids in America" thumped overhead.

"Push your way over to the side by that raised platform!"

"What?" Liam screamed at Zane as loudly as he could and tried to read Zane's lips as he repeated himself. Finally, Zane motioned toward the area where guys were dancing on a cube above the crowd.

After a few minutes of elbowed slithering, the group of fourteen runners hovered close together in the far corner of the dance floor. As soon as a drunk dancer stumbled off the makeshift podium, Zane jumped excitedly and veered to-

ward the platform. Just when Zane broke through the crowd
and reached the stage he had been eyeing, Gene planted his
foot onto the wooden cube and hoisted himself up so that he
was hip-to-hip with the three other gyrating men reigning
over the sweaty dance floor.

Gary rubbed Zane's shoulder consolingly, and several in
the pack rolled their eyes as Gene tossed his thin-ribbed
tank top into the crowd in the manner of a guitarist appeas-
ing his adoring fans. Liam marveled at Gene's unchecked
self-confidence. If he had a rim of fat jutting out over his
belt, Liam would never have danced shirtless in front of
dozens of hot young men. But Gene had his eyes closed and
flailed his arms from side to side arrhythmically as though he
were alone in his living room.

Everything was just a little off with Gene's body. He carried only about three extra pounds (he was a distance runner,
after all), but his core did not hold this weight in a compas-
sionate manner and left the extra fat to wiggle around his
waist. And though it would be impossible to do tactfully,
Liam wished he could suggest a series of yoga poses and abdominal exercises to tighten up Gene's stomach. To add in-
sult to injury, Gene's chest caved in on itself, drawing the eye
to a little grove of hair that begged to be plucked. A wider or
longer frame would have forgiven these shortcomings, but
Gene had a short body that could not handle more than one
aesthetic challenge. Liam averted his eyes, not because he
feared making Gene insecure but because he knew Gene
would be searching out any sign of potential interest and encouragement.

Mitch and Gary each pulled out two beers from their back
pockets and split the Heinekens with Liam and Ben. As intense body heat enveloped the dance floor and all the different booze he had consumed flooded his system, Liam felt
the quick slip into drunkenness. "Bad Romance" bled into
"Freedom 90," and two friends who had been dancing to-

gether on the raised island jumped into the crowd. Zane grabbed Liam and bounded toward the platform.

The music raced through Liam's blood; his skin pulsed with the heavy bass. From the elevated vantage point, Liam realized that the crowd was not all beautiful. Amid the gorgeous men with gymmed bodies mixed bachelorette parties from Long Island who had read the recent reviews in *New York* magazine and wanted to play "edgy" for the night or seek some vicarious thrill or relive some misspent past. Liam replayed the video for "Freedom 90" in his head as he rocked with his arms waving up to the sky. The famous models of 1990—Naomi Campbell, Linda Evangelista, and Christy Turlington—lip-synched the words of the song while bathing in bubbles and fretting across apartment floors in oversized sweaters. As the chorus began, Liam lifted off his T-shirt in one quick pull and jammed it into the back pocket of his Diesel jeans. Now he *was* George Michael dancing to the music.

When he opened his eyes, Liam noticed that Ben had parked himself directly in front of him. Ben feigned a look of disinterest as soon as Liam realized he was standing there in patient rapture. Feeling the rush of the reverberating music and the clammy tingle of the sweat that rolled down his pecs and over his nipples, Liam felt energized by the moment and grabbed Ben by the hand and guided him to the quieter edge of the dance floor, far away from the deejay and the speakers.

"Look, I know I was a dick to you, but I am pretty messed up right now."

Ben raised him eyebrows in faux-amazement.

"We're all damaged, Liam. You wear your psychic plight better than most."

Ben ran his fingers down Liam's nipple, and Liam felt his dick swell in his pants for a brief moment. He swatted Ben's hand away.

"Oh, come on, Mister Liam. You rip your shirt off but you don't want anyone to touch your beautiful chest. What are you, some piece of art that we're just supposed to admire from afar?" Ben slurred his words a little and gulped down the remainder of his vodka tonic.

"Be careful not to mix too may liquors tonight. Tequila can really mess you up."

"Thanks for the helpful advice, Liam. You are so fuck-ing sweet. You are syrup. We should put you in a bottle and call you Aunt Jemima."

"Got it." Liam began to turn away. "I am getting another drink. I'll catch up with you later—if you aren't hurling in the bathroom by then."

As he headed for the bar, Liam noticed that the crowd had nearly tripled in size since the Fast Trackers had arrived. Sidling up to the bar, Liam heard a familiar voice boom from somewhere off by the dance floor.

"That's it! I'm taking you home!"

Liam could identify the words quite clearly, even through the thundering volume of the music and the din of the club. Gary stabilized Mitch momentarily, but then Mitch swayed again and fell into the group of young black men who now jumped up and down to "Vacation." The guys whom Mitch leaned into appeared oblivious, but Gary had mustered every inch of his paternal instinct to shepherd Mitch off the dance floor and back into the main bar area. Liam jumped off the stage area and followed them to make certain that every-one was okay. Ben and Zane were close behind.

Maneuvering the dance floor proved somewhat tricky. Groups of guys had banded together tightly to block any strangers from trespassing. As Liam tried to slither through a group of skinny Hispanic teenagers, three of the boys de-cided to trap him in their web by bumping chests with Liam and with each other. As he turned to move in an alternate di-rection, a different kid from the same group leaped forward with his chest bulging out and knocked Liam right in the ribs. Seven or eight people in the surrounding area joined in and transformed part of the dance floor into a makeshift mosh pit. By the time Liam had successfully extricated himself and found his way to the front bar, Gary and Mitch were no longer there.

"Jesus, it's a jungle in this place," Ben said as he made his way into the bar area. "Just my luck to try to escape while they're tempting the crowd with 'It's the End of the World As We Know It.'"

Apparently, Ben was still on speaking terms with him. Amazing what yet-another drink could do to the complexion of the evening. Liam stood searching for Mitch and Gary among the scores of patrons left, most of whom looked as though they would need to be ushered home in a cab at any minute. Zane had apparently made eyes with one of the mosh-pit gang and had no intentions of leaving the dance floor any time soon.

"I suppose they'll be fine," Liam mumbled, to himself more than to Ben.

"Please, the drunk get home more easily than the sober in this town."

Liam liked the pithy way that Ben reeled off aphorisms, even if half of the time, like now, they didn't make much sense. Ben lifted his shirt to scratch his stomach, exposing spotty clumps of body hair around his navel and across his slightly chubby belly. The feeling of sex rushed over Liam. With the lights off and another drink, couldn't Ben be a suitable pastime for the lonely hours before dawn? No, he needed to focus on something else—and quickly.

"Poor Gary!" Liam summoned a cautiously concerned tone; he wanted to seem legitimately interested without being reactionary. "One of us should have accompanied him. Taking care of wasted friends is never a good time. He could have used the help."

"Please. He would kill for alone time with Mitch. He's probably hoping that Mitch allows for some below-the-belt gropes in the cab."

Liam sensed anger in Ben's tone and could not help but think of their drunken cab ride home.

"Don't tell me you have not noticed the puppy dog eyes, Liam? Haven't you figured out Gary's MO yet? He built this team under the pretense of caring about gay running when all he ever really wanted was a harem."

Liam needed to get away. Feeling inundated by innuendo, he no longer knew whom to trust or what to believe.

"I'm going to step out for a smoke," Liam said, taking a pack of Camel Lights out of his back pocket. "I need some fresh air."

"Smoke? Liam, you're a distance runner. What are you doing with a pack of cigarettes?"

"It's a drinking thing . . . let it go."

"I'll head out with you." Ben rubbed Liam's neck, and the tension in his upper back began to dissipate. He almost moaned in relief.

A taxi had stopped in front of Sugarland as they walked out onto the street. Ben rushed to the door and held it open for the couple inside who were still waiting for change from the cabbie. Liam had a habit of lingering in taxis when people tried obnoxious moves like that to get him out faster. But the couple thanked Ben as they exited the car.

"So you want to share a ride?" Ben asked, still standing in the same position with the taxi door open. The driver shook his head and waved his hands before finally honking.

"You know that I am headed in a completely different direction than you are, Ben."

"C'mon, I'm putting myself out there." Ben put his hands in his jacket pockets and looked down at the ground for a second.

"I just need to clear my head. I am going to walk for a little while, maybe catch the subway home," Liam replied.

As Liam turned and headed in the opposite direction, he heard Ben bark at him to stop and listen.

"I should have known better than to stick my nose in the boy-nip."

"Excuse me?" Liam took a step back and gaped at Ben in confused disbelief.

"*Boy-nip*—the cute young flavor of the month that sends everyone into a tizzy but offers no real sustenance . . . A mirage not an oasis."

"Really, Ben? I am supposed to be a source of water in the desert?" Liam made no attempt to hide his disgust and anger.

"Ha! That's the message you would hear." Ben now dramatically hailed a different taxi and opened the car door. "Never mind, Liam . . . I don't beg for sex."

Ben stood looking at Liam, and Liam knew that Ben wanted sex more than ever. He could hear the desire hot in Ben's words and see the anger in his boxer's stance by the intersection of Ninth Street and Roebling. If they were to go home and fuck right now, Liam sensed that the hostility and disappointment would translate into a fantastic orgasm. But then he would be writing the script for another of these soap opera moments. Even if it meant losing a new friend and earning a bad reputation, Liam had to do the right thing. And this was the right thing for both Ben and him. Liam headed west for the solitary trip home.

MILE 11

"Liam, there are no extra-smalls on this rack!" Monroe catalogued through the tank tops one last time before handing Liam a small. "That's probably better anyway . . . you *do* want to be able to breathe in the damn thing."

"I want it to be snug across my chest so that runners can see my nipples . . . well, at least the suggestion of my nipples. This one will swim on me. I'm just going to ask the clerk if they have anything else in the back of the store."

The few gangly men wearing singlets who appeared to be the salespeople on duty had suddenly disappeared. It occurred to Liam that he and Monroe were the only two customers on the floor, which seemed odd for a Saturday afternoon. The economics behind running stores baffled Liam. They tended to occupy considerable square footage in premium locations and had to pay rent commensurate with their size, and yet how much money could an owner ever make on $120 pairs of Asics running shoes?

The three employees all emerged in unison, carrying with them the various stock and apparatus to build a display tower for some new polypropylene socks. As he walked over to ask for assistance, Liam noticed that the men looked familiar. Clearly, they were competitive athletes he had seen at races in Central Park. Turned off by their entitled manner, Liam wanted to remind them they were working for $10 an hour to help people try on shoes.

"I'm sorry to interrupt, guys, but I need one of those Nike singlets over there in an extra-small. Are there additional sizes in the back you can check?"

"Sorry, what we got in right now . . . it's all on the floor." It was the tallest of the three men who answered; his Island accent allowed him to appear more helpful than he was.

"Oh, can you order it from another store?" Liam asked.

"Sorry, Running Fever . . . it's not a chain, mon. What you see is what you get. We have plenty o' small t'ings here for you, though."

The racks of brightly colored running apparel made Liam giddy despite himself. Six months ago, Liam would have never believed that he could spend half an hour deciding which pair of shorts would allow for faster leg turnover or what materials breathed best for long runs or the appropriate socks to prevent blistering. But the days of ratty cotton shorts and stained college T-shirts had evaporated with a few months of Fast Tracker workouts and some successful races. Not realizing there were scores of invisible photographers out there on the race course, Liam was mortified to receive an e-mail message attaching a series of photos of himself grimacing through the final minutes of a race in baggy wind pants and a nappy fleece pullover. With the local running boom in New York City over the last decade, a cottage industry of photographers had cropped up to capture weekend warriors achieving personal victories on the race course. In the future, Liam would not be caught off guard. Today, Liam would purchase some tight singlets and running shorts with slit sides. When the weather got a little warmer, he would turn heads out there. With that thought in mind, Liam scooped up two pairs of sun-orange shorts and a few navy singlets—the Fast Tracker colors—all in extra-small, and carried them to the counter.

As the cashier began to scan the tags on the items, Liam remembered the club discount and pulled out his Fast Tracker membership card.

"This entitles me to twenty percent off," he said to the ostrich-necked man busily ringing up the purchases.

"Fast Trac*kers*," he said, a question mark rising in his voice as he spoke. "Our coach has a challenge out with your team this year. The point was to help our second string feel a little competitive spirit. You know anything about that?"

"We're in the thick of it," Liam said and laughed self-consciously. He hadn't a clue that he was in Urban Bobcat country. "I'm sure it'll be an interesting year."

Liam noticed a sprawling team photo taped to the wall behind the register. The picture had obviously been taken in the summer, as almost all the men were shirtless and glistening with sweat. Liam couldn't help but search out Didier. In the front row, fierce as ever, Didier stretched his arms across the backs of two friends, the pose tightening his stomach so that it was taut as a drum.

"That's us after the Club Championships last summer," the man offered. "We try to get everyone together at least once a year, but it can be like herding cats."

The expression stopped Liam. Since he was a child, he had a tendency to wonder about the genesis of sayings. Liam liked this one as it was visually evocative; he imagined the team photographer tracking down one long-limbed runner only to find upon return that three more from the pack had skittered off on their own.

The cashier threw in the latest issue of *Running Times* magazine along with a new flavor of energy gel that Clif Shots had concocted.

"These are on the Bobcats," the man said as he totaled the transaction. "You guys had a good showing at the first race. I know our men are hungry to keep their lead."

While Liam wanted to probe for more details, he could see that Monroe was growing visibly agitated by the conversation. This was supposed to be their makeup shopping excursion—Liam's penance for being even later than he had said for his meeting with Monroe after the race a few weeks ago. Liam knew that he should have known better than to think any Fast Tracker event—let alone a brunch with a gaggle of gay men—could happen in a timely fashion. Today, Monroe had agreed to hit one running store but the next three stops on their agenda were Bergdorf, Barneys, and Bloomingdale's, regularly referred to as "B-Cubed" or the "The Father, Son, and Holy Ghost" by Monroe.

"See you out on the course," Liam said, taking the large shopping bag into his hand.

"Thanks for catching Running Fever!"

Liam laughed at the tagline to be polite and then hurried out of the store to meet Monroe, who was smoking a cigarette on the sidewalk. As Liam approached, Monroe turned and began to walk ahead briskly. Monroe continued to sulk as they made their way east through Columbus Circle, heading along the southern end of Central Park. At the intersection of Seventh Avenue and Central Park South, Monroe raced across the street as the light was changing, and Liam broke into a light jog to catch up to him. A taxi honked and swerved to alert Liam that he had narrowly skirted an accident.

"Are you going nuts on me?" Liam asked as he regained his composure on the sidewalk. Monroe continued to motor along without looking back.

"What is up your ass, Miss Marilyn? I am not letting one of your tantrums turn me into roadkill."

"It's so like you to not even realize." Monroe was losing his breath from walking so quickly. "We can't even have one afternoon where racing and *the team* don't intrude."

"Look, I'll buy you a Cobb salad at Bloomies. You can't stay mad at me over Cobb salad. It's simply not possible."

Though Monroe was clearly trying to keep his jaw locked

in anger, Liam could see a smile creep across his friend's face. By the time Monroe was eyeing a row of overpriced blazers, all would be forgiven.

They decided to hit Bergdorf first and took a diagonal through the courtyard outside the Plaza. A boisterous crowd waited outside The Paris for the opening of some new film starring Daniel Day-Lewis. The night fell in amber over Manhattan and the buildings of Fifth Avenue twinkled like rubies. Liam felt overwhelmed by how romantic the city could be.

Once inside, Monroe played the proverbial queen in a couture shop, prancing around from the display of cashmere knit scarves to a wall of suede jackets on over to the case of Hermes ties. There were no other customers on the first floor of the store, which made Liam feel conspicuous, as though at any second a salesperson would pounce on them with over-zealous offers of assistance.

Monroe led Liam to an escalator hidden behind a tall mannequin in the corner of the floor. The second floor housed all the designer collections that Monroe wanted to check out that afternoon—Jil Sander, Theory, and rag & bone—and Liam sensed an immediacy to his friend's need for some retail therapy.

"Hold on, cowboy," Liam laughed as Monroe began bounding up the moving escalator.

"So many shirts, so little time, my friend," Monroe beamed.

Liam wanted to comment on how radiant Monroe looked when he smiled like this and to suggest that he do it more often but then thought better of it. Helpful observations like that had a tendency to be heard only in their negative, and Liam could imagine Monroe retorting with something along the lines of *"What, I look like a miserable troll most of the time?"*

The clerk in the Marc Jacobs section convinced Liam to try on the aubergine sweater he had been fondling lovingly. He figured he may as well occupy his time while Monroe was flitting through the Etro sale rack—even if he knew that he couldn't plunk down the better part of a month's rent no matter how good the sweater looked on him. He took it and some pencil-legged blue jeans into the expansive changing room. After spending what felt like five minutes shimmying the jeans over his hips and buttoning the pants, Liam emerged to view the outfit in the series of mirrors the store had arranged.

"Why, who knew that James Dean had been reincarnated and brought right down to earth in the center of the Bergdorf Goodman men's store!"

Liam detected the voice right away and then saw in the angled mirrors that his ears did not betray him.

"Oh my, G-Lo! Are you everywhere? It seems my friend Monroe is right. You can't turn a corner in this city without slamming straight into a Fast Tracker."

"And you listen to that tired queen? Where is she? Have her come over here, and I'll bitch-slap her right now."

After successfully smoothing things out with Monroe once already, Liam did not have faith that their daily excursion could weather this surprise intrusion by Hurricane Gary. Liam's mind buzzed as he considered appropriate ways to shoo along the ever-pleasant club president.

"We're having quiet time together, Gary. I'm sure you under-stand. I'm going to change out of this overpriced outfit and help Monroe replenish his spring wardrobe. I'll see you at the track this week."

"Those clothes were handmade for you, stud. You ab-solutely *have* to buy them. It would be criminal for anyone else in this city to be sporting those."

Liam laughed and looked back in the mirror. He did love the way the jeans hugged his butt and the way the sweater ended just at his beltline, exposing the veins in abdominals when he lifted his arms. This is precisely why he never al-lowed himself to grasp at things beyond his reach—in cloth-ing and in life.

"You're too kind, but my credit line is tighter than these jeans."

"Please, I'll get them for you, babe. Consider it a very belated Christmas present or an early birthday present or whatever."

"Don't be ridiculous, Gary. I just tried these on for fun."

"If you don't let me do it, then I am going to hang around here until Monroe comes back and torment you both for the rest of the day."

Liam looked around to see if he was in jeopardy of Monroe dropping by and then considered how much he would be compromising his principles to let Gary buy him an outfit. Given the outrageous lushness of his apartment, Gary could drop $600 for this outfit without batting an eye.

"Fine, I'll be right out, but this is only to appease you." Liam darted into the changing room and swapped his clothing as quickly as he possibly could.

When he returned a minute later, Liam saw the train wreck head-on. There, by the cashier, stood Gary and Monroe, decked out in an Etro sports coat, chatting uncomfortably. Liam handed the salesclerk the jeans and sweater and steeled himself for the turbulence.

"Wow, quite a shopping day for Mr. Liam. And here I thought you had overspent at the running store." Monroe eyed Liam defiantly.

"Oh, those are on me," Gary chimed in. "I like to help out today's youth whenever I can."

"That's quite a public service you provide," Monroe said, smirking. "All twentysomethings should be so lucky to latch onto a do-gooder like you. And it would help the flagging economy to boot!"

"Liam's already given so much back to me by supporting Fast Trackers." Gary looked off dreamily as he spoke. "More than money can buy really."

"I think I may need to take a rain check on the Cobb salad, Liam. I have suddenly lost my appetite." Monroe unbuttoned the jacket he had on and pulled it off in a huff. "I'm just going to find a hanger for this and get out of here."

"Come on," Liam said, trying unsuccessfully to get Monroe to look at him. "We're almost done here and we still have two more Bs on our agenda."

"After I pay, I'll be out of your hair," Gary offered. "I can tell you boys are having special alone time."

"Don't rush on my account," Monroe said. "Like I mentioned, I'll be leaving. It's been a long day, Liam. I'm just going to head home now."

Knowing the premium that Monroe placed on loyalty, Liam wondered whether he should make one final overture but decided against it. The day had been ruined and dragging out the embarrassment on the floor of Bergdorf Goodman would not help matters any. Some future penance would be in store for Liam.

"Well, I've seen some divas in my day but that one takes the tiara," Gary said as he signed the sales receipt dramatically.

"Don't sell yourself short, G-Lo. You can play royal bitch with the best of them."

"Oh, shut up and come with me. Now that your plans have been foiled, you're going to grab a drink with Mitch and me at Townhouse. The piano bar will supply us with laughs for days. And it's just a hop and a skip from here so I won't hear any kvetching."

MILE 12

A pack of kids in big puffy jackets flew out the doors and barreled down the ramp, knocking into Liam. He couldn't say anything given that he was clearly in the way. He told Monroe there were no good meeting spots outside the Armory, but Monroe insisted that Liam escort him into the facility. Liam knew that being a good friend meant dealing with these irrational requests from time to time. He certainly did not want to discourage Monroe. It was amazing, after all, that he had decided to run a track workout, and Liam knew he would have to do everything within his power to make sure the night went off without a hitch.

In their friendship, Liam understood that one of his primary roles was to anticipate any misgivings that Monroe might have and proactively handle them. When Monroe had broached the topic with him a few days earlier, Liam carefully noted that it seemed odd for Monroe to attend a Fast Tracker event given how much torment the club seemed to cause him. Monroe confessed that he had initially been jealous of the fact that the club stole Liam away from him for such huge chunks of time, but that he wanted to see what all the fuss was about and give Fast Trackers an honest chance. They seemed to have reached a détente, but Liam still felt uneasy about what the night had in store. Liam looked at his watch and realized the workout would be starting shortly.

"So this is quite the hellhole." Monroe motioned to the cardboard village that had been erected alongside the facility. Liam had neglected to mention the details of the local scene, the homeless shelter next to the track, the urine on the streets, the piquant odor of marijuana. Monroe had dressed in a cute spring outfit, the colors of which were so painstakingly coordinated that Liam wanted to ask if he had consulted a color wheel. But he kept his mouth shut and played the good ambassador.

"You bet. It's definitely a neighborhood to be passed through quickly. But the track inside is first-class." Liam gave Monroe a kiss on each cheek and then, feeling self-conscious, headed into the Armory.

"Where are the locker rooms?" Monroe demanded as soon as they entered the building.

"We're heading up there now. It's really nothing fancy." Liam had been afraid to tell Monroe about the facilities.

As soon as they entered the oversized bathroom, Monroe's eyes darted from person to person. A tall man sat in his underwear on the radiator by the window, fishing through his knapsack for his workout gear. A compact African American college student balanced his body against one of the stall doors while he laced up his running flats. And a sinewy older man in his mid-to-late fifties crouched cross-legged on the dirty tile floor assembling his work clothes into a neat stack. Monroe shot a glance at Liam who had begun to change into his workout gear. They both stood at the far end of the bathroom, past the urinals and right next to the lone window, under which the lanky man finished dressing.

Liam began his established routine. He took his shoes off first but kept his dress socks on to protect his feet from the grime on the bathroom floor. The pants and shirt came off in quick yanks and were folded into his bag. As he finished

putting on his running shorts and tank top, Liam quickly exchanged his dress socks for his microfiber running socks and
laced up his racing flats. He glanced over and saw that Monroe had taken out each article of clothing he planned to
wear—baby blue shorts, socks and headband, with a black
mesh T-shirt and black training shoes—and stared at the ensemble helplessly.

"Do you need me to help bring anything upstairs to the
track?" Liam examined the elaborate display of clothes that
now rested on bags and was draped over every clean surface
in the bathroom.

"No," Monroe barked, looking up as he attempted to re-
move the second leg of his pants. His back was bent as he
reached to pull the pant leg off. "Just wait here. I don't want
to go up alone." As his head turned to catch Liam in the eye,
Monroe lost his balance and hopped forward twice in a motion to recalibrate himself. In the second hop, Monroe's free
leg got caught in the fabric of his jeans, causing him to lurch
toward the ground. His hands stopped the fall in a puddle of
dirty water and piss by the urinals. Liam immediately
dropped his backpack and kneeled to help gather Monroe up
from the spill.

"Are you okay? Did you hurt yourself?" Liam tried to turn
Monroe's leg so that he could see if there were any open cuts
or bruises. Monroe slapped Liam's hand as he began to prod
at his knees.

"I'm fine," Monroe snapped. He then glared in the direction of each person who may have witnessed his pratfall. "I
just want to wash my hands, throw on my running clothes,
and get to the workout already."

"Don't let this get you down, babe. They really should
have a proper locker room in a facility like this. I know . . . "

Monroe frowned at Liam and then took his one free hand
and reached over and shut Liam's lips closed so that he could
not finish his thought.

In the aftermath of his wipeout, Monroe leaned up against the door of one of the closed bathroom stalls. Having been scolded, Liam was loath to say anything until he could hear the person inside the stall flushing and getting ready to exit.

"We don't want an instant replay," Liam said, grabbing his friend and moving him over by the radiator, which was now free of any runners. "Just let me help you."

Monroe threw his tank top over his head and scooped up his belongings before scurrying toward the door.

"We should get going, Liam. The workout was supposed to start three minutes ago, you know."

The group had already warmed up and was stretching in a big irregular loop when Liam and Monroe arrived at the track area. Liam walked ahead to the bleachers and showed Monroe where their bags went. As they approached the Fast Trackers circle, Monroe directed Liam to wedge in beside Gary and Ben. In a play to avoid awkwardness, Liam chuckled to Ben, who smiled back cunningly—*all is not forgiven*. As they leaned into the calf stretch, Liam whispered to Monroe: "Glad you're here."

"Hopefully, this fires up my metabolism," Monroe said, with a smile. "God knows I could use that!"

Before Fabio could inquire about the newcomer, Liam walked over to the coach and introduced Monroe, explaining that he was new to running and wanted to see what speed training was all about. Liam looked over the Fast Trackers assembled and assured Monroe that there would be two groups of runners for the workout and that he would not be the slowest one there. Every runner fears being the last finisher in a workout, still trudging around the track while everyone else stands around chatting.

"So did you see that Marvin missed the workout again tonight? I hear he's *dating* a nineteen-year-old Peruvian." Zane jumped up and down excitedly as he spoke. "He goes MIA anytime there's a piece of barely legal trade within whiffing distance. This will be your time to get faster than him, Liam. Stay sharp! Stay hungry!"

"You remember my friend Monroe . . . "

"Oh, of course. Good to have you here, Murray."

Zane had already flitted away before Liam had an opportunity to correct him. Monroe stood with his arms crossed at his chest, waiting for something to happen.

With his clipboard in hand, Fabio rallied everyone to the starting line with a shout and a whistle. He announced the workout to muffled groans. Four sets of one mile followed by a 200-meter sprint. Fabio insisted that the miles be kept to 10K pace—no faster!—and that the 200-meter sprints be run "all-out" and that they be completed after precisely one minute of rest. As Fabio divided the runners into two separate groups by speed, Liam attempted to explain to Monroe that he should just run at a comfortable pace so that he could finish the workout. Going out too fast would only lead to a painful and disheartening evening.

From the side of the stadium seats, Ferdinand waltzed toward the track, decked out in a suede anorak with diamond-studded fur trim. Off his right wrist hung a pink leather duffel bag. He hurried toward Fabio and whispered something in his ear. Fabio shook his head a couple of times and then shrugged. The man peeled off his street clothes layer by layer uncovering a mint-green running outfit. Everything, right down to his custom-made racing flats, was the exact color of a pack of Wrigley's spearmint gum. When the opportunity arose, Zane thanked Ferdinand for taking the Urban Bobcat challenge seriously by showing up for a workout. Everyone on the team knew that Ferdinand's work and party schedule prevented him from attending most weeknight runs. If he wasn't off to some cocktail party at a fashionista's house, he had to watch a late-night run-through of the Dolce & Gabbana spring line. Running drills rarely took precedence over the fabulous life, but he still ran at a pace competitive enough to prove a valuable asset to Fast Trackers. Fabio threw Ferdinand in with the first group of runners and immediately moved everyone to the track.

As Liam waited at the starting line, he looked over to Monroe, who smiled as he exchanged pleasantries with Gary. Liam held out hope that Monroe might actually enjoy himself and have a good workout. In his first mile, Liam followed a few steps behind Zane, feeling strong and confident. With each lap, Liam moved more nimbly. When Fabio called out the times as 5:38 pace—a full fifteen seconds faster than his actual best-ever 10K pace—Liam worried that he had failed to heed his own advice by going out too fast. He would try to ease off a little in the next interval.

"You bought that pace," yelled Fabio. "Now you own it . . . we have a no-returns policy here, so I hope you're happy with your purchase. Everyone better hit those times the next go-round."

After the second mile interval, Liam hunched over and prayed for the workout to end; he imagined what it might be like to fake cramps and stumble off to the side of the track. He wondered whether he could get away with not finishing. Liam liked to fantasize he might do exactly that, even though he knew he would stick through to the bitter end. Looking at the overhead clock, Liam counted how much time remained in the workout and then thought back to where he was that amount of time prior. These little mind games helped the time pass.

Liam sucked down his exhaustion as he toed the line for the next interval. As he passed Monroe on the track, Liam mustered the strength to cheer him on. Despite the encouragement, Monroe had slowed to a near limp and looked like he was about to keel over at any moment. Liam glided into a powerful stride to try and jump-start his body out of the stiffened pain he was in.

As he completed his first lap, Liam heard a solid thud followed by a shriek and a string of expletives. Maintaining his form, he turned his head and saw the aftermath of the collision. The muscular black hurdler stood over a felled Monroe shaking his fists and yelling something that Liam could not quite make out. Fabio had engaged the man and, at least from the opposite side of the track, the matter appeared to be under control. Liam could feel the burn in his legs and an ache in his abdominals from having worked his arms strenuously during the previous sprints.

When the interval was over, Liam hobbled over toward Monroe, who was sitting on the sidelines reading a weathered copy of Edith Wharton's *The Age of Innocence*. The collision had looked and sounded more dramatic than it really was. The damage was relatively localized, but the incident had clearly injured Monroe's pride. Monroe pushed Liam away when he asked how he was feeling.

"I'm just going to head home," Monroe hissed.

"Stay, we'll get something to eat after."

"Just let me go home and sleep this one off, Liam. Okay? I'm not angry. This just hasn't been my night . . . my week . . . my year . . . Take your pick."

"This is the one that counts," interrupted Zane. "We have to head over to the starting line now. You can't give yourself too much rest, Liam. Remember that in races, anyone can pick it up right at the finish line. It's mile three of a four-miler that separates the strong from the weak."

"Go ahead, Liam." Monroe waved him along. "I'm going to be fine. You shouldn't ruin your workout. Seriously, I'm fine. Appreciate all your help tonight!"

Liam took his friend at his word and headed over for one more interval. That meant one interval closer to the finish. To rest. To burgers and beer. Just eight more times around this tiny track, Liam thought as Fabio whistled to command the group to begin its third interval. But after the third lap, Liam began to heave and wheeze.

"Control your breathing!" Zane didn't look back as he shouted over his shoulder. "Never let the other guy know you're feeling weak."

On the fifth lap, Liam fell a few steps farther behind Zane, and as his friend (and new mentor) exhorted him, Liam wanted nothing more than to slow down even more. His body felt wrung out; his mind had turned to putty. In one final attempt at jolting Liam awake, Zane turned around fully and waved to him, yelling: "Bye, bye, Liam! Wave good-bye to Marvin now as he's passing you by!"

Feeling even more despondent, Liam looked over his shoulder and noticed that Riser trailed by only a dozen or so feet. A pack that included Matthew and Mitch followed closely behind Riser. To salvage his pride, Liam buckled down and staved off the pounding footsteps coming up now behind him. He knew his fellow teammates had sensed his vulnerability and readied themselves for the pounce. Even with his breakdown in form and composure, Liam still clocked a 5:49, which was a completely respectable per-mile pace in a 10K—or any other race—as far as he was concerned. But Zane looked on disapprovingly as Liam crumbled by the finish line, whimpering with just under thirty seconds left to the start of the 200-meter sprint.

"You should have stuck with me until your legs fell off," Zane whispered into his ear. "People always slow down when the pain sets in. The body can always perform through pain. Remember that. Don't teach your body to slow down when it's tired—teach it to speed up."

Liam did not have the energy to raise his head and look at Zane. It was less than ten seconds before Liam had to walk back to the starting line and complete his one-lap sprint. A 200-meter lap was something that he could muscle his way through no matter how tired he felt. As everyone in the group assembled at the starting line, Liam stared at Riser for a moment. When did he become so feeble, so hollow-cheeked and withered? Remembering the ominous conversation that he'd had with Riser the night of Zane's birthday—all the talk of weight and unhappiness over his physique—Liam resolved to check in with his friend after the workout. Matthew and Mitch kept their heads hung, perhaps to avoid processing and acknowledging Riser's skeletal frame or maybe simply to shut out everything around them and focus on the task at hand. Ferdinand stretched out a cramp in his abdomen in the seconds before Fabio signaled the group to run. Annoyingly fresh-looking, Zane sprang up and down in place as he waited impatiently for the start.

Liam zoomed out at full speed, dashing in front of Zane and not looking back over his shoulder. It was full steam ahead. His muscular arms propelled him, their motion forcing his legs to rise up and speed through the finish. As he crossed the finish line, Liam felt a flush of cold sweat trickle over his brow. He knew his body was revolting against the strain and the stress, but he ignored the sensation and kept repeating to himself that he had fewer than six minutes of running left. The faster he ran, the faster this workout would be over. And the sooner he would be able to enjoy a cold draft beer and an oversized hamburger and fries.

The three minutes of rest time vanished into these thoughts of escape. Liam nodded at Zane as they positioned themselves on the track, and Fabio whistled to start the last mile interval. Hugging close to the interior of the rubber track, Liam slid behind Zane within the first fifteen seconds of the mile and struggled to stay there through the first four laps. Fabio shouted, "2:45" as Liam and Zane passed the half-mile mark. Immediately, Liam had thoughts of failure. *We went out too fast for the first 800 meters and now I am going to pay dearly for the mistake. There is no way on God's green earth that after all the fast running I've done tonight I can pull out a 5:30 in the last mile.* As his breathing heaved, Liam noticed Zane glance over his shoulder, but this time Zane chose to remain silent. Focusing on correcting his posture and on swinging his arms freely, Liam managed to stay directly behind Zane for two more laps. Fabio called out a time of "4:10" at the 1200-meter mark, and Liam felt a clamping down on his chest. Zane now turned his stride over faster and faster. The pain writhed down Liam's shoulder blades into his spine; he felt a spasm through his abdominals. He attempted every visualization scheme and magic trick he had read about—imagining himself light as air and flying to the finish, barking orders to himself that he simply *had* to stay with Zane or else he would be lost in the wilderness, and repeating the simple mantra of his high school coach: "Run, run, quick, quick, step, step, fly, fly." Gulping like a drowning man being pulled from the ocean, Liam crossed the finish line in 5:28. Staggering off the side of the track, Liam found a garbage can where he wretched a clear acidic liquid that came from somewhere deep inside. He couldn't even remember the last solid food he ate.

Despite Monroe's minor calamity and the rigors of the workout, the evening felt like a success. Liam had achieved a victory of will. He wanted to smile but was aware that he needed to wipe the spittle from his face. As he picked up the edge of his shirt to clean his face off, Liam felt Zane's hand on his shoulder and wanted to turn around and hug him. He wanted to thank his friend for forcing him to finish strong.

"So we're not done," Zane said matter-of-factly. "Aerobic cooldown to keep our bodies trained to running fast when tired."

"Wasn't that the point of the whole workout? Isn't there such a thing as too much?"

"You need an edge, Liam. Edges distinguish the angular among us from the round ones—remember that."

"Yeah, right," said Liam. "Look at how much of an edge Riser has achieved for himself. He's got toothpicks for arms, and he's practically catching me in workouts. I guess we're in *anything goes* territory now."

"Don't get off topic. I have Ferdinand and Matthew checking on him to make sure he's eating. Those three are as tight as Junior Vasquez and the turntable. But what I want you to focus on, Liam, is that edges are mental as well as physical. It's the mental ones that can be a lot harder to sharpen, and standing around like your trick stood you up after last call never helps. So let's hit it. A 6:20 pace for two miles."

They ran along the interior of the track as everyone else chatted and laughed in the stretching circle. After the first half mile, Liam heard a light trot from behind and the familiar sound of supple, near effortless breathing. He turned his head though there was no need for confirmation.

"Do you mind if I join you guys? I need to run a little while longer at a good clip, and my team members have all left for the night."

Liam had been so focused during the night's intervals that he had not seen any Urban Bobcats—let alone Didier.

"Sure, we all like company—and a steady pace." Liam knew he had managed to strike just the right tone of nonchalance. Though the workout had left him depleted, Liam felt stronger and more limber as soon as Didier joined the cooldown. The truth was that a 6:20 pace was now a bit of a cakewalk for Liam, sufficiently slower than his interval training pace and seeming easy even after the pounding of a tough workout.

As the managers of the Armory announced the close of the facility, Didier peeled off and thanked Liam and Zane for the solid run. Liam could not help but follow the arc of his exit in the hopes of seeing the square line of Didier's jaw, the sculpted concavity of his cheeks.

"Sleeping with the enemy?" Zane looked at Liam incredulously.

Liam flinched and pivoted his shoulders away from Zane, knocking the quip somewhere up into the bleachers.

"Don't trust those guys, Liam." Zane pulled Liam close as if to reveal a deep secret. "The hot ones are always trouble."

"Please, Zane! He just wanted to run a cooldown. Why does there always need to be such drama?"

"Life is drama. Don't kid yourself otherwise."

"So what, we're going to be a self-contained, doesn't-trust-anyone-unless-they're-gay team? What's the point of acceptance in the athletic community if we're only going to ghettoize ourselves?"

"No, Liam. Actually, you're going to fall in love with Didier, and he's going to join our team, and the Urban Bobcats and Fast Trackers are going to host a picnic every year in honor of both you and Didier."

"I want a dinner cruise, not a picnic," Liam said, smiling at Zane's sarcasm. But Liam couldn't help noticing the other Fast Trackers heading out toward the exit, and he wanted to snag Riser before the evening devolved into the chaos of the post-workout dinner scene. Matthew had his arm around a snowy-haired man about a foot shorter than himself, which seemed to corroborate the gossip Liam had heard about Matthew's age fetish. Gary lifted an invisible mug to his mouth to get Liam's attention, and Liam nodded in his direction. Riser trailed behind, putting some sweaty clothing in a Ziploc bag and fumbling with his belongings. An oversized backpack towered atop his bony shoulders, making Riser look as though he would topple over if he took a turn too quickly or if the slightest breeze shot up.

Liam excused himself, telling Zane he needed to ask Riser something and would rendezvous at the restaurant.

Riser seemed flustered as Liam approached, as though zippering his parka had taken any energy he had left. Liam rested his hand on Riser's shoulder briefly to get his attention and then Liam's jaw locked when he considered which words to choose to express his concern. Remembering how touchy and self-flagellating Riser was at Zane's birthday celebration, Liam knew he needed to be gentle so as not to come across as criticizing his friend. Liam had read that people with image issues or eating disorders tended to distort any concern or commentary that came their way.

"Great workout tonight!" Liam offered, looking his friend directly in the eyes. "You gonna come out to eat with the rest of the crew tonight?"

"Think I'll skip it," Riser said. "It's already so late."

"They know us at the bar around the corner so we get served really quickly. And it's so much better than eating alone."

"I am not really hungry, Liam. I had a granola bar before coming to the workout so I'll probably just go home and crash."

"Riser, you burned like 1,000 calories during this workout tonight. Your body needs to refuel. It needs some protein. Plus, there is always hysterical karaoke at this place. Truly tragic. If we're lucky maybe some drunk chick will attempt 'Express Yourself'!"

Out of nowhere, from behind, a presence popped up. It was Zane bounding along. He must have gone to use the restrooms. Riser quickened his footsteps to get ahead of Liam and Zane and opened the doors to the Armory, folding his arms against his chest to warm himself against the chilly night air.

"I bet that Didier may have been eavesdropping on us tonight, trying to find out inside information about our strategy for the race on Saturday."

Zane continued the earlier thread of conversation as if no time at all had elapsed.

"Excuse me, guys, I am going to run to get the subway home." Riser had already begun to cross the street toward the subway. Liam waved and said good night to Riser as his friend blew like a wraith across the busy intersection and disappeared down into the subway terminal. Liam hoped that

Riser might grab a yogurt or have a piece of toast or something before bed but somehow doubted that would happen.

Zane prattled on about Didier and the logistics and machinations surrounding the team competition; Liam had trouble believing that Zane could possibly think that the Fast Tracker–Urban Bobcats rivalry ran so deep. If the last five-miler were any indication, the Urban Bobcats did not need to plot a strategic attack against the Fast Trackers at the Brooklyn Half Marathon this weekend to secure a victory. The Bobcats just had to show up. Wouldn't it be less painful for Fast Trackers to accept that now than to fight uselessly for the whole year?

Liam and Zane entered the noisy restaurant and spotted the Fast Trackers at a table far in the back of the establishment. On karaoke nights, the owner took pity on the running club and seated them as far away from the makeshift stage and blaring microphone as possible.

"Better watch out . . . " Liam said, teasingly, and patted Zane's bottom. "I'd bare all our club secrets for fifteen seconds on those Parisian lips."

MILE 13

The warmth of the teeny booth lulled Liam into a half-sleep. His heavy eyelids shut and then opened quickly in a baffled start. Someone was pounding on the door. Liam felt embarrassed and hopped up, pulling his tights in a single tug from his ankles to around his waist. How long had he been inside? It didn't matter. He would have to skulk out now, and whoever was waiting would know that he had taken refuge from the elements inside a smelly Portosan.

As Liam blew his nose one last time, he readied himself for the outside world. The temperatures shivered in the low twenties, but it was the wind skimming off the breaking waves that made the prospect of standing on the boardwalk without shelter unbearable. Glancing at his watch, Liam noticed that there was still half an hour to the start of the race. In a few minutes, he needed to meet Gary at the baggage check to pick up his number.

Liam had initially felt guilty for relying on Gary so routinely. But being taken care of proved to be an easy habit to fall into. Gary made it seem like the least-consequential favor in the world—he lived inches from the New York Road Runners Foundation where runners picked up their bib numbers and chips, and he planned on going for his own purposes anyway. Liam had heard from Ben that Gary only pampered the young, fast, and cute runners—a rumor whose truth was borne out over time. If Liam were being completely honest with himself, he would admit that he was flattered by his inclusion. Gary's coterie was small.

The waves surged in a procession of grays. One after the other they came, more forceful and dogged against the shoreline. The Coney Island morning provided a study in contrast as the serene blue sky belonged to some coastline in the Aegean, or so Liam liked to imagine, having never been. A sprinkling of nimbus clouds painted wispy eyelashes on the beautiful, fat face of the late March sky. Not a soul was on the beach, and there was neither a kiosk nor a storefront to hide in. Liam's face and neck burned as the wind lashed every inch of exposed skin. He decided to do a quick warm-up sprint to the baggage check area where Gary would be handling the bib and chip exchange.

Approaching the small roped-in area where a dozen or so well-insulated volunteers collected bags and placed them inside vans, Liam noticed Mitch, Matthew, and Ferdinand waiting impatiently. He had heard that Riser was fighting off a flu and would not be racing but had wondered whether maybe Riser's body had simply weakened from the recent weight loss. Liam had e-mailed and called to check in with Riser, but he just underscored that he had some seasonal illness that had made its way through the office.

Everyone stood silently to conserve their warmth. After several minutes and one megaphone warning from the officials, Mitch rolled his eyes and searched out Liam for some decision on a course of action. What choice did they have but to wait? Without bibs and chips, none of their times would be recorded, and the team would suffer in the standings against the Urban Bobcats. Liam was not about to race a half marathon solely for his health and amusement. Waiting for Gary was the *only* choice.

Ferdinand rubbed his face and walked nervously in a circle before announcing that he had to go take a pill in the Portosan. As he jogged away, Liam looked to Matthew for an explanation.

"You ride the E-scalator up, and you've got to ride the E-scalator down," Matthew reported mysteriously.

"He's coming down off Ecstasy." Mitch sounded annoyed as he answered Liam's confused expression. "Where in the hell is Gary?"

As if on cue, Gary's car screeched to a halt right by the baggage check. After parking illegally in front of the vans that were transporting the runners' baggage, Gary stormed from his vehicle through a thicket of iced-over bushes. His face was eggplant against the fire-engine red of his eyes. Gary threw the plastic bag with Mitch's bib number and chip onto the floor and stamped on it. He remained scarily silent.

"What the fuck? We have like three minutes to get to the start, Gary. Where are your running clothes?"

Mitch had regained his composure as he fixed his own race number onto his shirt and told Gary to hurry along.

"A half hour!" The veins in Gary's neck bulged at Mitch's nonchalance. His whole body now shook. "I waited outside your apartment. Rang your bell. Phoned you. Texted you. Worried that you overslept!"

"Liam, you better lace that chip on and bolt out of here with me if you want to get to the start on time," Mitch said, remaining completely calm. "There's been enough drama this morning without us missing the race, Gary."

"You selfish fucker!" Gary dabbed tears from the sides of his face as his voice quivered. "You couldn't give a shit about me . . . you did not return one of my messages last night . . . And I come here anyway, like a fool."

"Gary, this is about the team. Get it together. Liam and I are running for the team . . . Matthew and Ferdinand, if he ever makes it back from the john, are running for the team.

It's all about the challenge that you asked each of us to take up. It's about Fast Trackers. You go feel sorry for yourself. We've got a race to run."

A final indiscernible rant faded out as Mitch forced Liam along in a light jog toward the starting line. Matthew would wait for Ferdinand. The racing officials announced that three minutes remained until the gun would go off. The knot of runners along the Coney Island Boardwalk attempted to stop Mitch and Liam from moving toward the very beginning of the line, but Mitch slalomed through the bony runners like a seasoned mogul skier. The horn honked to start the race, and Liam jostled along with the pack until a moment came when he could break free.

The brisk air stung his face, but he glided along on the steady feed of adrenaline from the soap opera he had witnessed a few moments prior. As he passed the first mile marker in 6:04, Liam realized that he had let the moment get the best of him. He could not sustain 13.1 miles running just a shade slower than his 10K race pace. After consciously slowing his breathing and moving his arms more purposely, Liam began to settle into the rhythm of the race.

The course started amid the shuttered pageantry of the Coney Island Boardwalk, with the Cyclone and the roar of the ocean as a powerful backdrop. After the second mile, the race moved through a long stretch of dreary parkway. For seven miles, Liam watched as the avenues moved down the alphabet—"U" to "T" to "S"—at glacial speed. His eyes welled as the wind smacked from side to side through the flat, treeless stretch of paved highway. To ensure he stayed hydrated, Liam grabbed a Dixie cup from one of the volunteers at mile five and a ridge of ice broke against his lips, causing all the water to cascade down his chest. Feeling miserable, Liam directed his attention to the mathematics of the race. He hit mile 5 at exactly 31 minutes, or a 6:12 pace. After taking it out too fast in the first mile, Liam had now reclaimed his confidence, knowing that he could force his body to churn out 6:15 miles for the rest of the race. "Focus," he told himself as he watched the monochromatic apartment buildings pass by in a mural of concrete and brick.

Liam's thoughts turned to Gary and Mitch. Had they just dissolved into a lovers' quarrel? Mitch's face had contorted upon hearing Gary's indignant pleas, which made the likelihood of a romantic connection tenuous. Ever since Ben had planted the seed in his head at Sugarland, Liam questioned the boundaries of their relationship. If Mitch had no interest in Gary at all, why did he allow him to fawn and goo and crumble to pieces around him? Maybe they had slept together once and Gary wanted more out of it than Mitch? Or maybe Gary just needed someone to ogle and Mitch just needed to be admired.

As he weighed the possibilities, Liam noticed a runner springing by him. By keeping metronome-like precision to his racing, Liam had managed to run without anyone passing him for the last three miles. Now, someone was clearly gearing up to glide right in front of Liam, and he was not certain whether he had the energy to speed up with the seven toughest miles of the race still ahead.

Once the racer pranced by gazelle-like, Liam knew he had to at least muscle a little to stay abreast. Didier did not even turn his head to acknowledge Liam as he passed by. Liam knew this did not bode well for him. Didier probably had twelve Urban Bobcats ahead of him, and here Liam was hoping to be one of the top three finishers for Fast Trackers. At mile seven of the half-marathon, Didier ran unencumbered, perhaps knowing that the Bobcats had it made in the shade—that they couldn't lose no matter how resurgent and plucky Fast Trackers proved itself to be.

The thought enraged Liam, and he notched up his effort to stay one stride behind Didier. No matter how little consequence his effort would make in the overall challenge, Liam decided in that moment that he was going to beat Didier. Just past mile nine, they veered up a slight hill that curved away from the parkway and onto a rotary. Liam could see the entrance to Prospect Park off to the right and knew that once they passed through the gates, the final 5K would be underway. His speed training on the track would have to kick in. His legs were more muscular than the toothpicks that moved Didier along.

Prospect Park presented itself immediately in a series of rolling hills. Liam did not push the pace; instead, he waited patiently behind Didier. If the race came down to the final quarter mile, Didier did not stand a chance. In the middle of a relentless climb, the sign for the eleven-mile mark stood beside a huge race clock. The time read 1:08 even. *What time had the previous clock reported?* The ten-mile marker had come immediately after the park entrance, and the excitement of a small group of spectators had diverted Liam's attention so that he missed the time. *Were they still speeding up?* The pace now had to be smack-dab at six minutes per mile. Liam's legs suddenly twinged. His breathing careened as he fought for air.

Didier glanced quickly over his shoulder as he broke away from Liam. Feeling his resolve dissipate into the frosty air, Liam bowed his head and felt his feet slow to a shuffle. As he crested the next hill, he could see Didier just 100 yards ahead. They were well into the thirteenth mile, and Liam reminded himself that the race was not yet done. Zane always told him that anyone could do anything for a minute. If Didier stayed within striking distance, then Liam could simply will his body to race full throttle and best him at the finish line. Liam knew he needed to be smart. His stomach heaved, and his lungs burned with each stride. Once more Didier turned to assess the competition. Liam could tell that Didier had planned on coasting through to the end of the race and was annoyed that he needed to stay mentally and physically sharp. Didier had just passed the sign noting there were 800 meters remaining when Liam decided he could wait no longer. Closing his eyes, Liam leaned forward and concentrated on raising his knees in a sprint. Didier still appeared to be a full ten seconds ahead of Liam. The thirteen-mile marker came at the beginning of an uphill overlooking a placid lake that must have been Prospect Park's answer to the Central Park reservoir. There was only a tenth of a mile left now. Liam pumped his arms as quickly as he could, but his legs felt as though they were battling quicksand. He did not know how much ground he could cover on Didier in the distance that remained. Barely able to keep his head up straight, Liam leaned further into his stride just to do something different, to mix things up so that his body could persevere through this race. One more quick turn and the finish line was only meters away. Within a few seconds of glimpsing the finish, Liam saw Didier's bony limbs thunder across it.

Liam completed the race in an exaggerated tumble of tired steps. Unable to fully control the momentum of his body, he collided sloppily with Didier, who was standing in the center of the finish line chute collecting his breath. Looking like a deer caught in headlights, Didier grabbed a hold of Liam by the shoulders to help steady his gait. The two stood for a few seconds, caught in this unexpected embrace. When they disengaged, Liam took his wet hat off, shook out his hair, and wiped the sweat off his forehead.

"You ought to have a license to carry around weapons like those," Didier said, looking directly at Liam's legs. "They seem to have a mind of their own and a desire to attack people."

It took Liam a moment to collect himself and take register of Didier's tone. He definitely did not sound vexed, the way he had when he scolded Liam at the finish line in Van Cortlandt Park. Liam wondered if there was something vaguely flirtatious in Didier's voice.

"Well, this isn't the ladies' mah-jongg table, my friend. You stand around here at your own risk." Liam felt sick to his stomach but managed to smile as he spoke.

"Fair enough," Didier replied. "Maybe I am putting myself in the line of fire. I should thank you then for not completely knocking me off my feet."

"I would say that I'm saving something for next time around, but you do understand that the next time it's going to be me waiting to congratulate you for the solid effort."

"I'd be a fool to underestimate you." Didier extended his hand to rub Liam's shoulder comfortingly. "You made me work harder than I ever had to work out there today. Thank you for making me dig so deep."

A few more finishers now buzzed over the timing mats and were funneling through the chute. It was clear that they would need to move along so as not to hamper everyone else's race. Liam and Didier began to walk toward the vans that had transported their baggage from the start of the race in Coney Island. As they approached the area where the vans had parked, Didier pointed to his race number and noted that his baggage was at the opposite end of the field. He thanked Liam again and said good-bye.

"You know, if you don't have any plans, a bunch of Fast Trackers are having brunch at a member's apartment. He lives somewhere right off Prospect Park. The address is in my backpack."

It was a bold and impulsive move, and Liam immediately questioned whether he was going to get in trouble for it. The members had thrown the gauntlet down with the Urban Bobcats and now here Liam was inviting the nemesis to brunch. And judging from the scales that seemed to balance in Didier's eyes, there was the equal possibility that this straight runner bemoaned the fact that his cordial exchange of pleasantries had been reciprocated with a come-on.

"You're sure it isn't a members-only kind of a thing?" Didier asked, surprising Liam with his shyness.

"We're friendly people, Didier, and there's always a sense of community when you're around fellow runners."

"I *am* starving. Let me get my bag and meet you back here in a minute."

Liam stared at the thin straps of Didier's singlet, which jostled up and down with his stride as he jogged toward the baggage van. From the other direction, someone shouted his name. Liam spun around to see Zane suited up in his post-race outfit with his backpack on, ready to leave the park.

"I'm Popsicle city over here." Zane's lips had chapped and salt stained his face in zigzags. "I feel like I was waiting for you forever."

"Thanks, that makes me feel just wonderful."

"You know what I mean. It's just cold. What was your time, anyway? Did you break 1:23?"

"I broke 1:22. I had a huge PR today. I think it was a 1:21:15. And you?"

"I managed a six-minute pace. A 1:18 something or other. You know I hate these long-distance races. I only did it because of that dreadful challenge that Gary got us into."

"So what was the team order? Was I second to you? Did Marvin end up running?"

Liam had been so caught up in getting to the start of the race because of all the drama and then in staying neck-and-neck with Didier that he had forgotten about his goal of beating Marvin.

"He beat us both, my friend. He looked fully recovered by the time I dragged my sorry ass across the finish. He thought his time was 1:16 flat. He already scooted out of here to meet up with the new BF. Talk about a short chain."

"I totally pushed myself and he beat me by five minutes— that's a fucking coffee break!"

"Look, this is his specialty. You are built for speed. Pick a 5K or a 4-miler to beat him. It's never going to happen on a 13.1 mile course. I am in your corner; we just have to be smart about what's real and what's not. Hurry up and get your bag, I want to jog over to Craig's."

"Okay, but we have to wait for someone before we leave."

"Someone? All the Fast Trackers know where to go. No one needs an escort."

"This isn't a Fast Tracker."

"Don't tell me. Did you really invite that closet case from the Armory? You do realize how seriously Gary & Company are taking this competition bullshit with the Bobcats?"

Liam got his bag and hoped that Zane underestimated the warmth of the club. Would Gary even be there, he wondered, after the huge scene he had caused with Mitch? By the time Liam returned, Didier had joined Zane and the two were making small talk about their respective races.

It took less than five minutes to jog to Craig's apartment. Standing tall right on the edge of Prospect Park, the pre-war building had a regal façade of clean red brick and oversized windows. Craig's living room faced the park, directly at the tree-line level. With all the fauna still leafless, the view had a certain enchantment. It made Liam feel as if he could hop right out the window and swing from tree to tree through the park.

Because they had rushed out of the park after the race, Liam, Zane, and Didier arrived at the brunch a full twenty minutes before anyone else. Craig must have been up for days preparing his apartment for this feast—every brunch food imaginable had been placed strategically throughout the kitchen, dining room, and living room. Craig kept a meticulous home and his placement of each food matched its likeliness to spill or stain. His trays of pancakes and waffles, browned perfectly and accompanied by little pots of blackberry, raspberry, and grape jams, had been safely lined up in the tiled kitchen. Foods that did not beg for gooey toppings but could still stain if dropped on the floor, such as the trays of scrambled eggs and the mushroom, spinach, and artichoke quiches, sat on the dining room table. The dry bagels, bowls of almonds and cashews, and piles of cereal and energy bars—a race had just been run, after all—were artfully displayed on the end tables and ottomans, far enough from the sofas and settees, in the expansive living room.

Didier ate a banana and a piece of quiche while standing uncomfortably in the kitchen, explaining to Liam that he had to go meet weekend guests arriving later in the afternoon. Zane scurried around Craig's apartment helping him tend to the final touches—placing sprigs of fresh flowers in little bud vases and napkins with inspirational quotes etched in gold script along the edges. Liam's noted that "a journey of ten thousand miles begins with one single step."

As Liam apologized for the low turnout and explained that people must have lingered at the finish, the door to the apartment opened and a huge group—easily two dozen people— entered. Mitch and Ben were among them and immediately stormed over to Liam in uncharacteristically urgent form. Mitch's face was flush and his hands gesticulated wildly.

"Can you believe that queen?" Mitch yelled the words at Liam more as an assertion of fact than as a question. "After all we're doing for the club, he shits on us like that."

"Mitch and Ben, this is Didier. I don't know if you know him from the Urban Bobcats. He trains a lot at the Armory."

"Oh, I thought you looked familiar. Hope you don't mind hearing me bitch about the president of our club. He's been having Royal Diva Syndrome recently and every single one of his subjects has been in the line of fire."

"I don't know, Mitch, maybe he was just having a bad morning." Liam needed to defend Gary, not so that the president of the club would look normal in front of the competition but because he felt that Gary was being victimized for his kindness. While he had no iron-clad evidence, Liam sensed that Gary would give anything to be at the center of the club—and that there were plenty of people willing to take whatever goodwill he dispensed.

"Please, he gets off on the drama. If it isn't there, then he creates it." Ben stepped forward, speaking with command. "Who would think someone could have a hissy fit over dropping off race numbers? Would anyone on the Bobcats do that, Didier?"

"Dealing with big personalities is probably something you don't have to worry over, Didier," Liam interjected. "At Fast Trackers, it isn't all about the running unfortunately. But we can move this conversation along so that it returns to the running, right, Ben?"

Liam searched Ben's eyes to see where he was going with this line of questions.

"No need to protect me, Liam." Didier laughed, and Liam realized that it was the first time he had seen his gaunt face with anything other than a deadpan expression. Didier's smile dimpled his sunken cheeks and threw a mischievous sparkle into his chocolate eyes. "I've been around the block a time or two myself."

"So where do you get all those fast runners?" Ben asked.

"I don't know, really. We don't do any outreach or marketing, if that's what you're suggesting. I guess it's our reputation."

"But I'm curious," Ben continued. "Why did you join there, for instance? Is it because there is superior training?"

"I knew someone from the gym and when he heard that I was competing in the marathon, he told me I should run the race under his team's name. It was word of mouth. People like being around people who are like they are—fast people want to be part of the fast team. Surely you can understand that? All your runners want to be part of Fast Trackers because they're gay, right?"

"So how do the fast gay runners choose, then?" Ben asked beguilingly. "What would you do if you were both fast *and* gay, Didier?"

Liam realized that when Shakespeare coined the saying "Hell hath no fury like a woman scorned" that the famous bard must not have had the pleasure of witnessing a jilted gay man in action.

Didier swallowed the last forkful of quiche on his plate and used his napkin to wipe the crumbs from his face, which had started to redden slightly.

"That would be a quandary, I guess. I would love to entertain more of these questions, but as I just explained to Liam, I need to straighten up my apartment for some house guests who are traveling in this afternoon. I'll see you boys at the track. Thank the host for me. And Liam, would you take this plate for me. *Every*thing was delicious."

Didier disappeared within seconds. Liam took the plate to the garbage can in the kitchen. As he used the napkin to dust off the crumbs, he saw ink scribbled under the gold quotation ("To thine own self be true") on the edge of the paper. It said, "Call me if you'd like to run sometime. It's good to have someone chasing you," with Didier's phone number jotted down below.

MILE 14

Down the hall someone hollered something about the number of pepperoni pizzas that should be ordered. It was Loretta, the summer temp on break from Swarthmore, making her Thursday night rounds and demanding everyone report the status of their articles for the magazine's close. It was seven o'clock and copy had to be fact-checked and ready for the senior editors by 7:30 or else heads would roll. In just a few short weeks at the magazine, Loretta had canoodled her way into the front pocket of the executive editor and several features editors. Just this afternoon a rumor circulated through the *Entertainment Weekly* cafeteria that she had convinced an editor to run her article on celebrity pet collagen and Botox treatments.

"So what's the status, Walker?"

Loretta tapped her pencil officiously against Liam's desk as she waited for his response. Normally, Loretta would engage in "Little Ivy" banter about whether Amherst or Swarthmore would be at the top of the *U.S. News & World Report* ranking of liberal arts colleges, but today she was all business. Liam ignored her icy power plays by reminding himself that she had been drinking cheap beer in the quad less than six weeks ago.

"The Ryan Adams piece is finished and I'm tidying up Sinéad right now," he answered without looking up from his computer monitor.

"*Tout de suite* it along, buddy. You know who gets lulu when she's waiting to read copy."

"I just sent Ryan Adams to print right now."

"Did you give the new CD an *A?* I found it completely *brill*." Four or five r's rolled off her tongue as she enunciated her verdict.

"You'll have to read the review. I can't chat now, remember? I need to fact-check this Sinéad piece."

Why the senior staff agreed to do a retrospective on Sinéad O'Connor's life and music baffled Liam. He thought the artist herself would find it maudlin, and even a tad insulting, when she had decades more to record. The number of remote Irish towns and abstruse Gaelic names in the article had irked Liam. He had triple-sourced everything and was finally ready to print out his annotated copy and do one last read-through when the phone rang. He let it go straight to voice mail. The phone rang again, and he answered it with a curt, "Yes?"

"Don't ignore me! I need to know our exact coordinates."

"Look, I'll meet you outside the Williams-Sonoma in twenty minutes. Things are tight here. See you then." Liam hung up before Monroe had the opportunity to prolong the conversation.

Liam smiled as he made his way through the 900 words of copy—an encyclopedic length for an *EW* article—knowing that he had caught a huge number of spelling and factual errors (town populations, the names of cavernous Irish pubs). He always received the toughest assignments because he had a killer instinct for accuracy. And with this Thursday night magazine close out of the way, Liam could now allow his *evening* to begin.

He decided against taking a cab and jogged up the West Fifties to the Time Warner Center. The evening had the smack of perfection that only comes for about forty-eight hours in mid-May—the promise of summer without any of its ill humor and humidity. Possibility without disappointment. As Liam approached Columbus Circle, the dark plum sky reflected in the tall glass towers at the base of Central Park. Cars were just beginning to switch on their headlights as evening descended on Manhattan.

Monroe stood outside smoking a cigarette and doing 360-degree turns in the store front windows, assessing himself from each new perspective. The purple Izod polo he wore tugged slightly at his stout midsection, but his complementary houndstooth sports jacket and butter-colored summer trousers slimmed him somewhat. Liam fought off the smile that tickled the corners of his mouth, knowing Monroe would feel judged and infantilized by any positive comment on the outfit.

"Spare some nicotine for a friend?"

"I'll let you know when I see one." Monroe put out his own cigarette and lit one for Liam. "Don't tell me you raced over here only to become bedraggled, and you still ended up ten minutes late."

Liam had felt the trickle of perspiration for the past few blocks but didn't think it would be noticeable. Was Monroe testing him? Hoping to stoke his vanity to see what Liam might do? Moving closer to the glass front of the building, Liam could see damp, dark rings under the armpits of his new aubergine Marc Jacobs sweater. The high-priced tickets had set him back a week's pay, and now he would enter looking like a sweaty boor. Liam had looked flawless earlier in the day—and he knew it. All afternoon random people had been glancing at him for that half a second longer than is socially appropriate, as if trying to recall his name or remember how they knew him.

The invitation called for "festive" attire, and Liam felt it was the perfect occasion to don the decadent outfit that Gary had purchased for him at Bergdorf Goodman. The sweater worked perfectly against his ink-blue jeans. Liam had even gotten a fresh haircut to showcase the angularity of his cheekbones. Everything had to be perfect, so he would simply wait outside for his sweater to dry off.

"Don't worry, kiddo. They always look at you. Tonight they'll just be looking at you and wondering if you put on antiperspirant."

"Very funny. You know how much this fund-raiser means to me. We're going to wait until I'm presentable."

"We're already fifteen minutes into the cocktail hour and Mama needs to have herself some Grey Goose on the rocks."

"The third person? Monroe, we've talked about this."

"Don't ruin your evening, beautiful." Monroe's tone had naturally switched from sarcastic to soothing. "You spent 400 bucks on the tickets, so let's enjoy ourselves. No one inside is going to look as good as you. No one ever does."

While Liam knew that the statement was the type of thing that one friend says to another out of a requisite sense of politeness, he found himself oddly empowered by the idea. He straightened his posture, clamped his arms tight against his sides to cover up the sweat stains, and turned again toward his statuesque reflection. Maybe Monroe was onto something. Why not go in now and get their money's worth?

As soon as they walked through the doors of Café Gray, Monroe grabbed two flutes of champagne from a waiter circulating through the foyer area. Liam hesitated as he brushed the lip of the glass against his mouth and felt the bubbles pop and tingle.

"C'mon," Monroe insisted. "This is the perfect chaser to a cigarette buzz."

"If the desired result is a date with the toilet," Liam said, placing the glass on a side table that housed a cobalt vase filled with white orchids. "Now, let's go into the main room and mingle."

Liam's hands trembled, and he knew a drink would settle his nerves. The bar was quite small and had been set up in the back corner of the room, making Liam feel desultory for tracking down a cocktail. The windows by the bar looked east over Columbus Circle, and in the short time since they had lingered outside every trace of the day had vanished from Manhattan. Something forbidden hung in the dark curtain of trees outlining the borders of Central Park. Light zoomed out in every direction from the busy streets below, but it was as though someone had taken a blanket and tucked in the green expanse of Central Park for a good evening's rest. Liam felt safe and warm inside this beautiful, overpriced restaurant. He ordered a second Ketel One and tonic.

"Why I never thought you'd actually show!" Liam felt the hot breath of the words in his ear and turned around to face Didier.

"Well, it's for a good cause." The words had come out without any thought. A reflex.

"Some might say you're supporting the wrong troops, but I can tell you that the Bobcats all appreciate your contribution."

"Helping out coaches is something that transcends team lines. I am glad that your staff may get better salaries as a result of this evening." Liam had come for one reason only and that reason was standing before him right now as he made a complete jackass of himself with clichéd drivel.

"I'll say, I think we took in over $40,000 tonight." Didier's eyes lit up as he spoke.

"That *is* a hunk of change. I think I missed my calling as a coach." Monroe elbowed slightly in front of Liam as he spoke, finally extending his right hand in a miniature curtsey.

"You'll have to excuse my friend Liam here. He's frightfully rude at times. I'm Monroe."

"Lovely to have you, Monroe. I am Didier Vallois. God, every time I say my full name it feels like I am choking on too many accents." Didier played with the platinum wedding band on his left hand. Liam had never noticed it before. "You'd think I was from the Ile Saint-Louis not Hoboken."

Hoboken? Liam could imagine a man being both sexy and a resident of Hoboken—perhaps if he had the grit of a mechanic or the rough, unschooled accent of some south New Jersey town—but Didier had the high sweeping features found in the countries of Northern Europe. There had to be some mistake, something to keep Liam's fantasies alive.

"I've heard tomes about you, Didier. I feel like we ate paste together in the corner of Mrs. Daltry's first-grade class."

Even when he was at his most vulnerable and agitated, Monroe seldom employed such guerilla tactics on Liam. There was only the slightest chance that Didier would connect with Monroe's humor. And even if he was entertained, Didier would surely feel creeped out to know he had been picked apart by Liam. Or perhaps that would feed his ego.

"Well, I hope I live up to all the talk." Didier smiled at Monroe and then turned his head to look Liam squarely in the eyes during the pregnant pause that ensued. "I aim to please."

"I'm going to head up to the bar, Liam. I'll get you another Ketel One and tonic. And you, Didier?" Didier lifted his half-full glass of red wine, and Monroe nodded. Midway to the bar, Monroe turned around and shouted: "Don't talk about anything interesting while I'm gone!"

Just then Liam felt the buzz of his BlackBerry through the back pocket of his jeans. He scrolled through the incoming message quickly while smiling apologetically at Didier. It was not good. The words were very few and fragmented, but it was clear that he had screwed up.

"You'll have to excuse me, Didier. My work needs me back there right away."

"It's eight forty-five . . . At this point, anything can wait 'til morning."

"You'd think, but the magazine I work for closes on Thursday nights so there is no wiggle room. Final copy is needed by midnight, and one of the articles I submitted apparently needs some quick fixes. I seriously don't even have the time to be talking to you right now . . . Tell Monroe what happened and tell him not to kill me for leaving."

Liam raced out of the restaurant and, as he bolted down the escalator, he heard Didier short of breath behind him.

"I'm not playing games," said Liam. "I might be fired. I need to hop in a cab right now."

"Let me hop in with you."

Liam stopped and looked at Didier. They stood about one foot apart from each other on the atrium of the Time Warner Center. Most of the stores had already closed, and Liam felt as though he could grab Didier and kiss him and no one would notice. If Liam embraced him, the kiss would be deep and violent. Adrenaline coursed through his veins and he needed the release.

"I said this isn't a game. It's work and it's going to be intense."

"I'll wait for you at the Starbucks downstairs."

"You don't even know where I work." Liam could feel himself blush.

"You're telling me there *isn't* a Starbucks downstairs?"

Liam's nerves slackened as he smiled tentatively and walked outside to hail a cab. He heard Didier's footstep following close behind. The image of Didier twisting his platinum ring nervously flashed into Liam's mind as he spotted a taxi with its light on. A brisk rain had picked up out of nowhere, and Didier's body pressed up against Liam. They ducked quickly inside the taxi. As the driver sped downtown, Liam watched the speckled blur of the city through the dirty windshield wipers. Didier clasped Liam's wet hand inside his own and closed his eyes.

MILE 15

After about ninety minutes in the newsroom of *Entertainment Weekly*, Liam had addressed all of the sourcing issues that the senior editors found on his latest piece and headed for the elevator banks feeling depleted. He could not believe that he suffered through nights like this for near minimum-wage pay. He had dreamed of moving people through his words ever since eleventh-grade literature class. Liam entered the elevator alone and looked at his watch. It was almost 11 P.M. Hitting the button for the lobby, Liam wondered how many other twentysomethings at magazines or at publishing houses had been similarly seduced by those classic American novels. As a sixteen-year-old, Liam spent hours lingering over the first few pages of *Moby Dick*, fascinated that a man writing more than a century earlier seemed to have peered into his mind, felt his spirit and shared his thoughts. His narrator, Ishmael, speaking of that "damp, drizzly November in my soul . . . that requires a strong moral principle to prevent me from deliberately stepping into the street, and methodically knocking people's hats off." How often, as a teenager in suburbia, Liam had felt his skin crawling at the prospect of a life defined by inertia—filled with trips to local shopping plazas in a town strewn with split-level homes, fast-food chains, and strip malls. And so here he stood, a true adult who had graduated into big-city life, with more than $100,000 of fancy education to his name—a whipping boy to editors peddling pulp and gossip to the starry-eyed masses. The doors to the elevator opened, pulling Liam out of his self-pitying reverie, and he walked across his office building's marble plaza to the Starbucks where Didier waited with a tall coffee and a newspaper.

"You really did wait for me?" Liam spoke with a tone that expressed surprise and gratitude, in equal measure.

"I'm nothing if not a man of my word," Didier responded.

"Not just another pretty face, hunh?"

"Let's get out of here, Liam. The fluorescent lighting and smell of roasting coffee have started to have an ill effect on me. You are done with work for the night, yes?"

Liam gave a wan smile; he looked at Didier and could not believe how strikingly beautiful, how unearthly looking, he was.

"Then let's go celebrate," Didier said, punching Liam in the arm.

"But, Didier, it is so late—and I am exhausted."

"We'll have a nightcap at your apartment then."

Cars rushed along the wet streets of midtown; it was true that the pace never really slowed in Manhattan. Hopeful anticipation of what might ensue with Didier mixed with apprehension as Liam considered the time and the fact that it was a weeknight. A creature of routine, Liam liked to get up early so that he could hit the gym before work. At this rate, he would be a sleep-deprived wreck in the office tomorrow.

"I can hear the wheels of doubt turning in your head, Liam." Didier stood up from the table and walked toward the exit. "I can tell you're not a gambler. Your face doesn't mask one single thought or emotion. And I absolutely love that about you!"

"I would like nothing more than to have you over, Didier.

No reservations about that at all. I am just spent from the work snafu and worried about getting behind on things."

"You did not move to New York City to be safe, Liam. Why be here if you are not willing to shake things up a little? Don't you want to stir the pot? Take a chance . . . Live a little . . . And please, don't make me reach for another cliché—I am at the end of my rope here!"

Liam laughed and rushed his hands through Didier's hair. He imagined running his fingers down Didier's back and over his buttocks and could almost feel the blood drain from his head toward his groin.

"And then there's that," Liam said pointing to Didier's wedding ring. "That may be a little more than I can handle at this point too."

"It's a technicality. I can't tell you any more than that right now, but I will be able to soon. You need to take a leap of faith here."

As Liam and Didier walked to the subway, a heavy silence grew between them, the weight of which could be measured by the gravity of the decision Liam was about to make. Liam knew himself well enough to understand that he had set out on this evening, had coaxed Monroe to go to the Bobcat fund-raiser with him, solely to get closer to Didier. And now everything he thought he wanted was here before him, an opportunity to realize his dream. He could not let it slip away. As they approached the entrance to the downtown Number 1 train, Liam realized he had just learned that Didier was from Hoboken. He thought about the fact that he had never been to that little commuter town across the river from downtown Manhattan before.

"I am coming home with you," Didier said as they descended the long set of stairs toward the subway platform.

"Yes, I know that," Liam said. "But only for a nightcap . . . I don't want to doom our chances any further by sleeping with you on the first '*date.*'"

Didier looked at Liam defiantly as they stood alone on the empty subway platform at Fiftieth Street, awaiting the train. Out of nowhere, Didier performed a cartwheel and clapped his hands together in proud fashion upon sticking the landing. Didier's boyish delight at getting his way made Liam smile. He imagined the warmth of Didier's body next to his own in his queen-sized bed and felt content and at peace and a little bit scared—fleetingly but all at once. Liam did not embrace happiness with any amount of ease or certainty.

As they climbed the flights of stairs up to his apartment, Liam began to feel self-conscious. He could not remember the last time he had taken out the trash or whether he had left clothing scattered all over the floor. And although he loved the charm of his place, he knew that the warped wood floors and clawfoot tub in the bathroom would not suit everyone's fancy.

"I apologize in advance if anything you see tonight does not meet your standards of hygiene or décor, Didier. The artist-in-residence here is often overwhelmed by his own little existence."

Liam opened up the refrigerator door and pulled out a half-empty bottle of Sancerre. He fished two wineglasses out of the drying rack that, all too often, doubled as a storage unit for his dishes and cutlery. He split the remainder of the bottle between the two glasses and handed one to Didier.

"Cheers," Liam said. "I hope white is okay. I don't have much in the apartment right now. Believe it or not, I was not expecting a visitor tonight."

"White is fantastic," Didier said, clinking glasses with Liam. "I hope that this big gulp of a glass doesn't put me out for the night, though."

"Not to worry if it knocks you out, sweetness. Like I said earlier, we are just hitting the hay and nothing else is happening."

"I am all for protecting a lady's honor."

They carried the glasses over to Liam's bed and sat down on the edge. Liam reached over and hit the shuffle button on his iPod. The forlorn opening chords of "Wild Horses" began to play, and Liam reached over for Didier's hand.

"I read once that Mick Jagger wrote this about his love affair with Marianne Faithfull," Didier said. "It's an unbelievably gorgeous song, isn't it?"

"Iconic songs like this one lend themselves to a lot of folklore, I think," Liam said, threading his fingers between Didier's. "I saw something once that said Keith Richards wrote this as a lullaby for his son, a way to address the fact that he was on the road a lot. But I like to think it's about something more basic and undefined—a yearning that can't be easily named and one that may be impossible to satisfy."

Didier threw back the last two swallows of wine in his glass and lay back on the bedspread, stretching his arms luxuriously across the width of the bed.

"You certainly are an old soul, aren't you, Liam? I get the sense you've lived decades longer than you actually have, like you're carrying around the yoke of past lives or something."

"I seem like an old man, hunh?" Liam kicked his shoes off and curled up beside Didier on top of the bedding.

"Quite the contrary. The combination of your young stud body and that rugged old soul—your world-weariness, as my mother would have called it—make you so fucking irresistible. Well, I can barely stand to look at you."

"Then let's close our eyes and go to bed."

They fell asleep on top of the duvet with their clothes on and at some point in the middle of the night, Liam woke up to use the bathroom and stripped Didier's pants off to place him under the covers. Didier wore black dress socks that clung tightly to his hairy and muscular legs. Boxer briefs amplified the curve of his buttocks. Liam stood for a minute watching Didier sleep peacefully on the bed and felt certain that he must be dreaming. When he got back into bed after using the bathroom, Liam wrapped his body around Didier's and fell fast asleep, and for the first time, in as long as he could remember, Liam turned off his 6 A.M. alarm and skipped the gym. He lay in bed in a state of half-sleep, feeling the warmth of Didier's body next to his own. There was something so much more special and more hopeful about everything given that they hadn't had sex. They left the apartment together and wordlessly parted ways at the corner, with a tacit understanding that talking would only sully the moment. Liam felt like a new man heading into the office that day. He vowed, silently, to continue to surprise himself.

By late morning, Liam was ravenous with hunger. Instead of buying two cups of yogurt at the deli in the lobby of his building, he decided to stretch himself beyond his normal routine, write to one of his friends who worked nearby, and suggest a lunch date. As he sped through the contacts on his laptop, Liam realized that he needed to connect one-on-one with Riser. Perhaps if he met him face-to-face without the distractions of other people, Liam could cut to the core with Riser and find out if his new friend had become a strict vegan and was looking more drawn as a result, or whether he was slowly starving himself to death.

Riser wrote back immediately to Liam's e-mail and said that he would love to meet up for lunch; Riser even went so far as to suggest a great place for chopped salad where the owners charged a flat rate for all you could pile on rather than *à la carte* pricing. *It's these little niceties that create loyalties for me,* he wrote in the exchange. The care given to pointing out this banal detail comforted Liam on his friend's behalf. He had an overpowering sense of optimism and contentment when he left the office to meet Riser for lunch at The Raw Deal.

Arriving first, Liam snagged a table for two in the back of

the establishment, so that they would have the space and privacy to talk openly and honestly. Liam ordered some seltzer and cranberry juice and a platter of steamed edamame to keep his rumbling stomach at bay while he waited. With all the miles he had been running lately, Liam noticed that his appetite had increased exponentially to keep up with the additional energy needs he was placing on his body. After about fifteen minutes of waiting, Liam emailed Riser from his BlackBerry to make sure that all was okay and that they were, indeed, still meeting today for lunch. Riser arrived within seconds of Liam hitting the send button on his Black-Berry.

"You had me worried there for a second, cowboy," Liam said with a wide grin as Riser sat down across the table from him.

"What? This is New York City, Liam," Riser responded, visibly agitated. "Haven't you ever heard of being fashion-ably late?"

"I am familiar with the term, Riser, but—fashionable or not—I get a pretty tight hour for my lunch, so I will need to leave here in about forty minutes to get back to the office be-fore someone has a coronary. I just wanted to maximize my time with you."

Riser shifted in his seat and seemed angered at having ex-pectations flung upon him.

"Let's order quickly," Liam offered. "At least this type of food doesn't take long to prepare."

When the waiter came around to their little raw wood table, Liam scanned the menu one last time and thought how he would really love a juicy hamburger and fries. The concessions one makes in the name of friendship!

"I will have the hearts of romaine with egg and raw tuna," he said, in final capitulation to the sparseness of the menu.

"And for you, sir?" the waiter said, without making eye contact with Riser.

"Oh, just some hot tea with lemon," Riser responded. "I am getting over a bad fever and am still in the phase where I have absolutely no appetite."

As the waiter hustled off into the kitchen to place his last round of lunchtime orders, Liam stared blankly into his friend's eyes.

"Work with me here, Riser," he said. "We did not have to eat out today if you were not feeling well."

"But I know these types of outings are just as much about the social aspect as they are about the actual nourishment."

Liam could feel himself freezing up; he wanted to say something about how the rapid weight loss and sunken features had made him fear for Riser's life. But he didn't want to hurl Riser further into this defensive and self-deluding posturing.

"It is really good to see you without the whole crew around," Liam said to Riser.

"A rarity—right! I wouldn't be surprised if Zane or Gary or Ben parachuted down right now and landed at the table next to us. Not in the slightest."

When his salad arrived, Liam felt very self-conscious eating forkfuls of egg and tuna as Riser drank, stingily, from the small saucer of hot tea he had been given.

"Are you sure you don't want some of my dish, Riser?" Liam asked, in a last-ditch effort to speak to the skinny, little elephant that had been at the table for some time now. "As runners, we really need to take better care of our bodies than the average Joe. We burn more calories before noon than most people burn all day!"

"Look, if you brought me out today to give me a nutritional lecture, then I am heading back to my own place of work, because I have better things to do with my time. No offense, Liam, but I see my doctor regularly, and I know my own body. I mean, I have been running faster times than ever before, and I feel so much more focused at work. Eating now would just distract from all that focus and take away from all those well-earned accomplishments."

Liam knew now that he would only be digging himself into a larger ravine of faulty logic and spurious facts if he continued to point out the gaping flaws in Riser's thinking. Instead, he ordered the check and told himself that he would enlist the help of some of the Fast Trackers who specialized in social work and health issues. Maybe a professional opinion and a learned voice was what would ultimately yank Riser out of this abyss he had fallen into.

MILE 16

Liam had snoozed through the first Sunday morning wake-up call and squinted at the digital blocks of time on his clock radio three times in a row before frantically recognizing that he had only twenty minutes to get uptown. Having spent the last two days guiltily sneaking around town with Didier, Liam wondered what he would say to the Fast Trackers about him. They seemed to monitor his coordinates within the city on a daily basis. While he liked the familiarity that had been established in recent months, he craved a little privacy—at least while he discovered whether or not something real might transpire with Didier.

In a hurried fit, Liam threw on the clothes he had laid out the night before and paced back and forth on the cool wooden floor trying to devise a game plan. He knew he was wasting time. But he also knew that the gang would not leave without him. As he raced out of the apartment and leapfrogged over the sets of hallway stairs, the pesky old lady one floor below him creaked open her door and called out Liam's name.

"Not today, Mrs. Scalabrin . . . I'm running late."

"I'll say you're running. Sheesh, what's the rush? You'll break your neck on these rickety stairs."

A pang of guilt hit Liam; he knew the old lady was dying for a cigarette and was afraid to leave her apartment and venture to the corner bodega by herself. For the next few hours, she would be listening for a willing neighbor on his or her way out of the building. On a Sunday at 6:30 A.M., she could be waiting for a very long time. Liam had moved to Manhattan, in part, for the anonymity but found that living inches away from strangers sometimes provided enough glue to form the invisible bonds of family. People crept into your life even as you tried to shut the door in their face. Almost every weekend Liam found himself running some small errand or other for Mrs. Scalabrin.

The cab rocketed up Sixth Avenue, the streetlights all turning green in perfect time with Liam's taxi ride uptown. As he approached the corner of Eighty-sixth Street and Fifth Avenue, Liam saw Gary's big red Range Rover idling in a stretch of road designated for a city bus stop. He glanced down at his watch. It was 6:45 on the dot; he could not have been more punctual. Gary looked relieved as Liam waved to him from across the street.

"I'm so happy that there is one in my flock who I can count on," he said and gave Liam a tight hug. He held Liam in his arms for a noticeable amount of time, as though searching for an answer in their embrace. "I am so happy to see you that I am not even going to ask why you didn't return my phone calls the last few days."

There it was—the inevitable. Liam's life had been handed over to the Fast Trackers, and he had willingly cast off almost all ties to the past and to other friends. But as he thought of Didier's hot breath in his ear and the rush of the forbidden, Liam felt his tongue twist over itself and did not attempt anything more than a feeble smile and a coquettish batting of his eyes at Gary.

The air still hadn't shaken the cold of the night before, but the strong shards of sunlight across the perimeter of the park and the stench of fertile soil hinted that today was going to be beautiful. It was almost June now, after all. Liam initially had reservations about forfeiting the Sunday of his Memorial Day weekend for this trip, but Gary lobbied so strongly that Liam found it impossible to say no. Succumbing fully to the persuasions of the Fast Trackers had become the norm for Liam of late, as Monroe had noted snidely the last time they met.

"Do I have time to get a cup of coffee?" Liam asked.

"Given that we're waiting on Zane and Mitch, you definitely have time."

"*Mitch?* Talk to me, Gary."

"Oh, shush." Gary giggled nervously. "Everyone knows that I'm dramatic. That's part of my charm. I explode inappropriately and then apologize profusely. Create mess. Wash. Rinse. Repeat cycle. We'll be fine. That scene at the Brooklyn Half Marathon is SO yesterday!"

"Alrighty, then," Liam said. "I just wanted to make sure all would be peaceful for the two-hour car ride."

"Of course, sweetie. Now make mine dark and stormy. And hit the Dunkin' Donuts on Lexington. It's a bit of a walk but the best coffee in this neighborhood."

By the time Liam returned with the two coffees, Zane and Mitch had arrived and had managed to cozy themselves into the car, with Mitch riding shotgun and Zane sprawled out across the back bench. He moved his feet a few inches so that Liam could squeeze into the back and then they flew off on their adventure.

With few cars on the road, Gary pressed down hard on the gas and hit seventy-five miles an hour by the time they reached the Triborough Bridge. A honeydew glow covered the island of Manhattan, making all the buildings look like cardboard pieces in a Candy Land game, and Liam thought about how small and manageable the massive city was from a distance. The driver behind them honked wildly and stuck his head out the window to shout an obscenity at Gary for cutting him off on the way to the E-ZPass lane. The incident pulled Liam out of his quiet reverie.

"A lightbulb just went off . . . Car game! Car game!" Zane exclaimed as Gary settled into the left lane of I-95.

"Ugh, I'm not looking for North Dakota license plates," Mitch groaned.

"Can't we just listen to my iPod? We can synch it with the radio here," Liam offered.

"I'm game for a game," said Gary. "It'll help keep my mind off the day. Distractions can be an old man's best friend."

"Okay, we'll do a few rounds of 'I Never,'" Zane announced.

"That's really more of a drinking game," Mitch chimed in. "I don't think I can play that before 8 A.M., Zane. Sorry."

"Of course you can. We'll keep it honorable. We'll keep it tame. In fact, we can keep it a drinking game. Everyone has Gatorade on them. Every time, we do an 'I Never' proposition, those who *have ever* can drink a sip of Gatorade. Remember, you have to make true statements, so you can't have done the things you claim to have never engaged in. Gary, you start."

"I never lost control of myself while running."

Everyone in the car looked at each other, and then Mitch took a swig of Gatorade.

"I was in Queens on a long run and got lost," he implored.

Zane then took a sip as well. It was unclear to Liam if that was an act of honesty or one of solidarity. Either way the game moved on, and it was Mitch's turn.

Mitch took a moment before speaking.

"I never cried myself to sleep at night," he then said.

Mitch looked straight at Gary, who turned to Liam, who looked up at Zane, who was staring off into space.

Gary drank first, followed by Zane and Liam.

"What did you expect, Mitch? We're gay men!" exclaimed Gary.

"Okay, onward and upward," Zane said. "Liam, it's your turn."

"I never drank too much and puked—since graduating college."

"I think we're all going to have to stop on the road to whiz at this rate," Mitch complained.

"You don't see me drinking, do you?" Zane smirked.

"Fine. Your turn now, Zane," said Mitch.

"I never slept with a Fast Tracker," Zane said, barely containing himself.

"No one drink!" Gary shouted from the front seat. "Zane, you know better than to pull this shit. I mean, even among good friends this is dangerous territory."

Liam studied Zane's face for some sign, to see if he was being mischievous or just plain mean. When he had confided in Zane about the Ben incident, Liam made it crystal-clear that the story was top secret. Deciding to give Zane the benefit of the doubt (gay men often did things without thinking or for humorous effect), Liam also saw this as an opportunity to change the subject and talk about another topic that had been on his mind. Riser.

"So, on a completely different note," Liam began, "what do you guys think we should do about Riser's current state of emaciation?"

"Has that girl dropped more weight?" Mitch asked. "She's always been a twig in my book."

"We all go through phases with our weight," Gary said, switching lanes and passing a small minivan with palpable vexation. "I hope you are not monitoring the spare tire inching across my midsection!"

"I think he has switched his diet to become macrobiotic," Zane said. "That could be part of it. He's still running strong so he must be okay. Have there been any other changes in Riser's mood that you have witnessed, Liam?"

"Well, I had lunch with him last week, and he got really miffed at me for pointing out that he should eat something when he only ordered a hot tea."

"Now, that seems like unhealthy behavior," Zane said, repositioning himself in the seat and looking straight at Liam. "Why didn't he order food?"

"Some excuse about being sick. I don't really know that I believe it."

"Look, I struggled with this in college, Liam," Zane offered. "Sometimes it is dangerous if people point out or harp on the issue of weight or eating patterns. Guys with eating disorders are already being really hard on themselves, and genuine concern can come across as unwanted criticism— which he does *not* need right now. I will feel him out next time I see him. Don't worry, I will be subtle. I deal with a lot of people with body image issues in my practice."

Feeling comforted by that promise, Liam curled into the nook of his seat and gazed out the window as the flat screen of Connecticut suburbia rolled out before him.

"Come on . . . come on . . . " Liam opened his eyes slowly to see Gary emptying the car. He had brought along a cooler and a first-aid kit and several changes of clothing for everyone. While Liam found the paternal instinct in Gary to be endearing, he wondered if he had gone more than a little overboard in his preparations for this day trip. They were parked in the corner of a well-manicured football field, alongside a handful of other vehicles.

"Where are Mitch and Zane?" Liam asked as he stretched awake. He looked for something to cover his arms. Sleeping had chilled him.

"They went for a warm-up jog," Gary replied. "You should too. This race starts in less than half an hour."

After having reconfigured his entire weekend to suit this

whim of Gary's, Liam chafed at the curtly delivered suggestion. Gary had sold the concept of a fun race away from the
suffocating crowds of Central Park effectively (the man
could proselytize with the best of the Bible thumpers), but
the antics of the morning had worn away Liam's patience.
Running a 5K around the West Hartford Reservoir could only
provide so much stimulation. Liam knew that he could have
spent the afternoon at a beer blast on the roof of Eagle Bar
with Monroe. He poured himself out of the car and hopped
up and down on the crunchy grass of the football field to
wake his muscles into action.

"I'll see you at the start of the race, Liam," Gary said. "I
have to check in with some of the local officials and organizers. Make sure that they remember to do everything correctly."

Despite his reticence to talk about the specifics, Gary had
made it clear that this race meant the world to him. He had not
missed the event in any year since its inception and had twisted
the arms of his three favorite team members to make certain
that fast runners participated and that the race remain competitive. Liam assumed that Gary was friends with the race
organizers or had some sort of community ties to the region.

Seeing that he had only fifteen minutes until the gun went
off, Liam stripped down to his shorts and tank top and
headed off for a brisk jog. He needed to move his head into a
place where the fierce competitor within him might awaken.
All the Gatorade from the car ride had snaked its way
through his system, and he headed into the wooded area behind the football fields to urinate against a tall evergreen
tree. The air between his legs and the smell of freshly shorn
grass added to the feeling of release. It was something that
he would never have dared to do in Manhattan; the Parks
Department had cracked down so much on public urination
that it seemed safer to fornicate in the rambles than to re-
lieve yourself on the Great Lawn.

Only about 150 people congregated by the makeshift starting line. Two guys with clipboards and megaphones stood next to Gary on a raised podium. The temperature had shot up about ten degrees since they left the city, and Liam could feel beads of sweat dampening his forehead. He sidled up between Mitch and Zane at the start line as the organizers read a brief list of instructions. Before sounding the horn, Gary cleared his throat and addressed the runners.

"I'd just like to thank everyone for gathering out here today for a really great cause. The Greater West Hartford LGBT Center was founded in 1990 by my partner, Malcolm, and it is through your support that queer and questioning children in this area will know they are not alone. When my partner, Malcolm, who extends his deepest regrets for not being able to attend the race today, was growing up gay in West Hartford, he had no place to turn and suffered many years of depression and self-doubt from that scarring period of his adolescence. Let's keep moving into the future fast, strong, and proud. Everyone have a fabulous race."

Before Liam had a chance to ask Zane for clarification on the back story to this event, Gary blew the horn and the racers jockeyed into position. Accustomed to elbowing through a chain of adamant runners at the start of every race in Central Park, Liam sprang out to the front of the pack to discover that he led the race for the first few minutes. Zane ran just a few steps behind him, practically on his shoulder, and the next runners were several hundreds of yards behind them.

Racing ahead of Zane made Liam nervous, like he had chosen an unsustainable pace or was simply defying the natural order. As they crested the first hill in the course, Zane challenged Liam by breaking out a few feet in front of him. "Pace yourself," Zane admonished as he strode past. They hit the one-mile mark with about five minutes, thirty seconds on Liam's watch. A canopy of cherry blossoms lined the next stretch of the course; the air was redolent with overripe flowers as they ran through the white tunnel. Liam noticed how free and unlabored his breathing was and decided he would catch up to Zane before the two-mile point, which he guessed would be coming up within the next minute or two.

As they turned onto the dirt path that hugged the low wall of the reservoir, Zane turned his head to peer over his shoulder. Liam knew now that if he focused he could beat Zane. Monitoring your competition was a sure sign that your confidence had been stolen from you. With the two-mile mark appearing at the end of the reservoir path, Liam moved to his left and pushed hard until he was running up alongside Zane. The paltry margin of dirt afforded the runners very little room to maneuver safely, and Liam apologized as his arm brushed into Zane's torso. Sensing the brevity of the 5K, Liam dug deep and sprinted out ahead.

Looking down at his watch, Liam computed the amount of time he would need to ignore his pain in order to finish in first place. He had never won a race in his life. Even back in third grade during his grammar school's track and field day, Wayne Snipes edged him out at the finish line to take home the blue ribbon in the 100-yard dash. Liam redoubled his efforts and pumped his arms to sustain his newly quickened pace. He struggled to keep his thoughts from sinking into the depths of self-doubt and refused to move his head one inch to the left or the right even as he heard Zane's breath behind him. With each slight twinge of a stomach cramp, Liam looked to a focal point up ahead on the road and resolved to reach that marker as quickly as possible. Exhaustion pressed down hard on his chest. The loop forked to the right, and Liam could see that a long decline led to a straight passage that would certainly deposit the racers at the finish line.

Determined not to take any chances—a sprinter by design, Zane would fare better in the final moments of the race—Liam used the downhill to generate a fast and forceful turnover that he parlayed into a sprint down the last quarter mile of road that led to the arch of bright helium balloons that served as the finish line. His legs stiffened as the finish approached; he could feel his insides writhe as they conspired to squeeze him into submission, cajoling him to stop so that all of his organs could take a mandated rest. Liam leaned forward and attempted to change the angle of his stride slightly so that he might work some unused muscles; he had read in a magazine months ago the importance of engaging one's entire musculoskeletal system when mining the hidden reserves of the body's racing resources. The sun splintered off the red and silver of the balloons, and Liam closed his eyes and staggered into the finish. As he stumbled toward the gentleman who was clocking the finish times, Liam finally looked over his shoulder to see Zane collapse in tears just under the sparkle of the finish line. Once he regained his faculties, Liam shuffled over to Zane. He placed his hand on the small of Zane's back and Zane stood clutching his knees.

"Let's walk it off," Liam said.

Zane nodded his head in a defeated but willing fashion, and they headed off the course.

"I just, I just . . . " Zane choked on his words, still heaving deeply even as he walked off his exhaustion.

"Don't say a thing, Zane. Just let your body adjust. We all have races like this. Just let yourself recover."

"This, you know," Zane started again. "You know, this was a fast race for me. You were just flying, Liam."

Liam looked down at his watch to see that he had broken seventeen minutes. He had managed to run faster than a 5:30 pace. He could not even remember what his fastest previous time had been, but he knew that he had smashed his old PR to bits. The urge to jump up and down swelled inside, but he resisted. Zane needed him now.

"My God, my God, my goodness!" Gary leaped in front of Liam and Zane and embraced the two runners in a bear hug.

"We snagged first and second place! And Mitch came in around fifth. Tremendous! You guys make me so proud."

Liam attempted to deflect the comment with a nervous chuckle and a shoulder shrug. Zane kept his eyes focused on the ground.

"No, you guys are the future of this club, of this movement. It *is* a movement, you know." Gary then paused to reflect a moment before continuing. "People think that I am over the top, but these things matter, guys. When Malcolm was a kid, he never tried to succeed in sports because of fear and because he did not believe in himself. You guys show how far we've come. Who wouldn't want to be like you guys? You're young, you're fast, you're beautiful. You're . . . You're everything."

Mitch walked toward the group, chomping on a half-eaten banana as he spoke.

"Uh-oh!" he exclaimed. "Everyone is looking mighty long in the face . . . Must mean that Gary has been working his magic again."

"Oh, shut up, you. We were just celebrating," Gary retorted. His face had reddened.

"Nothing like tears to spread joy and satisfaction . . . "

"Once you're my age, you guys will understand me!"

"That's an even more frightening prospect," Zane quipped, seeming alive for the first time since the end of the race.

"Keep it up and you bitches are hitching home," Gary said, pretending to slap Zane in the face.

Liam looked out over the green football fields and noticed that families had congregated throughout the area to partake in the day, which was growing more and more glorious by the minute. He was overcome with joy.

"Let's have someone take our picture!" Liam exclaimed. "Does one of you have a camera?"

"We can use my phone," Zane offered. "It's got all the latest gadgets. The camera is almost professional quality."

Gary found a young mother on the field willing to snap the

photo, and the four men posed, arm in arm, against the thick green forest behind them.

"On the count of three, everyone make their most proper smile," Zane shouted. "One . . . Two . . ." He suddenly grabbed Mitch's and Liam's nipples. "Three!"

Everyone erupted in laughter.

MILE 17

"Wait, wait, wait, wait!" Liam heard the distant wail and turned around to catch the heavy metal door before it closed behind him. There was no mistaking the voice, but Liam found himself sticking his head outside to verify that it was indeed Zane rushing crazily toward him with three big boxes in his hands.

"What a fucking pain in the ass this event is turning out to be!" Zane exclaimed. He scooted into the cold marble vestibule and recomposed himself. "The latest errand was running out for a Charlotte russe, crème brûlée, and five pounds of baklava."

With the club still needing to raise almost $5,000 to fund the June Pride Run, now just three weeks away, Liam thought it in bad taste of Zane to find fault with the organizer of this fund-raiser.

"If last-minute dessert runs are the worst of the complaints, then I would say that Ferdinand did a terrific job," said Liam.

"I see *you* didn't have to explain this strange rush order to the sous-chef at Asia de Cuba. Where the hell have you been anyway, Liam? The party started like two hours ago."

For a second, Liam wanted to open up and confess to

Zane, to tell him that he had planned to arrive on time but something had detained him. He could not seem to make a sound. The elevator doors opened up, and Liam took one of the dessert boxes from Zane in an effort to fill the silence. Once inside the elevator cabin, Liam pressed "11" and the slow journey to Ferdinand's apartment began.

"You look like the cat who ate the canary, Liam. Just spill it. What kept you? You're never late."

Annoyed by Zane's immediate demands for information, Liam turned to his friend and smiled opaquely. After the incident during the game of "I Never" on the way to the Connecticut race, Liam had qualms about telling Zane any details about his time with Didier. But Liam knew he'd eventually share the secret with his good friend. Zane harrumphed as the creaky elevator crawled from the fourth to the fifth floor. Liam wondered if any of the tenants in these converted warehouse buildings were afraid to ride in elevators that hadn't been refurbished since the early 1900s.

"You know that I'm just making conversation, Liam. I don't care if you tell me anything. But you don't have to be a jerk about it either, giving me the silent treatment. If I let my imagination run wild, who knows what I'll come up with?"

"Jesus, Zane!" The elevator just passed the eighth floor. "I was looking forward to telling you all the details, but you're making me want to keep it a secret now. I was with Didier all afternoon. There! Are you happy?"

The elevator doors opened onto the eleventh floor, directly into Ferdinand's crowded living room. It was a shade past nine o'clock and the revelers had started getting frisky. "I'm Every Woman" blared overhead as Liam and Zane stepped gingerly into the festive atmosphere. The news had rattled Zane, who looked a little perplexed and possibly even agitated; Liam second-guessed himself for disclosing anything. From out of the sweaty sea of Fast Tracker faces,

Ferdinand sashayed over and kissed both Liam and Zane on the lips.

"You boys have saved the day." Ferdinand collected the edges of his kilt and curtseyed as he spoke. "Now, come follow me into the kitchen so we can slice up these delectables."

The apartment felt cold and empty even though there were more than fifty people congregating in the living room and kitchen. Ferdinand had not dressed the floors with area rugs, and no drapes or curtains hung from the floor-to-ceiling windows that wrapped the southern, northern, and eastern exposures of the apartment. Asymmetrical ottomans and some tall teak stools provided the only true seating in the apartment. Everything had been stripped away to draw the visitors' eyes to the views of the Empire State Building to the north and of the Flatiron to the south. It was majestic, but the architectural sparseness and aesthetic purity of the space reminded Liam of Roark in *The Fountainhead*.

"I'll show you the rest of the apartment when I finish dividing up this brûlée, Liam. Zane can circulate dessert among the guests, since he's already had the tour." Ferdinand handed Zane a tray of baklava and some sliced Charlotte russe. "It's a bit grandiose to call it a tour. There's just the bathroom and the bedroom, really."

"He must walk you through his closet, Liam. Don't miss out on that. The closet is pure Ferdinand."

And with that Zane circled around and began offering the drunken masses high-priced desserts. Even though he had known Ferdinand for more than six months, Liam felt a little anxious being left alone with him. It was all the decadent stories of party drugs. The bathroom glistened in silver chrome and black tile. The bedroom contained only a king-sized bed, a Bang & Olufsen stereo mounted on the side wall, and, quite bizarrely to Liam's eye, a lectern at the foot of the bed.

"Is that for Sunday morning sermons?" Liam asked.

"My father was a professor of religion at Harvard," Ferdinand spoke while smoothing over the crisp white duvet. "He left me that in his will when he died last year. I like to keep it close to me."

"Of course," Liam said, glad that the low lighting hid his blushing. "That's very sweet. But I don't see any doors. Where is this famed closet?"

Ferdinand walked over and studied the wall for a second before pressing his hand along a small ridge in the paint. An opening formed that was big enough for two people to walk through, shoulder to shoulder, and he motioned for Liam to come forward and enter.

"It's really no big thing for someone who is in the business," said Ferdinand, holding Liam in abeyance by the door, "but the non-fashionistas go wild."

Ferdinand had crafted a closet in what other renters would have used as an office or perhaps even a second bedroom. The twelve-foot walls had been divided into thirds so that three tiers of clothes could hang. Ferdinand explained that the current season was within easy reach on the lowest rungs and that he had a sliding ladder in case he wanted anything from the upper regions. It being early June, floral shorts, crisp madras pants, and raw silk shirts graced the bottom rows of clothes. Liam spotted a chinchilla poncho near the ceiling and smiled to himself. The center island of the room, an area large enough for a bed, housed shoes and accessories—everything from pony-trimmed boots to retro saddle bucs to high-tech Japanese sneakers.

"These are the items that are being offered in tonight's silent auction." Ferdinand pointed to four jackets hanging by themselves in the far corner of the closet. "They're last year's collections but quite fine pieces by Ferragamo, Zegna, Tom Ford, and, of course, Prada. I figured we needed something tried and true for people to sink their teeth into."

Liam stared blankly at Ferdinand.

"Speaking of the auction, we should go out and see how the bids are doing."

As soon as he made his way past the bathroom into the main space where the party was being held, Liam saw the regular cast of characters arrayed in typical fashion. A silver-haired gentleman in a velour sweat suit was satisfying Matthew's geriatric predilections. Gary held court with a small group of twentysomethings. Riser looked like an apparition as he showed a pretty young boy his catwalk strut. Liam wondered if Zane had spoken to him yet—had whatever heart-to-heart he was planning. Then Liam noticed Zane in the corner, looking sullen as Gene wagged his finger at him to demonstrate a point. Zane brightened as Liam approached.

"Now Gene, I want you to hold that thought because you're going to finish telling me about your victory against asthma to become Idaho state cross-country champ." Zane looked earnestly into Gene's eyes as he spoke. "But I promised I would talk to Liam here in private about something. Our conversation was interrupted on the way in. Please forgive the rudeness."

Zane grabbed Liam and bolted before Gene had a chance to say whether or not he thought anything was rude. Most people at the party had clustered close to the dramatic windows and stared out at the city hopefully, as though something spectacular might happen. Liam asked if they could meander over to the silent auction and talk for a minute about Riser's weight. Zane glowered at him and said that he had spoken to Riser and that Riser was experimenting with different macrobiotic cuisines and that he had consulted a physician. It might look severe, but his body would adjust and all would be fine. Then Zane whispered through clenched teeth that he needed to know the details of what had transpired with Didier. Liam promised to tell him everything as time allowed and Zane noted that he would check in again with Riser when circumstance allowed. This was *not* the type of thing one could force.

"I've been looking for you guys forever. I have been live bait out there with the geezers of yore. Everyone is having a piece of me," Gary said, embracing both Liam and Zane.

"G-Lo, what are you talking about?" asked Zane. "You've been canoodling with your boy toys all night."

"That was a fleeting moment, Zane. I've spent most of this fund-raiser listening to every queen who had a role in the club over the last thirty years tell me how much better the Pride Run was before I corrupted it with young kids and competition."

"I see you've found your bevy of beauties, Gary. You must feel so much safer now!" The voice came from behind Liam. It was Richard Pollack, one of the founders of the club.

"Let's just move on, Rick," Gary said in a defeated tone. "These guys represent the future of our club and of our race. Don't blame them for any hard feelings you might have about the past—or the future."

"You guys don't even know the history of this club." Rick looked squarely at Liam as he spoke. "What we were founded on and fought through. This here tonight is a god-damn dance party. Our cause isn't about bidding on some Italian jackets."

"A member donated those articles of clothing, Rick." Gary's eyes looked bloodshot, but he seemed determined to make his point. "The money that members spend tonight goes directly to the race—to your race. This isn't 1983. This shit costs money, and we have to move with the times or else we get swept away by them."

"And so the ends don't justify the means, Prince Gary. This race was ours and now it isn't. Someone told me that 3,000 people signed up for the Pride Run this year because of some corporate promotional raffle that you dreamed up.

Now people only care about getting extra points on their AmEx cards or some such."

"I can't argue about this any longer. I paid my $50 to enjoy this party, and from here on in that's exactly what I'm going to do!"

"Don't let him walk all over you, G." Zane angled his shoulder between Gary and Rick. "We're more respected than ever in the athletic community and that's because of you. What more could the founders of the club want? *That* is what this club is all about."

"I'll have you know I meet with Stephanie Reeves Bammer twice per year to discuss what this club is all about," Rick retorted.

"That fat lesbian who promotes all the cyclist events?" Zane asked, looking around for others to corroborate his disbelief.

"The author of *The Fast Track*. It's only the book that gave our club its name. Thanks for helping me prove my point." Rick smirked at Gary. "All sizzle and no steak. That's the usual for Gary's acolytes. It's good to know some things don't change."

Gary walked away and headed to the little bar that was erected by the elevator. Rick followed suit, heading out of the apartment with three other older gentlemen who had been watching the melee at near distance, wearing scowls on their faces. Liam's head swirled from all the action; he had, after all, arrived just a half hour ago.

"So, I've waited long enough, Sir Sex-a-Lot. Give me the dish on Didier," Zane demanded. "I promise not to judge you."

"Judge him for what?" Ben swooped into the conversation like a crow that spotted something shiny. "I would say there is no judgment in a place where they're hawking cosmopolitans like it's still the year 2000. But at least the bartender is hot."

Liam turned to take notice of the broad-backed man serving drinks just ten feet from where he stood and realized he was thirsty for a drink. As he approached the bar to order a drink, Liam battled aphasia, mumbling for a moment before the meaty bartender.

"To drink," the man said in the accent of some newly liberated Eastern Bloc country. "Sir, I am asking you what you want to drink."

After managing to stutter the words "Seven and Seven," Liam watched the exquisite and fine muscles of the bartender's back rise and fall, pop and fade, bulge and recede as he fixed the drink. At about six-foot, four-inches tall and 220 pounds, the man managed somehow to appear statuesque and not oafish. His body had been issued by good genes and a blue collar living; he did not have the trim waist and volcanic veins sported by the twinks working out in David Barton gyms across Chelsea. As he turned to face Liam again, the bartender topped off the glass with some Seagram's and slid the drink along the countertop without saying a word. Liam noticed the thick bridge of the man's nose and the fat curve of his lips and felt himself instantly turn rock hard. He wondered how all men could be classified within the same species when the genetic pool churned out people of such unfairly different type and proportion.

As he walked dreamily away from the bar sipping the bittersweet mix of whiskey and ginger ale, Liam again felt Zane's insistent tug. This time Zane demanded to hear the details of what happened with Didier immediately. Liam dreaded that now there had been too much lead-up to the story. And he still felt that things were too new and too uncertain with Didier to have recent events served up as club gossip.

Liam flashed back to that first night in the cab and the sensation of Didier's tongue coming impossibly close while never touching the nape of Liam's neck. Liam had initially decided not to have sex with Didier when he felt the cold tremble of Didier in his arms, near tears saying that he could never tell his wife about their encounter on the evening of the fund-raiser. On that night, Didier had shown himself to have boyfriend potential, waiting like a saint for Liam during his work snafu.

Since then they had several real dates. This afternoon they had strolled through the West Village and were lingering by a construction site on Jane Street when Liam reached over and ran his hands through Didier's thick black curls. After kissing on the sidewalk for a minute, Liam led Didier around the edge of the foundation of a new apartment building and settled in behind some rafters. Liam dropped to his knees and unbuckled Didier's thick cowboy-style belt and unbuttoned the fly on his indigo blue jeans. Didier mumbled some words of protest as his cock stiffened inside Liam's mouth. Almost instantly, Didier pressed past his fears and dug into Liam's body desperately, and Liam could not stop. He loved sex too much. It sounded strange to say, he knew, being that everyone enjoyed having sex, but Liam had a wide-eyed wonder about how someone new might feel, sound, and look, where their hairlines were, how their hands might grope and grasp and grab.

"So start at the beginning and talk fast, already." Zane had walked Liam into Ferdinand's bedroom and plunked himself down on the king-sized mattress when all of a sudden a shriek rose from inside the closet.

"Someone call an ambulance!" screamed Ferdinand as he pulled Riser through the closet door. Ferdinand leaned over Riser's limp, alabaster body and stuck a small mirror under his chin. A look of relief registered on Ferdinand's panicked face as fog spread across the bottom of the glass.

"One glass of Chardonnay would throw this 110-pound kid into a coma, Ferd. What were you thinking? . . . Now, Riser will be just fine, but we need to be smart about dealing with him from here on out," Zane said. "He is on a diet of no carbs, no meat, no dairy, no eggs. You can't go from snacking on raw okra to knocking back alcohol."

"I know, I know, I know. Shit! He could die, Zane. He could die in my apartment. That would be awful and messy and really, really bad karma!"

"I think we need to move for just one second away from what this is doing to your fine leopard skin rugs or porcelain toilet bowls," Zane continued. "Our response right now will define us as his friends . . . As a club . . . Mark my words."

Liam decided that Zane had been able to focus on what was important when the chips were down—despite any left-over irritation he had over not hearing the whole story about the hookup with Didier.

Matthew flew into the bedroom with a cold cloth in one hand and a lit cigarette in the other.

"This always works," he said. "The cold rouses him enough to open his mouth and take a nice drag. The nicotine handles the rest."

Sure enough, within sixty seconds Riser was sitting on the mattress rubbing his hollow raccoon eyes with his long, bony fingers. As he sucked on the cigarette, Riser's cheeks looked as though they might be swallowed into his frail body.

"You need help," Ferdinand said, flatly. "You scared the life out of me. You can drain every drop of vitality from yourself, but you sure as hell ain't taking me with you."

Matthew wrapped his arm around Riser's shoulder and mouthed the words "shut up" to Ferdinand.

"Alcohol on an empty stomach . . . I should know better by now," Riser said, in the crackle of someone eking words through a breathing tube.

"We should all know better," said Zane, mirroring Matthew by placing his arm around Liam. "But we don't. But we will always, always, always have one another."

"Jesus H. Christ, Zane!" Riser said with a smile. "I think you have gone and turned into Gary!"

MILE 18

"Liam! Oh thank God you got here early. I swear, you are a godsend. I'm going berserk. Come help me hang the club's banner."

"Sure thing, G-Lo. Where would you like it to go?"

Gary answered the question by dashing off in the direction of the finish line and gunning through the litany of tasks he needed to accomplish in the hour and a half before the start of the race. The medic had to be briefed on the details of the course, the announcers needed to be informed of the sponsors of the event, and the club's volunteers needed to line up to marshal all the runners as they arrived. Liam may have missed an item or two in Gary's breathless rundown.

Within the next half hour the East Side Drive and the meadow flanking the 102nd Street transverse were transformed. A group of Fast Tracker men in sequin gowns and stilettos offered people the goody bags for the race behind large tables arched by rainbows of balloons. A squadron of muscle-bound cheerleaders pranced across the start line in a flurry of kicks and jazz hands, shouting: "We are proud of you! Yes, we are proud of you!"

The morning unfolded as though scripted for a race. The sun hid behind a fringe of clouds keeping the intensity of the late June day at bay, and a light breeze sifted through the park. Groups of runners warmed up along the dirt trails that twisted around the reservoir. Erasure pleaded for a little respect from the stadium speakers as Gary buzzed around from person to person, making sure that the final touches for the Pride Run were going off without a hitch.

At 8:30 A.M., Cosimo Villanueva, an injured runner who had become the de facto club photographer in the last month, corralled the team under a canopy of trees. Almost everyone Liam had met during the past eight months was there—all the avid racers, the men of the infamous "judging circle," and several groups of women who had been attending more and more events of late—and many whom he had never before seen. Cosimo clicked away capturing image upon image as he directed the runners in a series of ridiculous poses and faux-candid groupings.

"Gary! Where is that Gary Loblonicki?" A short man with a face runneled by age or disease raced all around the hilltop looking for Gary. "We've got business to settle, Gary. Rick cued me into the mockery you've made of this event."

From the innermost nucleus of the photograph-readied herd, Gary emerged in a fluster. His hands offered the conciliatory gestures of one who has just learned unfortunate news for which there was no recourse. The raisin-faced man pushed away Gary's attempt at an embrace and shouted loudly enough for pedestrians as far away as Fifth Avenue to hear: "That quilt tells our story. You want everyone to forget our fucking story! Well, we can't let people forget . . . We can't."

As the old man trailed off into tears, Gary pulled him in close for a generous bear hug. The man allowed himself the offer of comfort, but roused again after a few seconds to shove Gary into the assembled crowd. Zane materialized from out of nowhere and stood beside Gary in a show of solidarity; Mitch and Ben followed in quick succession. The soldiers were lining up to protect their leader. By the time that Liam pressed his hand firmly against Gary's shoulder in support, Gary had moved off by himself so that he could explain to those gathered what had sparked this conflagration.

The teeny man with the deep wrinkles had founded the Pride Run with Richard Pollack decades ago, and he came back every year to present the AIDS quilt to the runners at the end of the race. In 1984, a coterie of about a dozen runners had found themselves on the losing end of the fight against full-blown AIDS infections. It was long before the days of quick cocktail fixes and protease inhibitors, and many people were just learning that their sexual liberation would levy a heavy price tag. To celebrate their club experiences and friendships, these Fast Trackers knitted little squares that depicted their plight. One Midwesterner who had never seen the beach before traveling to New York City for fashion school made a large square of a white wave against a blue background. An older man who fancied himself a theater aficionado—a lover of Tony-award winning performances as well as the back-row pleasures of Times Square theaters of the past—wove the fragments of old ticket stubs and playbills into a beautiful gray mosaic. Throughout the eighties, those who succumbed to the virus added their stories to the growing quilt. Henry Duvall, who stood now before Gary with the tired agitation known only by those who have fought long for lost causes, had watched his lover die of AIDS and vowed to make the quilt an integral part of this annual event.

Many in the group of gay men and women clustered around Gary listened intently, hanging on each detail of the story. A few of the older members had begun to weep. Someone interrupted to ask if he could see the quilt.

"Some other time. Anyone who hasn't seen the quilt before can view it on some other occasion." Gary spoke with compassion but also with a quickness that would not allow for challenge. "This day is a celebration. I want us to look to the future and not get bogged down in the past. Now we all have a race to run. The gun is going off at nine whether we like it or not so trot-trot, people! Trot-trot!"

As Liam did his final sprint stride-outs toward the starting line of the race, he bumped into Monroe stretching on the side of the course. An immediate look of relief beamed from Monroe. Despite the fact that Monroe had vowed to come out and run, Liam doubted his friend's ability to get up and out of the house before 9 A.M. on a Saturday. With surprising lightness, Monroe sprang up from his calf stretches and bounded over to Liam.

"Sweetie, I have been wilting here, worried that I would not recognize a soul," he said.

"Oh, please stop the drama queen routine. If you don't see people you know today, then you're standing around with your head up your ass. I'm not indulging the woe-is-me Monroe this morning."

"It's gay pride weekend, Liam. Show a little love—with a capital *L!* I have a fun suggestion . . . Let's you and me run this thing together. We never get to run together."

The vagaries of Monroe's ironic humor made it impossible to tell whether he was kidding or speaking in earnest. Liam knew the consequence of not taking his friend seriously; he also knew that his competitive nature and the contest with the Bobcats mandated that he race his heart out today. But the idea of just jogging easily and enjoying the scenery with his best friend enticed Liam. He could never admit to any of his Fast Tracker teammates the dread he had each and every race day, the unalloyed fear that overcame him as he waited for the gun to go off, the sense that he would disappoint everyone— especially himself—with every performance. What would it be like to slip off the radar, to put the loyalties of his friendship with Monroe above the endless demands that Fast Trackers put on him? Liam knew the pointlessness of pretending he had any choice in the matter.

"Don't worry, sexy," Monroe spoke as if in answer to Liam's interior monologue. "I won't put you on the spot. I know you're in a pickle . . . what with your club reputation as the hot, fast young thing."

"I have to get to the start. Check the histrionics, Miss Marilyn. We'll brunch after . . . Promise!"

"You and me—or 'the club'?"

"I'll meet you at baggage check after the race. Good luck."

Why did there always need to be so much ado over racing? The essence of running could not be more pure or simple. That's what Liam loved about the sport. When removed from ego dramas and pettiness, running was one person testing the limits of his body in concert with his fellow competitors. Everything else fell away. But lately so much other nonsense had been getting in the way.

Runners had already jammed the starting corral by the time Liam arrived. Zane waved to Liam, urging him with frantic hand motions to move up toward the lead pack. Hiphigh metal gates blocked Liam from the corral with the local elite runners. The officials refused to let Liam hop over the barrier and instead directed him to the back of the long line of competitors now assembled. Liam scanned the first few rows of runners to see what the Bobcat presence looked like. The day belonged to Fast Trackers, and it was all blue and orange pageantry. The team was well represented at the front of the race, even if Liam had been relegated to the back of the pack. Pace signs from five-minute down to eleven-minute miles instructed runners as to where they should line up, but casual racers blatantly disregarded them. Liam snuck into the pack by the eight-minute pace marker and began to wiggle his way through the forest of men and women stretching and doing their last-minute race preparations. As the national anthem began, a surly man about sixty-five years of age scowled at Liam and told him to show a little respect for the country and for his fellow runners and stand still. Liam's blood boiled as he focused on weaving through the next cluster of runners; he was still about fifty rows back from the lead pack.

As he feverishly maneuvered through a trio of women wearing headphones, Liam heard the gun sound and he assumed running motion. His knee immediately collided into the back of the short middle-aged woman in front of him. He moved toward the extreme right to pass people along the edge, but the barricades made movement nearly impossible. Everyone inched along. It was like a monstrous traffic jam, and there were no openings in the hordes of people. Liam felt trapped and claustrophobic. After about thirty seconds, enough people had begun jogging that Liam could begin to speed through the masses to reach those who were actually running his pace. He wondered how the back of the pack runners dealt with this chaos each week. Why wake up at 7 A.M. on a weekend to be stuck in a dense, hot mass of people?

Liam crested Harlem Hill, where the first mile marker was, in 6 minutes 50 seconds. The bad start had added about a minute to his pace—that might as well have been an hour in a five-mile race. And he expended more energy than usual in the frustrating fits and starts of skirting around people. There was no way that he could now make up fifteen seconds in *each* of the four miles that remained.

Letting the pull of gravity speed him down the sharp decline of Harlem Hill, Liam thought about all the people in the club who had told him that running changed their lives. Feeling his feet propelling into short bursts of flight, Liam knew what they meant. For almost all of our waking lives, we sit or stand or move in cautious observance, afraid to disturb the balance. But flying down this hill, Liam had the sense of himself as a dangerous vector. He was accelerating to the point where he might lose control. Run off path. Collide. Intersect. It was exhilarating. As he reached level ground, Liam straightened his back and tightened his abdominal muscles to motor through the straight-aways and mild uphills of the west side. He concentrated on the beauty of the fields and on the foliage along the interior of the park instead of on where he might be amid the competitive herd.

Liam felt at one with the moment—singular and strong. This very sensation had hooked him on running. It all came down to these times, all too evanescent and ephemeral, when nothing else existed or mattered in the world but the air on his skin and the endorphins pumping through his veins. All care and worry and fear over job satisfaction and social status and money and the enormity of an unknown future evaporated into the sensation of adrenaline and sweat. This was competing. Not with another person but with himself, allowing the sport to erase all memory of disappointment and heartache. Liam had always wondered why some people were weighted down by the burden of heavy thoughtfulness and self-analysis, plagued with pity and doubt. An Art History teacher at Amherst had told him, somewhat capriciously over coffee one day after class, that he had the fragile soul of a poet. Liam knew she had meant it as a compliment, given that this professor was, herself, married to a published and highly regarded poet, and still he wished he had the easier lot of those without any rearview mirrors in life—those complacent souls who could forge ahead happily and with total confidence. At least there was running. The sport simply allowed him to quell his inner demons, to move beyond himself, to transcend. Even if only for a short while.

After rounding the southern end of the five-mile loop and heading up the east side drive toward the finish line, Liam finally began to see some of the Fast Trackers who had gotten off to better starts. In the last mile of the race, Liam passed Riser, who appeared sleek and aerodynamic but looked as though he may have continued to lose more weight over the past month. Liam knew he had done all that he could to help Riser. And perhaps everything really would be fine. After all, the excessive gauntness did not seem to impair Riser's athleticism; Riser raced with an intensity and fierceness that Liam had not seen in him before. Next, Liam caught up with Ben, who ran very smoothly and seemed to be having the race of his life. Liam knew his time would be disappointing but relished the easy feeling he had now gliding past other racers. Knowing he could now catch more of the people who were still ahead, Liam ratcheted up his speed. With less than 800 meters to go, he noticed Gene racing toward the finish and directed all his focus, every drop of energy in his now-depleted body, into turning his feet over faster and faster. As soon as his toes hit the ground, he thrust his legs forward. He worked his arms faster and faster as a side stitch throbbed along his rib cage. Liam ran side by side with Gene as they approached the finish line—too close together to declare either the victor. Liam barreled over the timing mats and smacked right into one of the race officials.

As he gathered himself together and apologized for the incident, Liam glimpsed at Zane, smiling and daisy fresh, off to the side of the race course, wordlessly savoring the turn of fortune since their last head-to-head.

"So did you see any Bobcats?"

Liam waited for Zane to wipe the smirk off his face and answer the question.

"Uh, no. But I know there weren't any in front of me. This was my best finish in a while—top ten finisher overall."

Giving a quick survey of the area, Liam did not notice many finishers at all.

"This place is a ghost town," Liam announced. "Almost everyone must have been behind us. I bet that Fast Trackers cleaned up today."

"What about your new *friend?*" Zane asked wryly. "Surely he must be here."

Liam knew that Didier had been crushed with work the past few weeks, and so they had not seen each other and had spoken only sporadically. Still, the race held some symbolic importance to Liam, what with its ties to the lesbian and gay rights movement, and he had secretly hoped that Didier would understand that and represent the Bobcats. Liam wanted not to care but had been eyeballing the crowds all morning, looking for Didier.

"Nah!" Liam paused and looked into Zane's eyes. It was one of those penetrating looks that can cause people to do the wrong thing, to say too much. "Let's go cheer for the Fast Trackers, Zane. That's what today is about after all—us."

Liam and Zane had made it back to the finish line in time to see Riser and Matthew cross with their hands clasped above their heads in victory. Ben came through next, followed by Ferdinand. And then a jumble of unfamiliar faces made their way to the finish line. There were old Fast Tracker men with their sagging chests painted in rainbow flags, and more women than Liam had ever seen before at a club event, all wildly shouting as they completed the race. As Monroe hobbled through the finish line, Liam screamed his name so loudly that his vocal cords ached with soreness. Zane picked up on Liam's chant and shouted: "Make us proud, Monroe!" On his way through the finishing chute, Monroe turned and raised a fist in solidarity, making Liam well up with affection. The race meant so many different things to so many different people. For the next twenty minutes, the team proceeded through the finish in a beautiful tidal wave of blue and orange.

MILE 19

There was nowhere to hide. The midday haze hung heavy in Central Park, and the mature treeline along the East Drive offered no shade. Liam's shirt clammed to his back and his head went light. He had suspected a run in these conditions was a bad idea and decided now to cut his loop of the park short at Engineers' Gate and walk the few blocks south along Fifth Avenue to visit Gary. His door was always open, and Liam knew that Gary would want to relive the details of the Pride Run and the convincing win that Fast Trackers had over the Bobcats. Improbably, Fast Trackers had come within inches of the Bobcats with half the racing year completed. Keeping the momentum through the summer and fall would not be easy, though, especially since the Bobcats would surely redouble their efforts in future races. But Gary would choose to rejoice in the now. The promise of air-conditioning and an ice cold beverage quickened Liam's pace.

Liam did not think anything of the two police officers stationed at the corner of Eighty-fifth and Fifth or of the rope of yellow tape partially blocking the entrance to 1040. Prepared to waltz in past the doorman as he had so many times before, Liam fell speechless as the porter on duty grabbed his arm and said: "Only residents allowed in the building today."

Feeling humbled and apprehensive, Liam walked back outside and dialed Gary's apartment. No answer. He then tried Gary's cell phone; it went straight to voice mail. Liam began to worry. Who else could he call? In the months since their stormy fight at the Brooklyn Half Marathon, Mitch and Gary had appeared closer than ever. Liam dialed Mitch's number frantically.

"Yeah, yeah, yeah." Mitch answered the phone in a quick and distracted manner. "It's a mess. Gary's staying at the Surrey. Hold on, Liam. There's a beep."

Mitch spoke as though he had been fielding calls all afternoon. What type of mess involved policemen, a closed-off apartment, and the yellow tape of a crime scene? Liam tried not to let his mind wander into worst-case scenarios. Clearly, Gary hadn't plunged to a sidewalk death; he was taking a sojourn to the Surrey Hotel. Two minutes had gone by and there was still dead silence on the line, and Liam gave up on waiting.

Feeling too invested in the mystery to turn around and go back to his own apartment, Liam straightened out his running clothes and fixed his hair as best he could in the dark windows of a Porsche parked by the corner of Eighty-fifth Street. The doorman in a neighboring Fifth Avenue building pointed Liam in the direction of the Surrey, on Seventy-sixth Street. The prospect of bad news intensified with the blinding afternoon heat. Not sure if it was curiosity or concern that sped him along, Liam had transitioned from a brisk walk into a light jog, his head pounding and his mouth sandpaper dry. The Surrey Hotel blended in so completely with the sedate town houses on the street that Liam at first missed its recessed entrance. He ran his fingers through his hair once more to look as presentable as possible before walking into the lobby and approaching the concierge.

"I'm sorry, but that guest has asked for no visitors, no calls, no disturbances," the man said without ever looking at Liam.

"He would definitely let me up. Trust me."

"They don't pay a thousand dollars a night for me to disregard their requests, young man. I suggest you leave a handwritten note. If and when Mr. Loblonicki comes down, I will be sure he receives it. Have a wonderful afternoon."

The concierge managed a level of respect despite his complete lack of eye contact with Liam. In his clearest penmanship, Liam jotted a simple and concise message on the hotel stationery. He wrote, "Call me. I'm worried, G. Yours, Liam."

As he walked through the Village from the Bleecker Street subway station, Liam imagined himself at home, facedown on crisp bed linens with the air-conditioning blasting. Even the kids playing in the makeshift yard between the Silver Towers on LaGuardia wilted in the mid-July steam. Before heading back to the apartment, Liam bought a six-pack of Sierra Nevada Pale Ale from the local bodega. He cringed at the thirteen-dollar price tag but couldn't wait to suck one down. He still hadn't figured out how the deli kept the beers so cold given its high customer traffic.

He swung the door to his building open with a thrust of his hip before realizing someone stood directly inside the teeny vestibule that housed an intercom system and a stack of unwanted telephone books. The man pivoted around quickly, knocking Liam backward into the street.

"Well, I have to say that I was hoping for a different reaction."

Perhaps it was the heat or maybe just the surprise, but Liam found himself stumbling over his words and grasping for a name.

"Now, stop the theatrics, Liam. I don't bite—that is unless you ask me to."

The context was askew. Without his running shorts and athletic singlet, Didier did not have as many sharp angles. The dark jeans and knit polo shirt that he wore masked his slimness. After not hearing from him for the better part of a month, Liam had placed Didier firmly in the "go fuck yourself" file, which involved a deletion of all contact information so that he would not accidentally drunk-dial him on some particularly lonely night.

Didier pulled Liam back into the vestibule and moved as close as possible to him without actually touching. Liam could feel the tingle of Didier's warm breath as he exhaled. The plastic shopping bag knocked against Liam's leg and the bottles of beer rattled in place.

"I have drinks. It's hot. Do you want to come up for a cold one?"

Didier continued to stare Liam down. He remained silent and pressed his heavy lips against Liam's, mashing their mouths into a kiss. Liam resisted at first but then separated his lips and let Didier's tongue glide into him. As the buzz of the kiss wore off, Liam realized they were making out in the entryway of his apartment building in broad daylight. He grabbed Didier by the arm and led him upstairs. Between the third- and the fourth-floor landings, Liam thought to ask why it was Didier hadn't called and what had brought him back. He decided not to spoil the moment. Liam's heart raced as he fumbled to get his key into the lock, trying to appear calm and nonchalant.

Liam had forgotten to crack the kitchen windows open before leaving for his run and, as if part of a chemistry experiment, the static apartment air had become charged and electric. Embarrassed by the inhospitable temperature, Liam ran through to the living room and cranked up the air-conditioning unit that hung in the window. With sweat pooling in the small of his back, Liam could think of nothing less inviting than having someone press into him and make him even hotter. He cracked open two bottles of beer and put the remaining four in his freezer.

"You better watch out there; those bottles could burst right open. You know—the pressure and all."

"You're mighty big on innuendo this afternoon." Liam did not want to expend energy on games.

"I'm just trying to help you avoid a mess."

"Is that right? Then help me drink the beer before we risk catastrophe."

The icy beer coated Liam's throat and helped keep his appetite at bay. Runners never advertise the fact that a cold pint of beer is the best elixir after a hard run, beating any energy drink or fuel bar hands down. The sense of fullness and the feeling of euphoria were immediate and incomparable.

They moved onto the second and third bottles within minutes, racing through the beer as if it were sport. Liam quickly felt invincible, and he knew as well as Didier what would come next. They drank in greedy swallows, with only the occasional exchange of a pointed look slowing the guzzling of the beers. Didier finished his third beer before Liam and smacked the bottle victoriously against the Formica countertop by the dishwasher. He gazed longingly into Liam's eyes.

"I'm going to take a leak. The facilities are down the hall?"

Liam nodded.

The air-conditioning had made the living room slightly more bearable but the bedroom still felt like a kiln. As he drifted from room to room in the railroad apartment, Liam heard a clamor from the bathroom, as though something had been knocked over.

"Is everything okay?"

"Can you come in here for a second?"

As Liam approached, he heard the hard drizzle of water and slowly opened the bathroom door. On the floor in a neat little stack were Didier's jeans and his polo shirt. Behind the closed plastic of the shower curtain, Didier's shadow moved, his arms raised up high and his head swinging in circles under the shower nozzle.

"What do you need?"

"I needed to cool off but now it's so chilly under here that I need some body heat."

Liam took off his clothes and gingerly poked his head around the shower curtain to glance at Didier.

"Why the fuck are you so shy all of a sudden? It's nothing you haven't seen before."

Liam climbed in and felt the icy spray of the water off Didier's body. He reached to adjust the temperature of the faucet, but Didier slapped away his hand. Feeling the alcohol high full throttle, Liam grabbed Didier around the waist and let his hands massage Didier's butt while the brisk water poured over their heads. The intensity of the coldness gripped Liam, and he bit into Didier's shoulder for relief. Pulling away in pain, Didier glanced at the teeth marks and drew Liam in tight for a deep, long kiss. Water slid between their lips as Didier moved in and out of the kiss in a playful, teasing fashion.

Feeling numb from the shower, Liam disentangled himself and hopped out to wrap himself in a warm, dry towel. Didier turned the water off and joined Liam on the little square bath mat. They shared a large beach towel, which Liam hoped had looked like a romantic gesture rather than a hint at the sad state of his linen closet. Didier's bony limbs clung to Liam as they dried off. A brief recollection of their last encounter—the hurried kisses on the construction site and the quick ejaculation that followed—sped through Liam's mind as he led Didier buck naked through the apartment to his bedroom. The air-conditioning had taken full effect, and Liam looked forward to the warmth of another body against his skin. He stirred at the thought of sex, and Didier quickly took notice and knelt down on the hardwood floor in front of him.

With the shades up and the early evening light filtering through the trees outside his bedroom window, Liam let Didier take his penis further and further into his mouth. He looked across the street to the strip of ritzy town houses where the owners prepared themselves for the night's activities. A woman in a gingham dress dotted some perfume onto her wrists as she danced from room to room getting ready to go out. A tweenage girl in the building next door paraded an army of friends into the television room where lights had been dimmed and a large blue glow irradiated all the young faces. And in the peach town house almost out of view—the one rumored to be Anna Wintour's residence—a long good-bye embrace was shared before a tall, thin man exited the building and flagged down a taxi.

Liam began to feel alone and unattached. Didier asked if anything was wrong, whether what he was doing was plea-surable. What was there to say? No one wants to hear about solitude or existential ramblings. And so Liam committed himself more fully to the sex act, falling onto the bed and po-sitioning Didier on top of him. He instructed Didier to take a condom out of the little nightstand drawer and then helped roll it down Didier's shaft. Liam asked him not to use lube, to force the whole cock in at once regardless of how much he winced in pain. This would be the act—like running itself—that jolted him out of his melancholy; this would be his atonement for never being able to settle, for navel-gazing and not allowing himself to be whole. Liam accepted himself for who he was—highs and lows—and could never be sure whether his life was richer for always being a little de-pressed. Happy people had their happy outlook and a palette of bright and shiny colors. People like Liam had so many shades and tinctures, subtle hues and tones in their lives.

Didier thrust himself quickly and forcefully into Liam. The pain was exquisite. Liam lost his breath for a few sec-onds but once he relaxed, the motion of Didier rocking in-side him made him feel weightless, not of this world. Didier took Liam by the waist and lifted him off the mattress, look-ing for a way to probe deeper inside him. As he watched Di-dier focus and concentrate, Liam gently moved his foot against Didier's chest, pressing his toes against his nipples.

Didier jerked back in surprise and wrapped his mouth around Liam's foot. Somehow it was now almost seven o'clock (the red squares of Liam's digital alarm clock blinked the time), and the black branches of the tree outside grew sharp in contrast to the purple sky. In one quick yank, Didier had removed himself and proceeded to strip the condom off and masturbate on Liam's chest. The cum sprayed out in long, clear strands, and Liam felt relieved that it was over.

When Didier started to stroke his penis, Liam gently stopped his hand and stood up from the bed. He foraged around in his closet for something to wear, and Didier came up from behind and kissed his neck.

"It's your turn. I won't feel satisfied unless you get off."

"You don't owe me anything, Didier. This is what it is."

"What are you talking about? This was amazing."

"Yeah. But will you still love me tomorrow?" Liam picked up Didier's hand and turned his wedding band tight against his flesh. "This doesn't seem to be going anywhere."

"You saw that ring the first time I met you. It's only becoming a problem now? Do you want to hear all the boring details about the loveless marriage that's a dull arrangement of convenience?"

Liam pulled away. He felt the alcohol cloud his ability to reason.

"I can change into someone good," Didier said. "But do you really want someone good?"

Didier began to whisper curse words into Liam's ear. The warm, wet curl of his tongue drove Liam into a fit of goose bumps. Didier took a hold of Liam's engorged shaft and then massaged the head of his cock until he came uncontrollably all over the floor.

The next morning Didier left early to go into his office and finish up a project due first thing Monday. Liam laid in bed until the sheets were no longer warm from Didier's body and then decided to put his robe on and fetch the Sunday paper from his doorstep. The white morning light managed to make even the cruddy linoleum in the kitchen hall look full of promise and possibility. Liam thought of his first cup of black coffee and a long run alone up the Hudson River. He could still feel Didier inside him.

And there it was as plain as day. He noticed the headline before even stooping down to pick up the newspaper, in big block letters on the front page of *The New York Times:* "Upper East Side Gay Socialite Found Dead in Fifth Avenue Penthouse."

MILE 20

"I think that's the last of the boxes. Marvin, could you stack those in the corner by themselves? I don't want my Wonder Woman collectibles to get ruined. They're about all that's left now."

Marvin dutifully followed the order. Everyone had been tiptoeing around Gary all morning. His world had capsized and the least his friends could do was pamper him for a while. With all of his belongings—a whole life—crowded into one room, Gary looked small and shattered. Liam had only known Gary to be a leader and a rock and hadn't a clue what to do with this withered version of the man. He found himself clumsily lining up boxes along the edge of wall to avoid falling into awkward conversation.

"I'm going to head out to buy some pizza and beer." Ben rose from his seat on the dusty floor and wiped the film of sweat from his brow as he spoke. "I think we can all use a break and a stiff drink."

The services at 1040 Fifth had been sublime. With porters chipping in and one of the service elevators devoted solely to Gary's move, all the boxes were out and neatly stacked in the U-Haul within an hour. Gary's new building offered no such amenities, and though the help of eight Fast Trackers made the work go faster, the long flight of steps leading from the street and the series of narrow door frames caused the move-in project to take about three times as long as the move-out. Everyone's shirts dripped with sweat by the time it was all over.

"Thanks, Ben. Let me give you some money." Gary searched for his wallet among the papers and keys and general clutter on the kitchen counter.

"It's on me, babe. You sit tight and make this place feel like home."

Liam wished he could join Ben, but the situation between them was still strained. But for Liam the prospect of getting loose from the claustrophobia of this twenty-foot-by-twenty-foot box, of escaping the woe that had beset Gary, was appealing. Marvin and Zane and Liam exchanged sympathetic glances. Matthew helped Riser count the number of veins protruding along the pale surface of his wiry arms. Ferdinand busily typed on his BlackBerry, absorbed in the drama of his twenty-two-year-old fuck buddy *du jour*. Cord Vespers had just graduated from Syracuse University where he had a stellar lacrosse career coupled with the sad, angry social life of a repressed closet case. Ferdinand joked that he had taught Cord the proper way to release energy. The secret was apparently found in a fistful of poppers and a tube of lubricant. Despite the distractions of his daily life and wanton habits, Ferdinand had worked tirelessly for Gary since Malcolm's death. Within days, he had pulled strings with a former trick in real estate for one of the city's top rental agencies to secure Gary a studio in Chelsea for the unheard of price of $900 a month. Until something more permanent came along, Gary would be temping at an event planning outfit that Ferdinand held a minority position in. Hourly pay and bare bones health insurance, but it would pay the bills.

"I guess I should get used to people taking pity on me now," Gary said. "It's funny how you do the right thing—or what you think is the right thing—for your entire life, and one day you're back at square one. Not even square one . . . completely off the board, totally out of the game."

Gary paced in circles around the high columns of boxes that formed an obstacle course in the tiny studio apartment. It felt as though he was performing a monologue, playing the patient on the proverbial couch in therapy and not really expecting a response to his diatribe.

"You guys should stake your claim to your own lives now. You're young and beautiful and talented. Don't sacrifice and give up your potential for anybody, for any reason—least of all in the name of love."

Gary stopped and looked thoughtfully from box to box, as if weighing the pieces of the past to see if the measure was something he could bear. After inspecting the magic-marker description of the contents of one cardboard box, Gary opened it and removed a handful of old Polaroids. His shoulders began to shake, and he cupped his head in his hands as he sobbed long and deep. Zane came up and wrapped his arms around Gary. Liam could think only of the suffocating heat and wondered when Ben would be back with the provisions.

"I turned down the role of Ralph in *Fame* when it was on Broadway." Gary looked at Zane as he spoke. "I know I could have done something on the stage. Everyone said I had a quiet power, a radiance."

And from out of nowhere, Gary stepped away from Zane and began to sing. At first, he sang low, almost inaudibly, but by the end of the first verse, Gary was belting out the lyric.

> *"I sing the body electric*
> *I glory in the glow of rebirth*
> *Creating my own tomorrow*
> *When I shall embody the earth.*

> *And I'll serenade Venus*
> *I'll serenade Mars*
> *And I'll burn with the fire of ten million stars*
> *And in time*
> *And in time*
> *We will all be stars."*

Tears speckled Gary's face as he performed the number, not to the Fast Tracker friends assembled in the room but to something far beyond the confines of this studio apartment, something deep into the past or far into the future. Zane joined Gary first and then Marvin and then Liam joined in a final verse of "I Sing the Body Electric."

> *"I sing the body electric*
> *I celebrate the me yet to come*
> *I toast to my own reunion*
> *When I become one with the sun."*

Gary glowed by the end of the performance and stood before the guys in the room like a pastor before a congregation, a father approaching his long-lost sons. He told them that he had to share what had happened to him, not to lay his burden down on others but so that they might learn from his own bad judgment.

Liam had tried not to absorb the fleet of rumors traveling around about Gary. The old men of the judging circle took perverse pleasure in the fact that the "high living G-Lo" got knocked into the gutter where he belonged. Some of Gary's closest friends made opaque references to his "situation" in tones that conjured, equally, images of mercenary gold digging and of ceaseless self-sacrifice. Being president of the club, Gary had always emanated an imperviousness to the slings and arrows of Fast Tracker folly. Since his partner's death, Gary kept a decidedly lower profile, but still the cracks in his armor showed.

"When I met Malcolm, there wasn't this mountain of cash," Gary began. "I guess there never is in these stories. Anyway, I went with a guy in one of my theater classes for drinks some random night in the early eighties. We went to The Townhouse. Don't roll your eyes at me, Riser; Townhouse was the sun in the gay universe back then. Anyone who was anyone met up there. It was instant with Malcolm . . . aided, of course, by a sprinkling of martinis. This was back in the days before Cosmos, when real men—even gay ones— sipped gin martinis at night. Ah, that night. The first week, the first year, it was all paradise. I rehearsed and washed dishes in a little German restaurant on the Upper East Side, and Malcolm trained as an analyst at Goldman Sachs. We spoke different languages, but what does that matter when you are twenty-three and having the best sex of your life? And the gravy was that Malcolm engineered many of the market changes in the mideighties, complex financing schemes that involved leveraging companies with all different grades of debt. He was hedging back when that still meant bush trimming. The paychecks grew exponentially with time; his bonuses went up tenfold each year. By the early nineties, we were in our little perch on Fifth Avenue—about as high as you can go in this town and probably the first openly gay couple to get there. Now, isn't that a nice little success story? Then the blight came down. For some reason, Malcolm got it and not me. God only knows why. I cried so much, you'd think I was the one infected. He sweated and tormented next to me, the sheets constantly damp and soiled. Malcolm Dodd, who had never missed a day of work, had to craft elaborate excuses with his office, and he dragged himself in looking half dead on many a morning. He eventually resigned to protect his name and his legacy, and I tried to keep up appearances and manage the finances but was in way over my head. Still, I wanted him to keep all that he had struggled to attain for as long as possible. The bills began to swallow me by the end, but I kept all the dreary details from Malcolm."

Zane had already begun to weep when Ben walked in with a big shopping bag and two pizza pies. All eyes turned to the apartment door and then just as quickly back to Gary, begging for more of the thread.

"It's just my life story, Ben. It'll be over in about three more minutes. Put the pizzas down and have a listen."

Ben followed the instructions and sat on a cardboard box.

"Taking care of someone, giving your life over to them, is a funny thing. At first, you get a high and are utterly grateful. It's like they've given you this supreme gift of purposefulness, and you have no idea what your life even meant before. Then I went through a questioning phase. I would stare at Malcolm while he was sleeping, his mouth a hoary mess, and I would wonder why the earth needed *me* and not him. And I would clean his sheets as a way of cleaning my soul, rubbing my hands raw to open the skin up, telling myself I'd let the disease come in and enter me. Each time I chickened out, wanting to live more than I wanted to understand what my lover was going through . . . But the days pile into years and your thick waves of black hair recede and gray, and you look at the sack of nothing in the bed all day, and one day you stop sobbing and you pray for it to end. You pray to God for your lover to die. I resented him and then I resented myself for being nasty and brittle with him. That's when the sickness had us both in its throes. You guys already know what happens next."

Marvin raised his eyebrows at Ben, who looked at Mitch, who turned to Zane, who chastised Matthew and Riser, both still angling in front of the only mirror in the apartment, with a look of disapproval.

"You silly guys," Gary went on. "This whole battle made me join Fast Trackers. This club saved my life. Or rather it helped me save myself. Running brought me face-to-face with each and every demon that haunted me, every insecurity and doubt and lie I harbored inside. The first time I tackled Central Park, it was middle March and a damp, brutal wind pummeled along the West Side Drive. The park was desolate and the naked trees swayed ominously, and I told Horace—yes, crazy, eccentric Horace, all dressed in purple, though he hadn't started running with those ridiculous little weights yet—that I needed to stop and exit the park. And he didn't throw any grand philosophical gesture at me about perseverance and success. He just reminded me that everyone was going to Mallory's—a tragic piano bar in the west Seventies but a destination nonetheless—after the run and that I only had twenty more blocks to get there and that the beer never tasted so good as when you had really worked for it. I panted and cursed on those hills along the reservoir, but I got stronger and changed my body image, and I cured myself of this disease. And now Malcolm is cured too. He deserves the peace more than anyone I've ever known. I don't mind that paying down all his medical debts and those Fifth Avenue expenses means that I have to more or less start from scratch. God help me, I am strong and I know I can. Ferdinand found this fabulous gem of a studio for me. And I get to live in a far hipper quadrant of town than the corner of *Uptight* and *WASP*. The $20,000 in personal savings I had squirreled away in case things really went south mean that I won't starve to death. Hey, young dreamers come into this city in their twenties with far less and live with endless possibility and unequaled joy. Maybe I'll end up having to work until I'm eighty-seven—but we can just keep our fingers crossed that I don't make it that long."

The room had fallen so quiet that the sudden sound of a cat shrieking for attention in the flower bed outside Gary's window caused everyone to pop out of their seats. Ben passed around the two pizza pies and opened several beers for the tired crew collected on this hot August night. Liam asked everyone to wait before guzzling down the ice cold lagers.

"Everyone here owes something to Gary," Liam began, raising his glass to alert everyone in the room that the gravity of a toast would ensue. "To some of us, he has been like a father figure, to others he has been a leader and a guide, and to some he has just been a really fun guy to hang out with. For me, he has been all three."

Ben rolled his eyes, blushing slightly when caught by Liam's glowering glance.

"Today, I want to wish Gary all the best in what is not the ending of a chapter but the beginning of a whole new book. A new residence, new happiness—a new life!"

"Here, here," shouted Zane and the room all clinked glasses and drank furiously in the heat of the crowded apartment. Though cramped with boxes and overrun with people, this studio felt so much cozier and more hopeful to Liam than the austere grandeur of the Fifth Avenue manse.

MILE 21

The summer felt like an afterthought, a rushed intermission between spring and fall. It was only mid-August, but Liam had never been able to wean himself of a school day's sense that Labor Day was a rain cloud at the edge of the bright blue morning. The 8 A.M. sky matched his mood, as a gray blanket rolled out slowly over the city. The humidity hovered over Central Park, and the runners peeled off layers of clothing to get as comfortable as possible before the race. Soon everyone was covered in a thin sheath of perspiration. Not a branch on a tree, not even a leaf, moved in the eerie stillness of the muggy morning.

As he jogged through the fields that zigzagged behind the tennis courts, Liam saw Didier's figure bent over the lazy drip of a broken water fountain. In all the heightened drama since their last rendezvous, Liam had neglected to return a few of Didier's phone calls. Liam sensed there would be trouble now. Once they made eye contact, Didier started jogging backward, away from Liam. The yellow and black of Didier's Urban Bobcats singlet stung Liam's eyes. No promise of switching teams was ever formally made, but Liam saw this as a bad sign.

"Look who's playing hard to get now." Didier shadowboxed playfully at a distance as he spoke.

"It's been a wild two weeks, Didier. Believe me when I tell you that you've got to trust me there."

"It's always something. Not that you care—or even asked—but I have had a rough couple of weeks as well. Oh, you know, with my life as I had known it dismantled and some other minor shit, but nothing for you to lose any sleep over."

Liam was mildly aroused by Didier's petulance but dared not smile.

"Finish your warm-up. We'll talk after the race." Liam was trying to be diplomatic without sounding dismissive. "Use whatever anger you have right now to your advantage out there on the course."

"Don't worry, I will. My whole team will." A demonic look lurked in Didier's eyes.

As Liam turned toward the rustle of footsteps at his back, Didier sped off. Zane and Marvin were jogging toward Liam; they had come to escort him to the race start. There were only three more races in which Fast Trackers were going head-to-head with the Bobcats so the team had to get the best start possible today. Zane tried to pump up Marvin and Liam with high school track visualization techniques, methods of knocking off runner after runner by breaking the race down into small segments and never thinking beyond what you could see before you.

"You need to get out from under this crush," Zane whispered in Liam's ear as they inched through the crowds to position themselves at the head of the starting line. "And then you crush him."

"This isn't a soap opera." Liam looked around as he spoke, embarrassed that a runner from another team might overhear their conversation.

"Isn't it? Look, we've got one minute until they start singing 'Oh, say can you see' and the gun goes off. Just remember that you've spent months killing yourself at workouts. You can beat *any*one."

There was an awkward pause, and some runners pushed to angle ahead of Liam and Zane.

"That's right," said Zane said, as if in answer to himself. "Anyone."

After completely blocking out all the runners around him for the first three miles of the five-mile course, Liam brightened to see that he managed to maintain an exactly 5:40 pace. The clock read 17 minutes flat. There were 12 minutes left in this race if he allowed the tired feeling in his legs to slow him, and only 11 minutes if he swung his arms with more determination and forced his legs to pick up the pace. Through the canopy of trees by the Central Park Boathouse, Liam saw a yellow and black singlet and focused solely on bringing himself closer to this runner. As they edged up Cat Hill—the deceptively long rise on the east side where the black statue of a lioness pounces out from a rocky lookout— Liam confidently passed the runner, whom he had never seen before. Maintaining his concentration on what lay ahead, Liam accelerated through the peak of the hill so that his momentum carried him through the downhill that ran behind the Metropolitan Museum of Art. As a burning pain edged up his torso, Liam glanced at the pavement and studied the white painted cutouts of bikers outlining the cyclist lane. He began counting the strides between the figures to take his mind off the pain and the awful thoughts of defeat that flickered through his mind, the creeping knowledge of how good it would feel to slow down, to stop.

The four-mile marker was right in front of him—22:29 blinked into 22:30 and Liam forced his body past the clock as it switched over to 22:31. His stomach clenched and he couldn't control his breathing. He heard the wretched wails coming from him as he attempted to move his mind off the pain and onto something else. Anything else. By the reservoir, he could see not one but two blue and orange singlets about one hundred yards ahead. Liam bit the inside of his mouth to wake himself up; it had felt for a moment as though his mind had left his body and was watching over him haplessly. Snapping out of this daze, Liam could tell that he was gaining ground on the runners ahead of him. There was less than five minutes left in the race. Liam kept telling himself that. Even if his body staged a mutiny on him, he could surely churn out four and a half minutes more of solid running. A sign directly ahead announced that there were 800 meters to go. How many times had Liam run a half mile at the end of a long track practice and finished it faster than any of the intervals he had run while fresh? Countless. He lengthened his posture into sprinting form and passed the first Fast Tracker ahead of him. Liam did not turn his head toward Marvin; he wanted to remain strong and feared that Marvin might shake his confidence. A second sign noted that only 400 meters remained in the race, and Liam knew he could finish and that he would be crossing the line in under 28 minutes. The only question was whether he could pass Zane with just over one minute left.

Liam watched the orange star in the center of Zane's singlet grow nearer and nearer. As they approached the 102nd Street transverse, Liam came shoulder-to-shoulder with Zane and out of nowhere Zane slipped into another gear and sprinted madly toward the finish line just yards ahead of them. Liam flew through the finish line and immediately crouched over along the side of the chute. Everything in his field of vision turned a whitish blue. Was he going to vomit? The uncontrollable gulp of his breathing felt deep enough to vacuum out his insides. He hoped that if he just dry heaved something would come out, and he would feel human again. Liam stood up and walked for a bit. He drank two cups of the orange Gatorade being dispensed by the baggage claim, but the sugar didn't return him to his senses. Damp sweat beaded across his face and down his neck, and a chill ran along the length of his spine. Something was wrong.

"You need to eat something quick," Zane said. He appeared from behind Liam and already had his backpack over his shoulder, looking eager to leave. "You're a ghost. We need to get some color back into your face."

Zane ripped open an orange and stuck two sections right into Liam's mouth, as though he were a diabetic in need of an insulin boost. The tart flesh of the fruit shot through his mouth, and Liam licked his lips to remove the sticky remnants of the orange. Next Zane forced him to scarf down half a cinnamon raisin bagel. A feeling of equilibrium began to resurface but then a different drama rose up around them.

"Where have you guys been? I was looking for help out on the course and no one came. No one. He was just lying there, and I couldn't get anyone to stop racing this fucking five-miler. Zombies. Fucking racing zombies."

Matthew had become teary as he spoke, and it was still unclear what had him so upset. Woozy from race exhaustion, Liam tried to piece together what had happened but left Zane to ask the questions.

"Who was in trouble during the race, Matthew? Come on, you've got to spell this one out for us." Zane spoke calmly and placed his hand in Matthew's hand for reassurance. "We didn't see what happened and we don't have ESP. Just breathe in deep and start from the beginning."

Through some fragments and asides and an occasional welling into tears, Matthew managed to cobble together a crime scene of sorts. As he was accelerating past the reservoir and imagining the finish line before him, Matthew noticed a body—a tangle of bones in a modified fetal position—over by the brush that lined the eastern edge of the park drive. He veered off course to examine what had happened, to see who was in distress. As soon as he saw the knobby knees and spindly thighs, he knew it was Riser who had been injured. He called out to the runners who flew past, looking nowhere but straight ahead and hearing nothing of his shouts for help.

Even men in Fast Tracker singlets just cruised along on auto-pilot. Riser moaned plaintively but could not elaborate on what had happened to him, which only heightened Matthew's anxiety.

"Eventually a race official heard me caterwaul like a sissy and came over. A medic took Riser to Cornell Hospital. He had the nerve to blame the collapse on Riser . . . said something about people needing to eat to survive. Fucking fat medic bastard. If he knew what he was talking about, he would have become a doctor instead of riding around in an ambulette."

"So he's alone at the hospital?" Zane shifted his bag on his shoulders to punctuate the accusation that Matthew had neglected his friendship duties.

"You've seen enough sad gay movies to know that they never let the friend or lover stick around for moral support. They thought it was just heat exhaustion and that some fluid replacement would do the trick, so I promised to stop by in two hours to check up on him."

"And you think that'll make him right as rain?" Zane's eyes bulged with incredulity. "I know you guys are BFFs but wake up."

"He's fine. Everyone is just jealous because he looks like a model now and is faster than ever."

"Matthew, I realize that you are worked up right now and very emotional," Liam said, placing his hand on Matthew's shoulder. "And maybe you are too close to this situation to see clearly, but Riser has not been well for some time. I know that I have tried to speak to him. We can't make him well, but if we speak to him with a unified message, there's a greater chance that one of us will get through to him."

"Exactly, Matthew—these are cries for help!" Zane shook Matthew as he spoke. "Don't mistake these clues, princess. Riser is in sad, sad shape."

"Zane, go easy now," Liam said, knowing the last thing

Riser needed right now was for his friends to be fighting over this.

"Riser was right about the whole lot of you," Matthew said in a flat tone. "Nothing but a bunch of mean, little bitches."

After Matthew stormed off, Marvin jogged over to congratulate Liam on beating him in the race. After having dreamt about this accomplishment for months, Liam had almost forgotten about it in a matter of minutes. The personal challenge seemed so silly and unimportant given the situation that Riser now faced. Liam still had a strong belief that Riser would snap out of the anorexia that now had so firm a grip on him. While he knew that any literature on the subject would say the exact opposite, Liam felt that his friend had just pushed himself to an extreme and would now see that he needed to reexamine his life and return to center.

Liam reflected for a moment on the pushing of limits. In sports, being able to tear down any semblance of a limitation or barrier to performance led to excellence, achievement, and recognition. He himself had pressed against the inner walls of self-doubt to make a breakthrough at the race today. People need to dig deep and face their inner demons to grow. But it was such a fine line not to go too far and overdo it. Liam always hoped that he might learn from the pain and teach himself how to move within those awful sensations that came late in a race, but the truth was that as soon as he crossed the finish line, he could scarcely recall the struggle. He imagined that the forgetting was part of self-preservation. No one would ever run a race twice if they had even partial remembrance of the agony that came at the end. Liam guessed that the same amnesia afforded women the ability to have second and third babies. Riser had pushed himself to the brink for beauty and speed and the aesthetic trappings of young gay life in New York City—and that long, hard journey landed him in a hospital bed somewhere across town.

Maybe he had learned nothing from the struggle. It was impossible for an outsider to guess. Liam felt empty inside.

Marvin was surprisingly gracious in his praise of Liam. While countless other racers would have made excuses for why they had not run their best that day (it was the racer's prerogative, after all, to manufacture reasons, even before beginning a race, as to how illness, lack of sleep, or bad preparation would excuse a poor showing), Marvin spoke only of Liam's success. Marvin commended Liam on his smarter racing and on "looking more like a runner." Liam thought to ask Marvin what it meant to look more like a runner but realized that Marvin was referring to the seven pounds he had shed since training more seriously. The intense focus on weight today had already depressed Liam more than he could express, and he now wanted to shift gears.

Enough time had elapsed that the race results had been posted by the baggage check. Though Zane had been ready to leave for the last half hour, he could not help but corral every Fast Tracker within earshot to come and see how the team fared. It took a few minutes of mental calculation for Zane, Liam, and a few other team members to collectively realize that the Urban Bobcats had eked out a depressingly narrow victory over the Fast Trackers that day. Zane slapped his arms hard against his sides and stomped back and forth in protest.

"You know what I am going to say. Liam, you know I can't hold my tongue. No, not today. Not after we all worked so hard and gave it our all. I may ask you for forgiveness later, but right now I've got to say that if that closeted little trick of yours had run for us and not for them, we would have had this in the bag. *Nolo contendere.*"

It was too much to hear, too much emotion to follow all that had come before it. Liam shut down and drifted off inside himself.

"C'mon, you're giving that asshole the time of his life—no strings attached! The least he could do is run for us. Every gay runner in this city should be running for us. It isn't right."

"Just let it be, Zane." Gary gently put a hand on both Liam's and Zane's shoulders as he spoke. "People come to this club in their own time and in their own way. You can't force it. This competition with the Bobcats has brought the best out in all of us so far. We had at least a dozen PRs out on the course today. That's something to be proud of. Bet that didn't happen over there at Bobcat central."

Even after all that had happened to him in the past weeks—or maybe because of those trials—Gary was able to mend fences with a few sentences of life wisdom. Zane looked briefly into Liam's eyes as though searching for some sentiment but then turned away in embarrassment. Liam reached out to grab his friend's hand just as the skies opened up into a summer rainstorm.

MILE 22

"She was running the race with an iced coffee in her hands. I am telling you the God's honest truth . . . I mean, could I make that up?"

Liam embellished a few of the details. It seemed like the right thing to do given the circumstances. Bertha Kurtzel *had* been seen sipping an iced coffee at the four-mile mark of the Club Team Championships, but no one knew for sure whether she had been handed the beverage by a spectator or had been carting it around the entire race. Either way, it seemed like a minor setback for competitive running in the club. And Liam knew that Riser of all people would find the tale amusing. Slumped in the hospital bed, Riser looked more like a concentration camp victim than a twenty-six-year-old athlete. His skin was sallow and his eyes, deep and haunting. Every once in a while, perhaps out of sympathy for Liam's earnest effort, Riser would eke out a look of amusement and the misery in his hollow face would shift into a wan smile or the outline of a laugh.

"Even in mid-August that Bertha had a flannel shirt wrapped around her waist. I guess to cover her fat ass." Liam had to keep talking to deal with the stress of seeing Riser in this state. "More power to her, really. I don't think I'd bother to spend a full hour of my day running a five-miler. Someone should credit the slower runners; they are the ones who have to stay on the battlefield while we're back at the diner wolfing down the lumberjack special."

Unable to stop his rambling, Liam delved further into detail about the other heftier runners on the team and their slovenly habits. He knew going into the visit that his level of discomfiture would be high (he never had been good in hospitals) and had begged Gary to accompany him for that reason alone. But Gary would hear nothing of it. In his book, Matthew and Riser had become prima donnas and behavior like theirs was not to be rewarded. "Yes, you're the only queen bee," Liam had retorted during their heated phone conversation. Gary had voiced many strong opinions during Riser's bodily transformation. The idea of willful starvation deeply insulted him. Having seen the way disease steals the body of itself, Gary called anorexia an affliction of pampered affluence. He had reduced Riser to a sad cliché.

Liam could feel nothing but sorrow for the lost soul lying beside him. The harsh afternoon sunlight streaked the blue veins in Riser's neck and the deep gully of his collarbone. Liam searched unsuccessfully for something reassuring to say to his friend. All Riser could talk about was how stupid the doctors were. They claimed that his bones weren't strong enough to run, which he noted was clearly misguided given his string of PRs in recent months. Riser waited for a response, eagerly canvassing Liam for some sign of agreement. Hoping to offer his friend some perspective, Liam laughed and said that it had been a long summer of racing for Fast Trackers and that the whole team was taking a couple of weeks off. A lie, of course, but Liam wanted to help Riser slay the demons of his type A personality.

Months ago, the doctors had shown Riser the striations and cracks in his bones on an MRI. Through unflinching will and determination, he had pushed past the shin pain and continued to train and race, but at some point the body demands its due. He now had no choice but to rest. Riser nodded as the doctor explained the situation, but Liam could see his friend's eyes glaze over as the man spoke to them. The first thing that Riser said after the doctor left his room was that the physician, who was handsome in an avuncular way, should drop twenty pounds before telling other people what to do with their lives.

Random Fast Trackers had been talking behind Riser's back for what had felt like an eternity, offering a selection of theories as to whether he was healthy or unhealthy, sane or insane, going to live or destined to die. Watching him in the hospital bed now, helpless like a child, Liam began to resent the jeering onlookers who had turned Riser's illness into sport. *Could Riser die?* A human could only make it for a few days without water. Longer without food, clearly. But what was the threshold? In many religions, starvation was a rite of passage or a cleansing ritual. Maybe Riser had ascended to a higher plane of being that none of his friends could yet understand. Life offered many a yin-yang tension—abundance and scarcity, satisfaction and yearning, completion and emptiness. The dualities swirled in Liam's head when he was suddenly ambushed from behind.

Sets of hands grabbed at Liam's rib cage, fingers fiddling under his armpits. He caved into a helpless ball of laughter, writhing on the cold hospital floor. As he wiped the tears from his eyes, Liam saw Gary and Matthew standing above him. Given his relief at their presence, Liam sloughed off his embarrassment and hoped that Riser had been entertained by their folly. In truth, Liam suspected that Gary might be the only person who could wake Riser up and help him reclaim his life. For a Fast Tracker, not having Gary on your side was like being abandoned by your father. No matter how many times you told yourself that you didn't care, that the old man was a loser, you never really shook yourself of

him. A Fast Tracker—at least a male Fast Tracker—needed
Gary's acceptance to be whole. It was just one of those annoying yet unassailable truths. Gary knew it better than anyone and deftly used it to his advantage within the club,
maintaining what some of the bitchier women and bitter old
men called his "entourage" of cute, fast boys.

"Why do they always make hospital rooms so dreadful?"
Gary circled around Riser's bed and drew open the blinds,
exposing the dirty brick of the neighboring building. "A
pretty pastel yellow or subtle pink paint could be purchased
at Janovic Plaza for the same price as this penitentiary white.
The chalkiness makes me think of Imodium A-D."

"Gary, I love that you still carry that Fifth Avenue haugh-
tiness even though you're now a dirty Chelsea boy like every
other queer in Manhattan!" Riser lifted himself out of the
bed to pat Gary on the back. "I hope to be just like you in
thirty years."

"Bitch, I came up here just to throw sunshine up your
sorry ass." Gary spoke with feigned indignation. "And FYI, if
you lose any more weight, *you're* going to look fifty-five years
old. Emaciation has a way of aging you. The pounds drop off
and the years pile on . . . "

Liam and Matthew looked at each other nervously. An uncomfortable silence followed Gary's punchy assertions.
Would his quips help Riser take himself less seriously?
Given his increasing fragility, Riser might take it personally
and recede into the inner world he lived in more and more
these days.

"Matthew, can you hand me the mirror that's on that
nightstand by the door?"

Matthew reached over and handed the small glass oval to
Riser. Gary, Liam, and Matthew turned their eyes in unison
toward the floor as Riser began to carefully study his reflection. Everything that Liam had ever read about anorexia
clearly stated that those who succumbed to the condition

could never see themselves as others did. Liam worried that Riser might hate himself more now that he knew his friends thought he looked wizened and that he might restrict his diet further as punishment.

"I think I just need a good night's sleep." Riser pressed his two index fingers into the bruised pockets under his eyes to see if they would change color. The skin only reddened. "Once I am back in my own bed and fully caught up on shut-eye, then I'll be perfectly fine."

"Brand spankin' new," confirmed Matthew.

"The cat's meow," Liam said, wanting desperately to believe it.

"Like a million bucks," Gary agreed with a gentle nod of his head.

It was as though they had all repeated the words of a responsorial psalm in mass. Everyone in the room had made a pact to move on from this moment, even if that meant pretending that a lie was the truth.

The nurse, a young woman who looked hardened by the realities of life, poked her head in and testily told everyone that visiting hours ended in *precisely* ten minutes. Catching Gary rolling his eyes, she informed the group that visiting hours were a privilege not a right and her only concern was that her patients got the proper rest they needed to survive. *How did it get to be that we put our lives in the care of strangers?* Liam wondered if Riser's parents, wherever they might be on the other side of the globe, knew the desperation their son lived with, if they had any idea that their little boy might starve himself to death for acceptance or for the whims of fashion. Gary moved closer to Riser to say good night and rested the palm of his hand on Riser's forehead, as though he were trying to tell if the boy had a fever.

"Good night, sweet prince." Gary leaned over and kissed Riser on the forehead in the administration of a sacrament. "And flights of angels sing thee to thy rest."

Liam wanted to cry. He knew the scene was overly maudlin but wanted nothing more than to throw his arms around Riser and beg him to be alright again. After all the tantrums and the petty bullshit, Gary could still make a man believe in things beyond himself. He could imbue you with a sense of hope and power. If Gary could sustain his partner through a decade of decay and the ravages of AIDS, then surely Riser could find the strength to take care of his own health and find a reason to live again.

MILE 23

Liam looked at his watch one more time. The big bill-board with all the track locations for the departing trains flickered with new information. While he realized that fif-teen minutes did not qualify as extraordinarily late by New York standards, particularly those employed by gay men in the city, Liam considered whether it was worth pulling out his cell phone from his beach bag and calling Monroe. Of course, if Monroe was already on a train heading downtown, he would have no cell phone service, making the attempt fruitless.

Liam had initially phoned Didier to invite him to this Labor Day party. But Didier did not allow Liam the chance to reconcile differences and rekindle their romance. He re-sponded to the voice mail that Liam had left with a short, mysterious e-mail. Didier wrote that he would be in touch soon, that he had some loose ends to tie up with his wife. Liam was glad that Monroe was available at the eleventh hour to fill in.

A collage of sad celebrity makeovers papered the news kiosk in the little store across the way in the train station. Liam caved in and bought a $5 oilcan of Foster's from the stand in an effort to busy himself and perhaps stop the beads of sweat gliding from his forehead down to his shirt. His mouth scratched with dryness, but he knew his bladder would regret this decision during the ninety-minute train ride out to the beach. As he leafed through the new issue of *Vanity Fair*, Liam felt a hand brush down his spine.

"You're so moist already . . . You are going to dissolve by the time we get out there." Monroe tipped the Panama hat that clung to his balding head.

"I've been waiting—or should I say sautéing—here for the last twenty minutes so forgive my indelicate state."

"C'mon, I agreed to join you at yet another Fast Tracker event. I know you're not about to give me shit . . . Anyway, you must have known that I would need the extra time to choose an outfit. I can't very well be upstaged by you!"

Liam yanked Monroe to attention as the track location for their train was announced. The crowds made a mad dash for the stairwell in unison, and Liam bounded through the thick mass of people, dragging Monroe along behind him. He hated the idea that after paying $22 for a round-trip train ticket, he might get stuck standing on a overstuffed Long Island Railroad train. After they crammed into a little bench seat in the back car of the train, Liam relaxed and took stock of the fellow passengers heading out to eastern Long Island.

It appeared everyone was taking advantage of the fact that the last official weekend of the summer was a scorcher. A young mother wheeled her toddler son onto the car backward; he had zinc oxide on his nose and cradled a water gun between his leg and the seat of the stroller. Three teenage boys in sleek fluorescent wet suits carried on oversized surfboards and managed to block one of the train doors. The tallest in the crew announced that the passengers would be serenaded with doo-wop songs from the fifties and sixties and then launched into the opening sound effects of "The Lion Sleeps Tonight." Liam closed his eyes and wondered whether he would be too annoyed to sleep through the racket.

"Don't think that you're going to snooze through this trip,

Liam." Monroe elbowed him hard right under the rib cage. "I fully expect you to entertain me. You know my escort services do not come cheap."

After Didier had turned down his invitation, Liam had received several offers of lifts out to the beach party from Gary and others. But Liam looked forward to the one-on-one time with Monroe and truly hoped that his friend would let himself unwind with a cocktail or two and maybe even find a little romance at the Fast Tracker barbecue. Being that Horace was hosting this fête, Liam knew that there would be an eclectic mix of older gentlemen in attendance—not just skinny young runners.

"If I don't get my beauty sleep, things are going to get ugly." Liam eyed Monroe as his head bopped against the rattling train window.

"Run through the guest list again," Monroe said. "You know I don't like to be surprised. If there's anyone I will detest, please tell me now. I'd much rather know in advance so I can prepare my game face. Tell me, is that horrific old queen Gary going to be there?"

"C'mon! You know he's the president of the club. Of course, he's going to be there."

"I'm sure he'll be hovering nearby all day—a moth to your flame."

Liam let Monroe's snippy tone roll off him. He appreciated that Monroe felt threatened by his friendship with Gary. It even flattered him slightly.

"Now, now," Liam said, with a slight chuckle in his voice. "There's more than enough of me to go around."

"Don't be so vain, my lovely. It's unbecoming."

Liam retreated into Annie Leibovitz's elaborate photo spread of young starlets and wondered, halfway through the accompanying text about Scarlett Johansson's latest project, if his dream job really was writing copy for this publication. His eyes narrowed with the pages until he was out cold in his

seat. Monroe gently shook Liam awake as the train conductor announced the last stop on the line—the Village of
Greenport.

"That was enough beauty sleep for one afternoon," Monroe said as he pulled Liam back into consciousness. "Not to
worry, you'll be fresh as milk from the cow for the party,
Liam. I, on the other hand, was kept awake by some
tweenager with unlimited minutes in the row behind us.
How do I look? Please, lie to me if necessary."

"No need for fibbing, Monroe. You're a dandy in that outfit. I know you'll shine. Now, let's get out of this train and try
to catch a cab to the party."

Feeling more fatigued than before he had his ninety-
minute nap, Liam began to have doubts about the trek out to
eastern Long Island for a party that would last about as long
as the commute back and forth from the city. He wasn't certain he would have the energy to juggle all the personalities
at play but knew he needed to focus on Monroe's happiness
for at least the first hour of the event.

The ten-minute ride from the station wove through some
old farmlands and vineyards before hitting any signs of beach
life. As the cab wound through Lake Drive, a vista of dunes
rose up in every direction, and an army of little boys skipped
out onto the rocky beach with Styrofoam boogie boards. A
green snake and a purple dragon floated and dove around
each other in the cloudless sky; their masters fidgeting to
keep them airborne from the expanse of a beachfront deck.

Liam instructed the cabbie to turn at the mailbox marked
"No. 17." The house itself was not visible from the road, and
the driveway rose and fell several times before depositing
them at what appeared to be the guest cottage. Cars were
parked everywhere—in and by the garage, on the grass, on
the stone pathway that led around the property—but not a
single person was in sight. Only the sharp sound of The Ea-

gles singing "Take It Easy" offered proof that a party was taking place.

As they walked around the stone steps to the back of the house, Liam took survey of the landscape. A forty-foot-long pool overlooked the Long Island Sound, and everything was blue. In every direction. The water. The sky. Even the grass that offered sunning spots to some of the older guests had a regal blue tint straight out of *The Great Gatsby*. Large deck umbrellas freckled the scene yellow and red. Waiters in tight shorts and Fast Tracker singlets served daiquiris and frozen margaritas.

Rising out of the pool in a square-cut bathing suit of chartreuse plaid, Horace rushed over. Liam examined the fragmented slabs of Italian tile on the deck to avoid making eye contact with the spare tire spilling over Horace's waistline. Horace did not believe in cordial greetings and instead insisted on full-on-the-mouth kisses. Liam detected the taste of stale cigarettes and rosé wine on his mouth and hated himself for finding the combination appealing, even sensual.

"So glad you traveled all the way out to the boondocks, Liam." Horace shook out his mop of silver hair, christening Liam and Monroe in chlorine. "And who have we here?"

"Horace, this is my friend Monroe . . . "

"We ran together last year," Monroe quickly interjected, "on my first run with the club. Thanks for taking mercy on a slowpoke."

"You're very welcome, Monroe. Sorry, I didn't recognize you. Everyone looks so different out of running gear. Feel free to jump in the pool or take a walk around the grounds or a tour of the house or head across the way to the beach. Liam, some of your crew headed out that way—through the gardens and down to the Sound. If you go, be sure to keep your shoes on. We have rocky beaches here in the North Fork. The Hamptons got the white sands, and we got the wine and the rocks."

Knowing that Horace could chatter on all day if left to his own devices, Liam quickly excused himself by noting a dire need to use the facilities after the long train ride from Manhattan. Liam took Monroe by the hand and walked up the stairs to the deck, through the sliding glass doors and into the house. Even with Horace's invitation to take a tour of the house, Liam felt like a trespasser. By throwing a Labor Day party, Horace must have imagined the guests lingering by the pool, not poking their heads through the warren of rooms in his massive ranch house. The only art on the walls in any of the dozen or more rooms that Liam and Monroe walked through was documentary photographs of adolescent boys. While none of the subjects was ever naked, or even scantily clad, they looked self-conscious in their vulnerable positions in front of the camera. Liam wondered whether these were boys Horace had invited into his home but then suppressed the notion. He continued on with Monroe toward the far end of the house, where there were two small bathrooms opposite one another that they used.

"There is something creepy about this whole setup," Monroe said, finally, as they exited the house through a set of French doors that opened onto a breezeway. "I mean, I'm kind of intrigued and afraid at the same time."

"Let's chalk it up to his being eccentric," Liam said. "Getting to spend the last weekend of summer at the beach is a good tradeoff for dealing with a few questionable household details."

"Yowza, I had no idea you could turn kiddie porn into a simple question of taste," Monroe said, laughing. "Where did my little Liam pick up this political aplomb?"

Liam and Monroe stopped outside a small barn at the edge of Horace's property, just before the gate that led to the beach. As they drew nearer to the little triangular house, Liam and Monroe heard muffled voices. The two small windows at the top of the structure were at least twelve feet high, making it impossible for them to peer in, so they tip-toed around the perimeter in search of an entrance. Once they located the door, Liam and Monroe paused outside, looking to one another sheepishly.

"Do you think it's a sex party?" Liam whispered to Monroe.

"It's barely one o'clock in the afternoon," he replied. "I certainly hope not."

"But what then?"

"Maybe drugs," Monroe offered.

"With a crew of runners? I don't think so."

"Why don't we just crack open the door?" Monroe said. "What's the worst that could happen?"

The intense blue light inside the little house blinded Liam at first. After a few seconds of squinting to adjust his eyes, he noticed that about a dozen men stood transfixed in front of a fifteen-foot-high wall of stacked television screens. It was not dissimilar from an installation you might see in the Museum of Modern Art, except that each monitor showed footage of Horace having sex with a different man. Each sexual partner was beautiful and looked young enough to raise the question of legality or, certainly, moral impropriety.

Monroe leaned against the wall and his mouth went agape. The images on the television screens grew more graphic. A hairless slip of a man was ordered to bend over and expose his anus. A close-up of Horace's tongue circling the inflamed pink sphincter followed. Liam watched in awe, paralyzed by what he was witnessing. But in less than sixty seconds his macabre interest in the films turned into complete disgust and he motioned to Monroe to leave. As they turned to exit, Liam was stopped dead in his tracks at the sight of Matthew necking some liver-spotted man with steely gray hair. With a quick tug, Monroe pulled Liam out of the barn. In the high blue of midafternoon, Monroe blinked dramatically while addressing Liam.

"What kind of warped world have you taken me into, boy?"

"Oh please, like I could really shock a weathered queen like you."

Liam rubbed the buzzed fringe of Monroe's shaved head and felt very aware of how much he enjoyed hanging out with his best friend. Liam suggested they forget all the freaky goings-on and enjoy the beach. If it were possible, the day had grown even more beautiful in the hundred-yard walk from the gate toward the pebbly strand.

By the shoreline, tons of parents stood with their ankles in the water begging their kids not to venture out an inch farther. The water was very still and sandbars freckled its crystal blue surface, reminding Liam of the late summer tides of his childhood. Something final lurked under the shoals, and he began to feel melancholy without reason.

"You're looking pensive all of a sudden," Monroe said, taking Liam's hand into his own in a pure and platonic gesture.

"Endings, I guess." Liam smiled. "You never shake that back-to-school feeling, do you?"

"That yearning keeps you young," Monroe offered. "Try to remember that."

As they progressed another hundred feet or so along the beach, Liam saw the large contingent of Fast Trackers frolicking in the water. He considered checking Monroe's pulse on the gathering one last time but thought better of it as he saw Zane running toward them at breakneck speed. His skinny arms were wet with saltwater and a clump of seaweed stuck to his calf.

"You need to protect me, Liam." Zane gasped for breath. "Ferdinand keeps playing this game where he attempts to drown me. He took something when he went out to the barn earlier and has been acting like a reckless maniac ever since."

"Zane, you've met my friend Monroe before."

"Of course, of course, of course. Well, sir, if you have swimming trunks on under those shorts, I'd say you have to come join us in the ocean."

"It's the Sound, not the ocean." Monroe smiled in a feigned attempt to soften the obnoxiousness of the comment.

"Okay, smarty pants. I'll put it more simply—wet or dry?"

"I'll go back to the house, Liam. It's okay. You should enjoy the water."

"Don't be such a frowny-face, Monroe." Zane emphasized the instruction by pinching at where he estimated Monroe's nipple should be. "Go sit under the umbrella there with Gary. He's got a cooler full of alcohol, and he could entertain you well into the fall with his cutting commentary on everyone at this party."

"Oh, I'd love a beer," said Liam. "Let's all go over."

"We need you to be lean and clean for our last two races against the Bobcats, Liam. We can still win the competition against them." Zane lectured Liam as they all marched over to the striped sheet where Gary was camped out. "You also have to remember that the marathon is less than eight weeks away."

"My God, I've running my ass off for the last eight months. If I want to have a beer at a barbecue, you damn well better be sure that I'm going to."

Gary leaned over from his chair to pull out three bottles of Stella Artois from the cooler that anchored one corner of the oversized beach blanket. He wore denim shorts and a polo shirt. A wide straw hat guarded him against whatever sun the beach umbrella might miss.

"I'm with you, Liam," he said as he popped open the three bottles, handing one each to Liam and Monroe and taking a long gulp from the other. "Work hard. Play hard. It's one of the tenets this club was founded on."

"I had no idea there were principles behind this traveling circus," Monroe quipped back.

"Ouch, no one told me there were sharks in these waters," Gary snapped back.

"Looks like you've got company now, G-Lo," Zane announced. "Liam, finish the beer and join me in the water!"

Zane plopped an orange raft over Liam's head and dragged him out to the water. Liam glanced over his shoulder and could see that Gary and Monroe were already engaged in conversation. They clinked their bottles of beer together, and their bodies were angled toward each other. Liam thought he picked up the soft sough of laughter through the lapping waves. As the tide pulled him out farther, he tried to focus back toward the shore but could only make out partial shapes and movements on the blanket.

MILE 24

The city looked coquettish in the late morning light. As the road rose, gradually, the curve of downtown reflected in mirrors of glass and steel. Up ahead to the right, the redbrick projects of Chinatown stretched in succession toward the great heights of midtown Manhattan. The city revealed itself in flashes and suggestive poses. That was the way that Liam had always experienced the trip over the Manhattan Bridge; he would force cabbies to go out of their way to take this route into the city anytime he was in Brooklyn. Running across the bridge made the effort all the more rewarding. This was not an easy feat, with its slow but seemingly endless incline. Liam had to remind himself to keep a steady pace. This was just the second of five bridges in the day's twenty-mile run.

"That mile was 7:07." Gene heaved a little as he spoke. "We should probably cut it back a little. We're only about nine miles in."

Gene had just purchased a top-of-the-line GPS watch and now tortured anyone within earshot with an endless recitation of statistics. Between the chip on his shoe, the strap across his chest, the TV screen mounted on his wrist, and satellites in the sky, the gadget managed to report back exact pace, average miles per hour, his heart rate, and the total distance run. Everyone rolled their eyes as Gene used the device to order people to pick up or slow down the pace.

"I can't believe you spent $250 on that piece of crap, especially considering what a cheap bastard you are," Ferdinand spoke in a joshing tone that disallowed Gene direct rebuttal.

"Why are you even running with us, bitch?" Gene began to run a little faster to pull away from Ferdinand despite his edict that the group slow down. "You're not a high-fiver, and you're just going to fade and finish this run with the B-Group."

"You broke six-minute pace in a four-miler a year and a half ago, Gene. Are we plagued to hear about it forever? You're a high-fiver by technicality only."

Zane used the empirical data of racing to exact revenge on Gene whenever he had the chance.

"You may have the edge in short distances, my friend, but you've never even run the marathon." A collective groan rumbled through the silence before Gene finished his thought. "Let alone broken three hours in a marathon. All I can tell you guys is that I never could have done that last year without even pacing and discipline."

As his feet pounded along the steep decline of the bridge, Liam could feel a sharp pain dagger through his lower back. He bit his lower lip and focused on relaxing his breathing. Marathon day was just a month away now. He knew the race would throw even more discomfort his way—but at least he would not have to listen to the childish bickering of his teammates.

The long off ramp of the bridge came to a quick halt and spilled the runners out onto the congested streets of Chinatown. Zane, who was at the head of the group, stopped and waited for Marvin to direct everyone toward the Williamsburg Bridge. According to Zane and Gary and the entire nucleus of power at Fast Trackers, Marvin had ended his boy-toy fling after the nineteen-year-old he had been sleep-

ing with stole a fifty-dollar bill out of Marvin's wallet. Pre-
dictably, they said, after months of absence from the club,
Marvin returned to the fold as though nothing had happened. The lore was that you always knew when Marvin was
single again because he was back on the prowl, hitting on any
runner under the age of thirty. But no matter, everyone was
just happy to have him back. He could map a run through
any borough flawlessly and with just two more head-to-head
battles with the Urban Bobcats, Fast Trackers really needed
its top line in top form.

By the time they reached the Queensboro Bridge, no one
had any energy left for chitchat. Even Gene had stopped re-
porting the mileage and pace of the run. Ferdinand had, indeed, fallen off somewhere in Queens, and Matthew slowed
down to keep him company. Liam directed his thoughts in-
ward to steel himself for the marathon when man against
man, man against nature, and man against himself would all
roll together. He knew that the pain he felt now would be
nothing in comparison to the last 10K of the marathon. The
gabled rise of the Queensboro presented the next challenge.
At more than a mile in length, the Fifty-ninth Street Bridge
offered a mirage of Manhattan at its halfway point in the
shape of Roosevelt Island. This would be mile number sixteen in the marathon, he thought, the quiet valley right before the maniac masses of First Avenue. He felt suddenly
emotional and choked back tears. With the heavy part of
training over, Liam had only a half marathon next weekend
and two weeks of tapering before race day. And then the
performance would unfold before crowds of spectators.
Thinking of the race course sent goose bumps down Liam's
skin—almost 40,000 runners leaving Staten Island and weaving through Brooklyn, Queens, Manhattan, the Bronx, and
then snaking back through Manhattan again to end up at
Tavern on the Green. The course brilliantly exploited New
York's eclectic character and uneven terrain. In just a few

weeks, Liam Walker would be running the most famous race course in the world and maybe even helping to bring his team a much-needed win against its local rival.

Fast Trackers had dared not to think that far ahead. The club had inched so close to the Urban Bobcats but would need to score definitive victories in both the half marathon next weekend and in the marathon itself to have a shot. But the Bobcats had so many tricks up their sleeves and so many talented runners in reserve. By comparison, the Fast Trackers had been fragile in recent months. Riser did have good days but still struggled to keep his weight above 120 pounds, and it was out of the question for any Fast Tracker to suggest that he run strenuously given his illness. Matthew had lacked focus since his best friend had gone off the rails. The forecast for Ferdinand and Marvin, both flaky in their own right and subject to the lure of party drugs and boy nip, respectively, had brightened with their appearances at the long run today. No one had expected them to show. But, then again, there were still several weeks for a new diversion to sidetrack them.

Liam turned off the bridge and led the runners in his group through the northwest zigzag to the diner chosen for the post-run brunch. They had phoned ahead for a table of fifteen, but people were going to be arriving at vastly different times depending on what pace they had run. Catching a glimpse of himself in the mirrored walls of the restaurant, Liam immediately felt self-conscious to be in public with salt rings on his face and his clothes dripping with sweat. Now he would have to tell the hostess that fourteen more just like him would be dining in the big booth in the back this morning.

"We're the party of fifteen," he said to the old woman taking names by the door. "It's under Loblonicki. We called ahead several hours ago."

"Runners," she spoke in a thick Eastern European accent,

her words fraught with disappointment. "A lot of water refill. Not a lot of food."

"We promise to eat heartily. We just ran twenty miles." Liam tried to smile, but had begun to feel anxious.

"But I see only seven people here. You said you are a group of fifteen?"

"The others are coming soon. They were running right behind us."

"I sit your party when everyone is here. Please wait outside the restaurant until then." Her tone conveyed impatience.

"We're paying customers," Gene planted himself in front of Liam to make the assertion. "You sit us now, or we're going to go elsewhere."

"Good luck to you," she said.

"Never mind him," said Liam. "We'll wait outside for the others."

"What's with the ultimatum bullshit?" Zane yelled to Gene, once they were situated far enough from the window of the restaurant. "Can't wait half an hour for your eggs and bacon. You're such an ass."

"They should treat us like every other customer. That bitch wouldn't sit us because she saw us as a big group of flamers about to scare away the pack of breeders in there. It's typical Upper East Side bullshit."

"This whole plan doesn't make any sense," Marvin said, matching Gene's agitation. "We could eat our meals and get on with the day by the time some of those guys get back here. I mean, Liam, what pace was your friend Monroe running anyway?"

Liam had not computed the time differential between his twenty-miler and Monroe's. Normally, Monroe ran about two minutes per mile slower than him, but Monroe had never run anywhere near this distance before so it was difficult to know whether he would even complete the run. At least Gary had agreed to jog with Monroe, citing a sore Achilles' heel as the reason for slowing down his long run. The gesture knocked a huge weight off Liam's shoulders. It had seemed the two formed a bond of sorts out on Long Island over Labor Day, but Liam had been burned before for taking too much for granted with Monroe and so remained cautiously optimistic on how today might turn out.

"We've already been standing around for the better part of fifteen minutes," Liam replied. "I bet everyone's back here in another twenty or twenty-five minutes. What choice do we have now but to wait?"

As soon as he asked the question, Liam received an answer. His teammates quickly expressed an eagerness to get on with their day. Marvin excused himself, then Ben, then Gene, and within fifteen minutes only Zane and Liam waited outside the Silver Star Diner.

"I bet Ferdinand and Matthew headed straight home," Zane said, looking at his watch. "We can just leave a message with the hostess in case anyone comes by, but I have a feeling no one is coming, Liam. She can tell folks that we've jetted."

"If you feel like heading out, please go ahead, Zane. I'm a big boy. I'll stick around a little while longer. I want to hear how Gary and Monroe got along."

Zane began to laugh and threw his arm around Liam's shoulder. Liam felt something odd and condescending in the gesture.

"What?" Liam asked. His hunger disabled his ability to play coy.

"I am certain they got along just fine, kiddo." Zane smirked and patted Liam on the shoulder again.

"Please." Liam wanted Zane to know he wasn't in the mood for games. "I know the club loves this type of drama, but I really don't want idle gossip to cloud my friendship with Monroe."

"Are you really trying to tell me that Monroe hasn't told you?" Zane waited for Liam to respond. Liam just shook his head. "Let's just say that ever since that day out at Horace's place, Gary and Monroe have gotten to know each other— *real* well."

Liam stared at Zane for a moment to see if his gullibility was being tested and then excused himself. He began to walk away from the restaurant but did not know in what direction to travel. Zane's suggestion gnawed at Liam as he replayed the events of that day at the beach. But it could not possibly be true. Monroe told Liam every detail of his life. This was madness. Then again, why would Zane lie? Liam's head pounded. Perhaps Monroe finally opened himself up to another man. Maybe Gary actually took a liking to someone his own age. But they were both far too transparent to hide romance from a close friend.

Liam picked his cell phone out of the pocket of his shorts and dialed Monroe. He would leave a message for Monroe— tell him, calmly, to call as soon as he returned from the run. As he walked toward the train, Liam noticed a tall maple tree straight ahead of him. The only greenery on the block, somehow the tree had managed to survive under the cement and asphalt of East Sixty-first Street. A cluster of leaves on the top branches caught the sun in a brilliant flash of yellow and red. Liam wondered when the tree had been planted and for how long it had been holding on against the litter and congestion of the city.

As Monroe's voice came on with instructions to leave a brief message, Liam hung up the phone. He looked at his watch. It was not yet noon on a gorgeous autumn day in New York City, and Liam decided to walk west toward the subway to get on with his own day. As he crossed the avenue, he thought of Monroe and Gary doing the same—possibly together—and he smiled.

MILE 25

"Did you bring them?"

The desperation in Riser's voice was palpable. It was early morning and the sun swept through the room with determination and promise. The beautiful light and the smell of clean sheets made the sight of Riser crumpled helplessly in bed all the sadder. Liam handed Riser the crisp paper bag, and he feverishly opened it.

"I never would have guessed that a change of wardrobe would be your highest priority right now." Liam no longer knew what to say. He had hoped that Riser's initial stint in the hospital would shock him into reality and make him want to live again, but here it was just over a month later and he was back in the same hospital room festooned with tubes and monitors, looking more acutely sick than ever.

"These jeans were the Holy Grail." Riser extricated the dark denim from its tissue paper wrapping and held the pants up to offer the evidence to Liam. "Helmut Lang—$345. I refused to allow myself to buy these until I was a size 28."

"They're a very smart look," Liam offered clumsily.

"Help me up so I can try them on?" Riser raised his two bony arms in the air solicitously.

"But there are all these wires and tubes, sweetie. Maybe you should just lie there and rest."

"I've been in this same position all night long . . . I'll have bed sores soon, Li. Please just help me up. All this shit moves. Trust me."

Afraid Riser's bones might snap like twigs on impact, Liam gingerly shimmied his friend off the mattress. Riser leaned his upper body against Liam's shoulder, and Liam hoisted him up.

"Oh shit, the room is spinning."

"Just stand still with me a second and everything will come into place. You've just been on your back too long."

Riser squeezed the flesh between Liam's neck and his shoulder. The pain rippled through Liam, and he bit the inside of his lip to stay silent. He knew Riser was not in total control of his actions.

"I'll lift my leg, Li." Riser paused and looked as if he had lost the ability to form words. When had Riser taken to abbreviating his name? Liam wondered. "I'll lift my leg up and you can just slip the pants on. Okay, Li? It'll be a team effort."

The pin-legged pants glided over Riser's emaciated legs, and Liam helped button the fly so that the jeans were on right and proper. Any pretense of humility on Riser's part had disappeared.

"I nearly killed myself to fit into these." Riser turned to Liam and laughed. "I guess truer words have never been spoken, hunh?"

"You're going to be fine, babe. Stop being so dramatic. Let's sit down and watch some Saturday morning cartoons."

As he bent down to sit in the leather recliner next to Riser's bed, Liam's phone began to ring. There were signs every fifty feet throughout the hospital ordering people to turn off their cell phones, but somehow Liam had neglected to realize that his was still on.

"Who is it?" Riser sounded as though he was afraid to have an interloper steal Liam away from him.

"It's just Gary, sweetie. I can call him back later."

"Holy shit. Today's the half marathon in the park, isn't it? You missed the race against the Bobcats because of me. God-damn it! Bad enough that I can't run for the team. Now I am causing our best runners to miss key races. Once a fuck-up, always a fuck-up."

"Riser, we're a team. We take care of each other. We help one another out. There are *plenty* of Fast Trackers who raced out there this morning, and I am certain that they did us both proud."

When Liam had gotten the call from the station nurse just before midnight, he took a taxi to the hospital immediately. He was both concerned that Riser's vital signs kept fluctuat-ing so wildly and incredibly flattered that Riser had listed him—over Matthew or Ferdinand or anyone else on the team—as his emergency contact. The visit wore on through the wee hours of the night and then, just after daybreak, Riser asked Liam to trek over to his apartment and fetch his favorite pair of jeans. Liam conceded the morning's race to his friendship with Riser, though he did begin to worry over which Fast Trackers would show up to run the half marathon. Each time the thought entered his mind, Liam felt ashamed and tried to dismiss it. Now, Gary was calling—probably with the results—and Liam had to just look the other way, search-ing for old episodes of *The Smurfs* on the static-laden TV hanging from the corner of the ceiling.

"Liam, you should go enjoy the day. Please. I am the one who is bed-bound. You? Go out and have mulled cider in the park . . . It's autumn in New York, for chrissakes."

Something about the little blue men marching through the heavy snow of the old television set lulled Liam into a sense of peace. The volume was too low to hear, but Liam could easily figure out the one-dimensional plot—the Smurfs were scrambling into hidden brushes in the forest because the evil Gargamel had been spotted. Liam wished the divisions between good and evil were so clearly drawn in real life. Liam fought the heaviness of his eyelids and wriggled in his chair to shake himself awake. As he turned to draw Riser into conversation about the program, Liam noticed that the sleepiness must have been contagious. Riser's body was swallowed by the whiteness of the hospital linens. His hip bones jutted up sharply, exposing the largeness of the twenty-eight-inch waist of the Helmut Lang jeans. Riser had worked so hard to get into them, and the jeans now swam on his underfed body. In the honeyed morning light, Riser's skin had the cold alabaster quality of a marble statue. The veins in his hands and his stomach rose to the surface in a desperate but sensual way. Riser's mouth had fallen open as he drifted into sleep, elongating the concavity of his face. He looked ethereal and beautiful but almost like something imagined, something that had never inhabited the earth.

Liam pressed his lips to Riser's forehead and whispered the word *good-bye.* He would call Zane or Matthew or Gary after he left the hospital and inform them that they should visit. It felt important that Riser not be left alone. As he made his way toward the elevator bank, Liam ran into the officious nurse who seemed always to be consumed by hospital protocol. She smiled sadly at him.

"It's been a long morning," Liam said.

"I can imagine," she replied. "You're a good kid to come stay with your friend overnight."

"I'm his emergency contact." Liam chuckled uncomfortably. He didn't want to talk about Riser anymore and pushed the button to call the elevator a second time.

"That's quite a responsibility," she said and paused. "In this disease, there is a loss of perspective. You are going to be key in helping your friend regain his."

Liam looked to the ground in silence. He did not know why people felt a need to offer unsolicited advice.

"I know it's not my place," she continued. "But if you work in a hospital long enough, you feel like you can see into people. Your friend is a sensitive soul. I think he's lost. Someone he trusts—like you—can set him on the right path again."

"You try telling a gay man he needs to pack on ten pounds," Liam said. "No matter how obvious it is to us, he's just programmed not to hear that."

"Just promise me you'll help your friend by treating this like a disease and not a dieting fad."

The nurse stood waiting for a response as Liam entered the elevator. The woman peered at him for another moment before consulting her chart and walking down the hall to her next patient. She scribbled down notes as she strolled off. Liam filled with anger and fantasized about storming after her and pulling all the bobby pins out of the tight bun of her hair.

"My friend is strong!" he yelled to no one as the doors to the elevator closed shut.

As Liam made his way through the hospital corridors and onto Seventh Avenue South, the bolt of early afternoon sunlight punched him squarely between the eyes, and he had to hunch over for a minute to let his vision adjust to the daytime. The day had grown unusually warm for October. Liam slunk under the shade of a little florist's awning on the corner of Greenwich, where he dialed Gary's phone number.

"Liam!" Gary's urgent tone was jarring. "Liam, Liam, Liam! Where the fuck have you been all morning? I've only tried your cell phone about eight times in the last two hours. You know I'm not a patient man."

Liam remembered the incident with Mitch at the Brooklyn Half Marathon—the scorn, the tears, and the bitter accusations—and smiled at the understatement. It amazed Liam how easily Gary could laugh at his own zealous lunacy.

"It's been a crazy blur of a morning, G . . . "

Not waiting for Liam to finish his thought, Gary launched into the news that had prompted him to call so many times in the last few hours. Fast Trackers had obliterated the Urban Bobcats in the half marathon that morning. And that wasn't even the news that was going to knock Liam off his feet. No, there were several other surprises, Gary teased. He pressed Liam to guess, but the exhaustion of the protracted hospital visit had robbed Liam of any playful enthusiasm.

"C'mon, I'll give you a hint. Who do you think came in first for the team?"

"Well, I would have said Zane, but clearly the only answer I can be sure of is '*not* Zane.'"

"Fine, Mr. Grumpy Pants. I'll just tell you. The big shocker was that someone who normally would have been one of the top scorers for Urban Bobcats was the top scorer for Fast Trackers New York this morning."

There was silence on the line.

"Speechless, aren't you? I told you it was good, Liam. Now, I never lie . . . I may embellish, but I never lie."

Liam could not believe it. After all this time. And he wasn't even there to appreciate the beautiful gesture. Liam was overcome with emotion and quickly thanked Gary for the phone call. Before hanging up the phone, he mustered a few rah-rah words for the team. After the long year of ups and downs, they just might make it. The marathon would still be a huge test of their collective will, but they would actually be toeing the line with the Urban Bobcats knowing that this competition was anyone's to win. Maybe the exhaustion had caved in on him or maybe it was the immenseness of the news, but Liam could not bear to deflate Gary with Riser's sad tale. Liam crumbled into a crying jag after he hung up the phone.

Liam knew that he had to call Didier; he *wanted* to call Didier. But he hoped not to sound fatuous and fawning. Their roller coaster of a relationship these past few months had made the prospect of easy rapprochement seem foolhardy. Though his gesture was grand and romantic, Didier's racing for Fast Trackers did not necessarily mean that he had cast aside his other life. Who knew how long he had been married and the ties he had to his wife. Who knew what the cryptic "loose ends" that Didier had referred to in his e-mail really entailed. Did Liam feel strongly enough about this beautiful "Parisian" to risk . . . what? . . . What was it that he was risking? As soon as he considered the question, he dialed up Didier. Liam began to walk briskly to ease his nerves. He had made it almost all the way down Fifth Avenue where the foliage of Washington Square Park glittered like a pot of gold at the end of a rainbow. Didier answered after only two rings; he sounded groggy and far away.

"Sorry if I woke you . . . I can call back later. . . ."

"Are you shitting me, Liam? The race this morning may have knocked some of the wind from my sails, but I have been waiting for your call as impatiently as a five-year-old on Christmas Eve Santa Watch."

"That's pretty wound up," Liam said with a laugh.

"Where were you this morning? You never miss a race."

"Look, Didier," Liam began but was unsure how he wanted to finish. The story was too much to rehash. "There has been a lot going on for both of us. Should we really be doing this?"

"I have no choice in the matter, Liam. I've missed you more than I knew was possible this last month. I can't continue to be on-and-off with you."

"Come meet me downtown for a late lunch—at Otto on Eighth and Fifth." Liam would be able to sort this out better face-to-face. "The restaurant is just north of Washington Square."

"Of course, I know it. Isn't pizza and wine a little heavy for midday?"

"You've just run a half marathon, Didier; I think you deserve it."

Wrestling with a bad case of overtiredness and anxiety,

Liam drank two and a half glasses of Barolo while waiting for Didier at the bar. The day had cooled a bit since the early afternoon and had begun to feel more like autumn; the red and yellow trees outside the bar window helped Liam romanticize the season. Liam loved these early sunsets after the stretch of long days through July, August, and September. He knew that he would tire of the cold and the gray by the depth of winter, but now, here in this moment on this day in mid-October, he could fool himself into thinking that the perfection would last. The bartender came by with the bottle again and filled the wineglass quickly and without asking Liam's permission. At $15 a glass, Liam bristled until the man motioned that this one was on him. Liam knew that the free booze meant that he had already had more than his share. He strove for a toasty buzz, not a drunken stupor.

In a cloud of contemplation, Liam leapt out of his seat when Didier sidled up beside him at the bar.

"Glad you started without me, sport. There is nothing more depressing than sitting at a bar without a drink in your hand. I mean, can you think of anything more thoroughly useless?"

"Please join me then." Liam smiled from under the delightful veil of alcohol. "I have been waiting here for the better part of an hour to toast the great feats of our newest Fast Tracker."

"I did pretty good, didn't I? I only wish that you had been there to witness it."

"So you could have whipped me too? I hear you beat Zane. That's not an everyday occurrence at Fast Trackers."

"I really just went out there and ran my own race. I focused on feeling fresh and loose."

"And how did the Bobcats take your mutiny?"

"I don't care, Liam." Didier paused and dropped his voice into a low, deep whisper. "I just want to move forward. Onward and upward."

The dim light drew out the severity of Didier's features, exaggerating the soft fullness of his lips and the height of his cheekbones. Liam gulped two large swallows of wine to steady his racing heart. His phone rang and everyone at the bar turned to look at him; he laughed at again neglecting to heed the signs prohibiting cellular devices.

Liam excused himself and headed toward the exit as he answered the phone. It was the hospital, and he did not want to send the call to voice mail.

"What? What is it? What?" The lady on the other end kept asking if she had received Riser's next-of-kin.

"They don't live in the U.S. I am his emergency contact. That's why you have my number and that's why you've called me. Now please, what is it? Is something wrong?"

"I hate to be the bearer of bad news, Mr. Walker." She paused for a moment. "But your friend has passed on . . . He went so peacefully in his sleep, looks just like a baby, really. I am so sorry to be the one to have to tell you."

"You must have the wrong person. My friend is Riser Kolz. And Riser Kolz is a twenty-six-year-old runner. He isn't dead."

"You're upset. I understand. These things happen. Sometimes we do things to ourselves that our hearts can't take. If you would like to come to the hospital to talk with me or the doctor, please feel free."

"No, thank you," he said. "I've heard enough." Liam hung up the phone in disbelief. The ruby-orange halo of dusk lit up the brick buildings like fire, and a man and woman in heavy cable-knit sweaters clutched each other's arms to fend off the slight chill of the coming evening. A group of teenage girls asked a burly man in a tweed jacket to take a picture as they posed on the street. Perhaps this was the beginning of their first vacation to Manhattan or perhaps it was their last evening together before some life-changing event. The city was getting ready for another night filled with adventure and disappointment.

Liam pressed his face to the window of Otto and exhaled. A huge circle of condensation formed. Looking through the glass, Liam could see Didier smiling back at him, fidgeting at the bar and motioning wildly for him to come back inside.

MILE 26

Matthew wanted to run through the slides one more time, but Liam convinced him to relax and have a cocktail before the guests started to pour in. The bar looked sad and dusty with no one in it. The mild, coppery stench of Saturday night lingered in the air, making the cool, gray October Sunday feel even lonelier.

Liam quickly downed a tall pint of Sierra Nevada and ordered another. He had to quell his nerves and stop his hands from trembling. Matthew shuffled through some index cards between sips of Stoli cranberry. In the hour that they had spoken the night before, Liam told Matthew that as Riser's best friend he should give the eulogy. Matthew clearly wanted to do the honors and to share his impressions of Riser, but he realized his limitations as a public speaker. Just sitting and looking at his prepared notes caused him to sweat profusely.

"He'll have another drink," Liam said to the bartender and pointed to Matthew's glass. "Throw it back, Mattie," he whispered. "Trust me on this one."

With no time to plan anything formal and no sense as to the rules of decorum governing the death of a good friend, Liam and Matthew had decided to host an open bar at

Riser's favorite watering hole—the Gym Bar on Eighth Avenue. When the owners heard about Riser and his untimely death, they agreed to give Fast Trackers the entire bar from four to seven o'clock with drinks at half price. Matthew had been up for days scanning all the photos that he had of Riser and putting them to a suitable audio track. The slideshow presentation had caused Liam to sob the first time he saw it.

"I don't know if I can do this." Matthew looked as though any action, the touch of his hand or even a nod of commiseration, might vault him into tears.

"You have to, sweetie. You'll regret it forever if you don't . . . plus you'll help all the other guys in the club. They don't have all these great memories, all this beautiful detail about Riser's life at their disposal."

A tentative squeak at the front entrance announced the arrival of the first two guests. Gary and Monroe walked in at an odd distance from one another, as though neither was ready to commit to the idea, now plain as day, that they were a couple. Hugs were exchanged and Matthew handed each man a copy of the brief program that had been prepared for the service. A beautiful photo of Riser running in shorts and a tank top, taken a year or more before his body was ruined by starvation, graced the cover with two lines of text underneath: the years of his life (1986–2012) and a quotation from one of his favorite songs "Long May You Run."

"You men are doing a great, great thing," Gary said.

"I remember when I used to have to go to these memorial things every fucking month." Monroe's voice cracked, and he wiped a tear from his cheek. Gary reached over and rubbed his shoulder and kneaded the base of his neck with his hands. "Guess you never escape the past completely. And twenty-six will always be too young to die."

"Thanks for coming, G," Matthew said. "I know, given what you've been through with death this summer, the opening of unhealed wounds can't be feeling too good."

"I may never be a father, but I feel like I've lost many children through the years . . . never as senseless as this, though."

The door swung open again and a larger group entered the bar. Liam saw Zane and Mitch along with some older faces that looked familiar but which he couldn't quite pair with names. He looked up at the clock; it was 3:55. The quiet time had ended and now it would be a procession of greetings that would extend until the bar ushered them out at 7 o'clock.

"I never thought it would come to this." Zane placed his head on Liam's chest as he hugged him. "We should have known. It was our responsibility as his friends to watch out for him. That's what gay guys do for one another."

"There was no way any of us could have known, Zane. So many runners get so thin. It's the badge of honor in this sport, isn't it?" Liam stopped and reflected for a few moments. "Well, that didn't come out exactly right, but you know what I mean."

"How do we go on now?"

These were the banal and unanswerable questions left for the living to grapple with, but Zane stood before Liam and looked into his eyes as though he expected a real answer from him. It occurred to Liam that during the last year almost no one in the club had patience for the fits Riser would pitch and the drama that he had caused. The club was like that, part of what brought people together was their annoying differences, and the more nettlesome or gossip-worthy someone's behavior became, the more Fast Trackers understood and embraced them. There was a humanity to the club that made people forget their gripes and forgive their shortcomings. No one expected, or even wanted, you to be perfect at Fast Trackers.

By a quarter past four, more than fifty Fast Trackers had crammed into the back room of Gym Bar. Most had used the sad circumstance as an opportunity to drink judgment-free while the sun was still out on a Sunday afternoon. People laughed a little self-consciously as they shared stories about the club. Liam nudged Matthew to corral the group around the pulpit of his bar stool. As he fumbled through the cards one last time, Matthew patted some sweat off his brow with a damp bar napkin and cleared his throat.

"Thank you." He paused before starting again, much louder this time. "Thank you all for coming! Thank you."

The conversation in the crowd trailed off into murmurs and then to silence. Once all eyes were glued on Matthew, Liam thought he actually heard his friend's stomach growl beneath his pinstriped shirt. He looked Matthew in the eye and nodded. Matthew placed the index cards on the bar and spoke from memory.

"Riser Kolz was a good friend to me." He stopped and looked around the crowd as though he might identify someone to corroborate the sentiment. "I know that he wasn't easy to know and at first blush he rubbed a lot of people the wrong way. It's funny to me that he could come off as abrasive. The poor guy had no defenses against the world. He was so open that he just let everything in and that kind of poisoned him, in a way. I know that when Riser left his family back in Bosnia, he redefined himself in New York. This club helped shape who he was, and he loved, envied, and even worshipped so many of you in this room. I just wish he could have lived to see how much he meant to you guys. I wish he had let himself see that reality while he was here with us. We can all honor his life by spreading a little of that joy and love and admiration among each other today—and from today on."

Liam had anticipated a shaky and awkward speech, but Matthew had hit just the right pace and had punctuated the words *joy*, *love*, and *admiration* so that at least half of the men in the room now rubbed tears from their eyes. As soon as everyone had a few moments to digest Matthew's speech and to applaud his astonishing delivery, Liam walked over and hit the play button on the laptop to start the slideshow.

As the skipping, sultry beats of Fatboy Slim started to boom through the bar, photographs of Riser were projected onto a movie screen in the middle of the floor, where a pool table should have been. Matthew had strung together a few baby and childhood shots he had found while cleaning out Riser's apartment, but the bulk were from the last year or so. The transformation saddened Liam as he saw it play out to the catchy dance music. In a group photo from the club's New Year's Eve party the previous December, Riser and Matthew sported Depends as the babies ringing in 2012. Riser had the sinewy build of a lifeguard. His body would have inspired envy in almost anyone, the leanness of his frame looking natural and effortless. The lyrics "I have to praise you like I sh-ou-ou-ou-ou-ou-ould" pounded as winter moved to early spring, and Riser dashed long and healthy toward the finish line in several races. So many Fast Tracker events had taken place in the last year. Liam puzzled to think of what he did with his time before joining the club.

The music slipped into the mellower and more contemplative chords of Van Morrison's "Into the Mystic" as the photologue traveled into the months of May and June. With the warmer temperatures, Riser's outfits switched from long sleeves and tights to shorts and singlets and, finally, to no shirt at all. Looking at the photos now, Liam realized that the undressing was a cry for help, a way for Riser to show his wounds. His torso bore the vacancy of a carcass. The thinner he became, the more focused and intense Riser looked. If he were being honest with himself, Liam would have admitted a certain respect and even a jealousy in seeing Riser strain harder and harder to achieve what he so desperately needed.

"So sorry that I am so late." Droplets of rain glistened through Didier's hair. "I couldn't decide whether I should let you have the afternoon with your friends." Liam had told

Didier not to trouble himself given his limited knowledge of Riser but felt so relieved that he had not listened. It scared Liam to think of how happy it made him to have Didier here.

"It's amazing," Didier whispered, and Liam nodded.

Didier reached under the bar stool and grasped for Liam's hand. Feeling the cold, bony fingers clutching at his palm, Liam grabbed a strong hold of Didier's hand. A photo of Riser from a long run in early August popped up on the screen. His drawn and runneled face smiled amid a small group that included Matthew, Ben, and Mitch. Having run many miles before the photo was taken, Riser's body appeared breakable in its gauntness. That was only ten weeks ago, not enough time to receive a furniture delivery and yet enough time for a friend to slowly kill himself. Each photo brought the pointlessness home.

"I can't believe it's over." Ferdinand choked through his words as he embraced Matthew and Liam in a group hug. "You just don't prepare . . . "

"You don't need to say anything. What can be said? The best we can do is to remember and to rejoice in him."

"Life is for the living, eh? I know you're right on that, Liam," Ferdinand spoke tentatively. "This has scared me sober. No more fun escapes—no coke, no ecstasy, no anything. I'm going to let life ride through me like a speedball. Nothing could be more of a trip, more of a fucking trip, than taking this all in sober. I'm so grateful I have you guys."

Liam had expected some of the members who were older—perhaps Gary and some of his friends—to weep over the loss. The memory of the AIDS epidemic and the heartache it wrought still stung those who were members of the club in the eighties. But having one of the more self-absorbed and carefree members of the club break down overwhelmed Liam.

"Ferd, it's going to be okay. We're all going to miss him, but we can make it so he lives on in us."

"Oh, that's so trite, Liam. Are you listening to yourself?"

This began to sound more like the Ferdinand whom Liam knew and loved.

"We can help him live on by getting our act together and running like we believe in ourselves next Sunday!" Zane had sprung from out of the crowd to re-purpose the team.

"It would be an awesome distraction," Ferdinand mused. "I would love to have something else to focus on."

"We can do it!" Zane now exhorted an impassioned group that included Matthew, Ferdinand, Gary, Ben, Gene, and Liam. "Beating the Bobcats might be the last thing anyone would want to think about at a time like this. But we can't do anything to save Riser. This, this we can do. We can attempt greatness. If we're all willing to focus and face our fears, we can annihilate the competition."

"I'm in!" screamed Didier, much to the surprise of the other Fast Trackers. "This is why I came aboard. Let's do this!"

A rousing chorus of "Let's do this! We can do this!" ensued, and even the bartenders had begun to cheerlead along with the raucous chant. Didier excitedly bent over to kiss Liam, but Liam withdrew. He had butterflies over the Bobcat challenge and could not relax. It seemed like putting a lot of eggs in one basket. Who had appropriately trained for the marathon in Fast Trackers? How many more people would the Bobcats have? How far could faith and camaraderie take you? Liam breathed deeply and swallowed his doubts. Maybe he had never yielded to the workings of faith before, but this time he wanted nothing more than to believe in something greater than himself and to accept that something impossible could happen. He would run the marathon unfettered from the silly training laws that predicted performance. He would push himself harder than he ever had before and pray that he would finish strong. For the first time in many months, Liam *wanted* to race.

THE LAST 385 YARDS

Liam decided to get out of bed and go into the living room. The wind did not want to stop whistling around outside, and the branches of the gnarled cherry tree behind his building kept knocking into the bedroom window. It was four o'clock in the morning, and he tiptoed around the edge of the bed to avoid waking Didier. The alarm would not go off for another forty-five minutes, and Liam wanted time to himself in the apartment. He liked to perform his morning rituals alone.

Walking from room to room in the narrow, floor-through apartment, Liam tried to relax his body and let his mind go blank. The linoleum in the kitchen stuck cold to his feet. He wondered why the apartment had such an oversized kitchen window; the frame around the glass started just a foot from the floor and ran straight up to the ceiling. Five and a half years in the building, and he had never before stopped to think about this peculiarity. His mind bobbled between other random thoughts as he tried not to think about the wind. The *whirr* outside sped to a howl, and the panes of glass in the kitchen window shook in place. Every single room in the neighboring building was pitch-black. What a perfect night to sleep, he thought. It was a night custom-made for burrowing under the comforter.

Liam would check the Weather Channel to ease his mind. He turned the volume on the television as low as possible so that the noise would not wake Didier. After a series of commercials offering the successful removal of unwanted hair and an end to adult acne, a snippet of weather streamed across the screen. The gusts could reach thirty-five miles per hour by late morning. Liam thought about the Verrazano-Narrows Bridge and felt his stomach quake. He turned the television off and lay on the couch for a few minutes, staring out the window onto the blackness of the tenement across the way. He had lived just an arm's length from all these people for a large portion of his life and what did he know of them? The guy one floor down liked to cook shirtless in his boxers with a denim apron to guard against the mixing bowl spills and frying pan splashes. And once, Liam had guiltily watched the skinny stranger in the apartment at a forty-five-degree diagonal jerk off in an armchair. The wind whipped by again. Liam closed his eyes and visualized running easily, steadily, with a gentle wind at his back.

"We should get going in a minute or two." The words traveled down like the faraway murmur of a train conductor's voice. Liam opened his eyes only to have the lids succumb again to their own weight.

"C'mon, sunny. We've got a race to run." Liam felt Didier's still-warm-from-the-bed hands shaking him awake.

"What time is it?"

"It's five o'clock. We should catch the 6 A.M. bus to be safe."

"The wind . . . Have you heard it? This is going to ruin everything we've worked for this year."

"Liam, you're talking nonsense. Just get dressed and let's go. Everyone is going to be running the same marathon with the same sun and wind and temperature. That's the beauty of running; everyone faces the conditions equally. It's all about the given day. And who's tougher—*you* or the Urban Bobcats."

"You mean *us* or the Urban Bobcats." Liam realized he was in a mood to pick a fight. He felt groggy and superior.

"No, I know that I am tougher than they are. I used to be them, remember. And I know you're tougher too. The question is, what do *you* know, Liam?"

"I promise to be ready to leave in ten minutes as long as you swear to put an immediate end to the pep talk."

After some coffee and juice from the corner bodega leveled his blood sugar, Liam thanked Didier for being supportive and kissed him on the forehead in an attempt at détente. Now that he had Didier, Liam feared that he was going to take him for granted and mistreat him. He had done the same to his last three boyfriends, each relationship lasting three months, almost to the very day. Thus at this point in time, three months appeared to be the life span of any physical relationship for Liam. There was no gradual decay or petering out or period of bickering and evaluation, but rather a definitive end-point at the three-month mark. Ninety days proved to be a critical date for the expiration of product warranties and service guarantees and had an equal significance in the life cycle of a Liam Walker romance. *Had something formed or was it just sex?* Maybe three months functioned as the tipping point, the line in the sand where Liam had to classify a series of casual encounters or dates as something more vital for him to continue to find any meaning or derive any pleasure. Liam could not say for sure. His friends had always faulted him for residing too often inside the synapses of his own gray matter, wandering aimlessly through long corridors of thought and despair, mired in indulgent self-doubt and unproductive psychoanalysis. Liam yearned to be free— or at least he thought he did. He decided suddenly to stop thinking now and jump in headlong. Why not savor these early moments in a romance when everything still seemed possible? There was such goodness, such grandness even, in Didier's leaving the Bobcats to join Fast Trackers. So many club members needed this day to be great for the team.

The traffic inched along the Verrazano-Narrows into Staten Island. It was all charter buses dropping eager runners off at Fort Wadsworth for the start of the marathon. Thirty-nine thousand runners had gained entry this year. That was the most exciting part, the idea of partaking in a massive demonstration of sorts. The stop-and-go of the bus had caused Liam's head to pound, and he looked out the window for distraction. The crisp blue blanket of water below the bridge had been upturned in flags of white and gray by the wind. The sails on some early morning recreational boats billowed out in accents of green and purple.

"Why don't we just get out and walk the 200 yards down to the staging area?" Liam asked. "I can see it from here."

"No, they don't allow that. It would be bedlam if everyone ran from the buses at this point . . . The driver will never open the door for you until we are completely over the bridge."

"And then everyone is going to run for the Portosans at the same time."

"I told you not to drink the whole cup of coffee," Didier said with a smirk.

When the bus finally opened its doors, Liam ran out into the color-coded village looking for a bathroom. Because of the size of the event, the marathon organizers had split the race start into three different colors—blue, orange, and green—and all of the staging areas where racers waited before the start of the race were segregated by color. The runners would line up on the different levels and sides of the bridge based on the color of their start. Being part of the local elite, Liam had a slot at the very front of the green start, which was a wonderful thing except that the lines for the Portosans ran fifty to a hundred people long in the green start. Feeling the impossibility of the wait, Liam resorted to a racing trick he had picked up from a fellow club member. He walked over to the fence that outlined the edge of the field and kneeled down to tie his shoelaces. As he did that, he tucked his penis out of his running shorts and urinated on the grass. It was a completely brilliant technique, so long as no other runners got too close to you. Didier, who had been following at near distance, harrumphed when he saw the stream funneling through the grass where Liam knelt.

"It saved me time and pain," Liam said.

"If even just one out of ten people here did that, it would be a modern-day Woodstock."

"Don't be so dramatic." Liam playfully patted Didier on the chest, and Didier retorted by tickling Liam under his armpits.

"So I see you've traded up." The voice came from somewhere behind them. "Guess we never offered the whole rough play element . . . just a nice running experience."

The tall, lanky man who had just commented without looking at anyone specific, or seeming to direct his words at either Liam or Didier, jogged off and did not turn back.

"A bitter Bobcat?" asked Liam.

Didier nodded.

"Well, just fuck 'em."

"Hey, if I could have, I would have . . . but then I may never have joined Fast Trackers."

"Look who's being bad today!" Liam slapped Didier on the ass, and the two jogged off together to the starting corral.

The marathon event staff had truly tipped its hat to the local elite runners, offering a spacious corral with its own set of bathrooms and room to jog while waiting for the officials to start the race. All the top teams in the city were there. Many unfamiliar faces too. Long, lean runners with knitting needles for legs trotted back and forth, speaking in foreign tongues. Gossip had trickled down over the past week that the more established and moneyed teams had flown runners in from Africa to compete on their behalf. There were no rules against such practices. Liam looked around to see who had Urban Bobcats singlets on.

"Are you guys ready to do some damage?"

Zane emerged from one of the Portosans and stretched his calves out while talking to Didier and Liam.

"The wind has Liam worried." Didier rolled his eyes coyly at Liam as he spoke.

"The course goes in so many different directions, sweetie," assured Zane. "The wind will have to be at your back for huge stretches. It can't keep switching directions just to mow you down!"

"I just want everything to go right. We need to beat the Bobcats."

"Liam." Zane took his friend's hand. "You can't *make* us beat the Bobcats. You can only run the best race that you can today. It's as simple as that. Make it the run of your life. Enjoy the hell out of it. But it makes no sense in the world to worry about it."

"I get it. Careful, though, I already warned Didier about inspirational musings."

Liam knew he would be unable to ignore any yellow and black Bobcat uniforms in front of him, or coming up at his side, on the race course. But with 26.2 miles to travel, he would be in serious trouble if he sped up too soon on the enticement of another runner who may or may not have a smart racing strategy. Liam felt his head go dizzy and his stomach clench under the pressure. He was desperate for today to be a success. It wasn't that he believed Riser was out there in the universe looking down on the team, but Liam did have a spiritual need. He needed to believe in the power of togetherness, that the whole was greater than the sum of its parts.

The wind grew stronger, picking up the discarded wrappers from Clif Bars and energy gels that runners had tossed onto the lawn. A gust ripped open the roof of the big tent where trainers from Equinox gyms were encouraging anyone who would listen to stretch and stay loose before the start of the race. People panicked as the canvas tent toppled over.

Announcements were made that runners should huddle together for warmth; the officials emphasized the importance of preserving core body heat before a run of this distance. Zane quickly gathered all the Fast Trackers who had arrived in the corral and distributed extra sweatshirts that he had brought with him because of the weather forecast. Almost all the marathoners in this huge series of Staten Island fields had layered themselves in the ugly, old garments that are usually earmarked for painting or gardening projects. That was the standing-around gear. Under it, most serious racers wore shorts with netting—lighter and easier than having to wear cotton underwear—and a slit on the sides to facilitate movement, and a racing singlet made of a technical fiber that doesn't grow heavy with sweat. Once the gun went off, everyone would disrobe while crossing the Verrazano-Narrows. Serious racers were in as little clothing as possible by mile two of the race.

After the minor tent commotion, the distant hum of the national anthem signaled the start of the elite women's race. All of the men and all of the female recreational runners were told to use the bathrooms one final time and prepare to move from the staging area in the shadows of the bridge up toward the start of the race. In a quick survey of the corral, Liam could see Marvin, Gene, Zane, and Didier amid a sea of yellow and black. The Urban Bobcats looked long, lean, and hungry, and the Fast Trackers did not yet have its entire arsenal of fast runners on the line. Liam had seen Matthew and Ben milling around the complex earlier in the morning but worried that Ferdinand might have overslept or decided to bow out at the last minute. The top five runners from Fast Trackers needed to beat the Bobcats' second string runners, those placing sixth through tenth for their team. It did not matter if they had flown in a couple Kenyans to dazzle local spectators and further their image as the premier club in all of New York. But then, Liam thought, the usual Bobcat racers whom Fast Trackers did not have to compete with head-to-head would be pushed down from the top five to the top ten. His head swirled with the permutations, calculations, and the possibilities. *Oh well.* It was like Zane had said, the team would just produce the best that it could and not worry over what-ifs. But Liam had spent so much of his life mired in what-ifs. He had trouble keeping the bad thoughts at bay.

It was five minutes until the gun would go off. Marvin passed Liam an empty water bottle for him to piss in. Maybe it was nerves, but no matter how many times Liam used the restroom before a race, he always felt the urge to go once more at the starting line. He began to urinate discreetly into the bottle; the sensation was so freeing and so pleasurable that before he knew it the Evian water bottle overflowed with his piss. No one noticed as he dried his hands on his sweatshirt. For better or worse, he would throw the urine-filled bottle over the side of the bridge once the race started. Before final announcements were made, Liam wished Didier and Zane, who were both by his side, a good run, and he gave a thumbs-up to Marvin and Gene and scanned the crowd once more, noticing that Ferdinand had made his way to the start with Matthew and Ben.

Liam felt clearheaded and at peace as the starting shot fired and all of the racers jockeyed for position, a tangle of skinny arms and legs knocking into one another. He had hit his stride by the one-mile marker in the middle of the long span of the Verrazano-Narrows. The clock read 7:00, which was good. The first mile of the race went straight uphill, and adrenaline-fueled racers often killed their legs on the initial stretch of this difficult course. The bright sun had busted through the cloud cover, yellowing the shapeless mass of Brooklyn off to Liam's left. He would be running through Bay Ridge and Park Slope and Crown Heights and Williamsburg and Greenpoint—all in the first half of the race. He pushed the idea out of his head and kept a steady rhythm as he cut his way through a patch of runners to the first water station, just feet from the turn onto Brooklyn's Fourth Avenue.

Didier was running within a stride of him—something Liam had explicitly requested he not do—and they passed a small Dixie cup of water between them. It was an efficient buddy strategy, but Liam knew the many physical and mental hills and valleys he would travel in the almost three hours of marathon running and did not want to have to think about a fellow runner. Even Didier. He moved to the outer edge of the street, hugging a line of shade created by some five-floor tenements. This was the part of the course where Liam knew he had to breathe and move freely, expending no surplus energy. He would need to draw on his reserves starting at the bleak climb through the tunnel of the Fifty-ninth Street Bridge. But that was still almost eleven miles away.

They hit the four-mile marker at exactly 26:30. Perfection! A long-limbed runner in black and yellow Bobcat gear glided between Didier and Liam and spat over his shoulder. The wad of saliva grazed the side of Liam's face ever so slightly, but he decided to ignore the gesture. *Expend no energy. Expend no energy.* He kept repeating the mantra to himself. Didier had now inched in front of Liam, increasing his speed from about a 6:30 pace to a 6:20 pace. Liam felt his own leg turnover quicken in adjustment and noticed Didier eyeing the gangly spitter who had gotten a few yards ahead.

"No, no, no," Liam shouted. "Keep it steady, there's a lot of road ahead out there."

Didier nodded and slowed down so that they were again running stride for stride. A big group of Italian teenagers blasted Stevie Wonder from a boom box on the side of the avenue. Lyrics from "Sir Duke" cascaded through a torrent of applause. The kids were high-fiving runners and handing out wet paper towels and bananas. Someone had once described the marathon experience to Liam as being in your own movie. The training was the dues-paying, and the race was the reward. Novice runners inevitably got caught up in this hoopla during the first 10K of the marathon and flew through the crowds in an effortless wave of excitement. But twenty long miles lurked ahead after the 10K mark and promised to bludgeon runners with the potholes and warped pavement of New York City's merciless terrain. Liam kept his head steady and sipped on some Gatorade as they moved through the 10K mark in 40:42. They were on target for a steady 6:40 pace; Liam relaxed and enjoyed the spectators as they entered Park Slope.

The crowd lessened in volume and in spirit along the stretch of Bedford Avenue in Williamsburg. The pavement thinned from the wide expanse of Fourth Avenue to an uneven knot of road. For the next few miles the marathon toured unsung and relatively unvisited segments of New York City. There was the zigzag through the Polish shops of Greenpoint at mile twelve leading to the halfway point on the Pulaski Bridge, the charmless foot crossing that has the renown of being the only pedestrian bridge connecting the boroughs of Brooklyn and Queens.

The wind had died down by the time they reached the 13.1 mile marker. The less challenging weather conditions reinvigorated Liam. The road hooked sharply to the right as they ran down the Pulaski Bridge into Long Island City. A surprising number of spectators roared with delight, and Liam looked over to Didier and nodded. It was time. They both took a small tube of energy gel from the back pocket of their running shorts, ripped it open with their teeth, and quickly squeezed the contents of the packet into their mouths. Liam tried to gulp the thick Creamsicle-flavored ooze, but it stuck to the sides of his mouth, leaving an unnaturally sweet taste. He hated the energy gels but knew that he needed the quick sugar fix to fuel him for the rest of the run. Every runner used gels differently in a race, strategically positioning two or three of them throughout the course. Liam planned to take just one more, right before the dreaded twenty-mile mark.

As they crisscrossed between the old factories and hip new restaurants of Long Island City, the hulking shell of the Fifth-ninth Street Bridge loomed up ahead. The approach to this monstrosity was as endless as the bridge itself. Every few minutes or so, Liam noticed that Didier would gain a stride or two on him. Didier looked far fresher than Liam now felt; his skinny body was better suited to long-distance running than Liam's thin but more muscular build. The psychological burden of wondering whether he held Didier back was not something Liam wanted to shoulder. He motioned for his friend to pull ahead, but Didier looked befuddled and shook his head "no."

"Go, just go!" The speaking drained Liam of more energy. The sweat rolling off his brow stung his eyes.

"I'm getting you over that bridge whether you like it or not."

Didier ran ahead of Liam and grabbed a cup of Gatorade from the fluid station up ahead. The bridge was devoid of anything helpful to runners, except perhaps for the glimmer of Manhattan through its dirty girders. It was well over a mile and a half before the next opportunity to drink anything. Didier forced Liam to take two big gulps from the cup and to stick with him through the ramp leading up the bridge. Liam's calves cramped and a vise-like shock clamped down on the center of his back. He knew that he had trained well enough to collect himself and focus better on keeping his pace. But he let himself escape for just a few moments and thought of the wonderfulness of home, of being in the shower, and of lying on the bed watching the trees throw patterns on the neighboring tenements.

"C'mon, we're hitting the downhill. C'mon, this is where we're picking up the pace." Didier did not shout. He spoke in a matter-of-fact tone that announced that this was what must be. And Liam told himself that, at least at this juncture, following along with someone required far less of him than falling apart on his own. Liam gave himself over to Didier, and he believed that he was in quite good hands. His running form returned. The energy gel began to kick in as the swell of spectators along First Avenue announced the runners' entrance to Manhattan with a deafening thump. Everything looked up now, but Liam knew what was to come. This high feeling never lasted. No matter what the physical terrain, the marathon unfurls in 26.2 miles of hills and valleys.

As they passed Ninety-sixth Street, Liam noticed another yellow and black singlet coming up alongside Didier. The muscular man had a short but confident stride and clearly picked up his pace to make a commanding statement to the two Fast Trackers. Didier stole a look of disgust. Liam had no idea how many Fast Trackers were in front of him or behind him at this point. He figured that Zane and maybe Marvin were somewhere ahead of him, but barring divine intervention that would be all. And here was another Bobcat passing. Who knew how many were so far ahead that Liam had never even laid eyes on them? He couldn't hold back Didier. Even if the only thing gained was that some of Didier's old team members knew he had not lost his racing edge, that simple fact would be good enough for Liam. A true racer brought his soul out on the course, and it would be unconscionable for him to deny his training, his body, and his essence.

Liam looked ahead and pointed to the Bobcat who now ran a few feet ahead of them. When Liam caught Didier's eye, he nodded. Didier smiled and did not say a word as he went ahead alone. The nineteen-mile mark was within a block, and Liam felt more fortified than he had all day. Within a few minutes, Didier had made it far enough ahead to be beyond view, and Liam started to lose concentration.

To focus amid the thinning crowds of Upper First Avenue, Liam found an object at close distance, a bodega on the corner and then a jalopy parked ahead on the side of the road, and counted how many steps it took to reach it. Knowing that he couldn't allow his form to break down, Liam concentrated on the straightness of his back, the rhythm of his stride, and on keeping the equilibrium of his breathing steady and unstrained.

The dreaded Willis Avenue Bridge then presented him with another uphill. The climb was worsened by the aching throb of his feet against the metal grates of the bridge, which was covered ineffectively by a flimsy red mat. Liam stared down at the murky water beneath him, following it toward the silvery mud on the shorelines across the bridge. When he looked at the clock at the end of the bridge—the twenty-mile mark where runners famously hit the wall—it read exactly 2:15. Liam had just under forty-five minutes to complete the final 10K. Given a fresh start, he usually clocked about thirty-seven minutes for a 10K. What his body could do after running through twenty miles of uneven city streets was a different story. Liam tried not to get too far ahead of himself in calculating the mile splits needed to assure a sub-three-hour finish time. It felt so reachable and so easy. But a successful marathon is not about the easy or the safe. It's about the unknown, and it's about discipline. It's about the preservation of faith. As he watched runner after runner who had been ahead of him on the race course succumb to the pants and cramps of exhaustion, Liam reminded himself that nothing could be taken for granted. Nothing was in the bag.

A makeshift crew of rowdy teenagers break-danced to a surging remix of "Thriller" as the marathon course wound its way back into Manhattan. Liam tried not to think about how many street signs would pass by before he entered Central Park for the final two miles of the race. *It's just mental. Your body is trained . . . Let your head do the rest.* He raked his brain for any inspirational thought that might be available. The sun fell into his eyes. It was 129th Street. Seventy more blocks to Central Park South. *Stop that! You just need to keep your head in this for the next half hour.* Liam watched the shoulder blades of a taut man in an "Italy" singlet as he raced around Marcus Garvey Park in Harlem and then, after passing that runner, high-fived a gray-haired black woman singing in the Hallelujah Choir outside a church on 117th Street. Everything hurt at this point. His feet burned with the blisters between his toes, and the stabbing pain in his lower back came and went every few blocks. Distractions could occupy him for no more than seconds at a time. The twenty-fourth mile of the race, the one following the long upgrade through Museum Mile before Fifth Avenue deposited runners into Central Park at Engineers' Gate, proved the most difficult.

Liam had the slight boost of knowing that just inside the park, right behind the Metropolitan Museum of Art, the Fast Trackers had their water station. He refused to look fatigued for his teammates. When he arrived, the huge masses of people looked like a liquid wave moving in and out of focus. The jumble of empty water cups and the outstretched arms of his team members became an instant blur. He could not pinpoint one specific face, even as he heard scores of people shouting his name. What had lifted his spirit for about half a mile had gone by in about twenty steps and now two more miles of New York City came between him and his goal. From somewhere deep within he culled the resources to quicken his foot turnover and to move his arms faster. He had read once in a sports magazine that if you pumped your arms faster, then your legs would pick up the pace as well.

And then it happened. He could not believe his eyes. Zane was slumped over at the top of Cat Hill, just a few hundred yards beyond the Fast Tracker water depot. He was rubbing the tops of his thighs and whimpering in pain.

"Run with me, Zane!" Liam shouted out.

Zane looked up halfheartedly and shook his head no. He tried to shoo Liam on with a quick wave of his hand. Liam refused to leave his friend behind. After the months of training as a team, Zane needed to finish this race and to finish it with strength and grace.

"You can finish. It's less than two miles, Zane. I am getting you through this."

Zane was not moving, so Liam had to walk over to him. As soon as he stopped running, Liam felt a cramping through his legs. His feet were on fire.

"I'm not leaving you here. And you're not causing me to sacrifice my sub-three-hour marathon. So get a move on."

Liam took Zane by the elbow and started to jog. They were jogging very slowly at first, barely faster than Liam could walk, but before they reached the bottom of Central Park they had picked it up to about a 7:30 pace. The race clock at the twenty-five-mile mark, just before runners exit the park and make their way onto Central Park South, read just over 2:51. They had just under nine minutes to complete 1.2 miles. Now Liam did all sorts of mathematical computations. A 7-minute mile pace would be fine but not an 8-minute mile pace. He could feel his heart pounding.

"C'mon!" Coaching Zane through the last bit of the race was taking his mind off the myriad aches and pains of his own body.

"Just focus on Columbus Circle. Just keep your eyes up there, Zane!"

The crowd thundered with applause along Central Park South. It rivaled First Avenue for the volume and enthusiasm of its spectators. A sign along the road said there were 800 meters—one half of a mile—to go. Liam glanced at his watch. It read 2:56:15. Liam could not figure out exactly what pace they needed to run or at what pace they might currently be going, but he knew he was not going to chance it.

"We can't leave anything out here on the course, Zane! Just imagine two laps on the track. It's less than that!"

They made the sharp right turn at Columbus Circle and entered Central Park once again. As they approached the park's interior running loop, a final sign said 400 METERS TO FINISH, and they muscled through the last set of rolling hills toward the balloons outside Tavern on the Green. Liam felt splintering pain down his side and through his back. His body had stiffened so that it seemed as if his legs could not eke out one more stride. Cruelly, the last feet of the race were uphill. The clock ticked off as they approached, side by side. Liam yelled to Zane not to slow down but to hurl himself through the finish. Every second would count.

Liam finally stopped his watch after they had crossed the series of timing mats at the finish line. 2:59:15! Amazingly, they had managed a 6-minute pace for the final half mile. As his body relaxed for the first time in hours, Liam felt a stabbing throb in the small of his back and could tell that a series of blood blisters had formed between his toes. He offered his neck to a beaming volunteer who adorned him with a medal for finishing the race. Once they had cleared the crowded finish line area, Liam turned his tired body toward his teammate and hugged Zane furiously. They walked gingerly toward the baggage claim area, supporting each other, arm-in-arm, like injured soldiers.

THE FINISH LINE

As he finished dressing for the party, Liam splashed some water on his face and raced his fingers through his hair in the small bathroom of his Grove Street apartment. He maneuvered around the little marble sink and took a piss in the toilet before checking out his appearance one last time.

"You could not look any hotter if we chiseled your jaw out of some fine Italian marble." Didier stood at the bathroom door and presented Liam with a tall glass of Belgian beer. There was almost nothing more fulfilling or pleasurable than the pre-cocktail cocktail—also known informally as "apartment tailgating." Liam thought that he picked up this predilection from watching the movie *Swingers* too many times as a teenager.

"Don't give me a hard time, Mr. Man," Liam said, twisting Didier's nipple playfully. "And put on a nice shirt. We have to get to Gary's in the next hour or else we'll be well beyond fashionably late. He can be a little idiosyncratic when it comes to punctuality."

"I think I am going to stay in, Liam. I have been a little worn out from the spate of Fast Tracker events recently. Between the runs, the races, the social events . . . I just need a little downtime tonight."

"You can take a Fast Tracker sabbatical after tonight, dearest. Promise. I need you with me tonight, and this will be fabulous anyway. Gary throws amazing fêtes, and I am sure there will be a theme and some unbelievable food and holiday fare. I can't go without you. Plus, it will mean a lot for Gary and for Monroe to see you there. This is the first official event that they have thrown as a 'couple,' and they will need all the reinforcements and support that they can get."

"I am really happy for both of them, Liam. I really am. And I will do a double date with them any time that you choose, but these types of large parties where fifty people are crammed into a room meant for twenty are not my cup of tea—and they are awful for socializing or catching up."

"Look, I am not trying to win an argument with you here based on logic, Didier." Liam placed his two open hands around Didier's waist and could not fathom the tone or perfection of his boyfriend's body. No matter how many times he touched this specimen of beauty, Liam still managed to be surprised by each sinew and vein. "Would you please do this for me? It would mean a lot."

Liam heard himself say the words and realized how true they were. It *did* matter to him—and that fact alone sent a frightening chill down his spine. He thought about the fact that they were well past his ninety-day expiration date. The relationship had had its twists and turns, but Liam was proud of himself for giving it his all. Now he needed to know that Didier was in this too.

"It's just a party, Liam. You will know every single person there. You do not need me—not in the slightest. Those guys are your family. I am still like a hanger-on, an awkward guest at the dinner table."

"I can't believe that you are doing this to me now, Didier. You knew about this party for weeks. We should have left fifteen minutes ago and now you are pulling the rug from under my feet and expecting me to smile and enjoy the party on my own. Well, no! It is not that simple. People in relationships do these types of things for one another."

Didier's eyes widened and he took a step back, looking uncomfortable in the incandescent light of the hallway.

Liam realized that he had said too much. Neither of them had placed a definitive label or elaborated on their personal expectations of their time together. Liam felt raw and exposed and alone in the strange silence that ensued. Turning and walking toward the bedroom, Liam took three successive gulps of his beer. The Chimay tasted cold and bitter in his mouth.

"Liam, don't walk away . . . It really is *just* a party. And I will be here waiting for you when you get back."

"It just might be that I need more than that, Didier."

"More than someone who wants to be with you? More than someone who will be here when you come home late at night? Is there anything more than that?"

"I saw the way your whole body contorted at the word *relationship*. I may be a little younger than you are, but I am no dilettante. I am not a novice at these games. And I know what I need, Didier."

"Liam, it has been a ridiculous and tumultuous year for me. My marriage has fallen apart; I switched running teams; I upended my entire life; and I know that I want you. Isn't that enough?"

"I don't know. I want it to be, but I know myself too well. I deserve something more here. Oddly, Didier, I think you deserve more too. When it is right, it is right. I may be a hopeless romantic or just hopeless, but I happen to believe all that."

"You are just tired and worked up over this party and what people will think, Liam. Who gives a fuck about what other people think, Liam?"

"I know. I know . . . But this is not about what other people think at all, unfortunately. It is about what I think. Good-bye, Didier."

****

Someone had left the door to the apartment building ajar, and Liam walked through the main hall without ringing the buzzer. The party had started over an hour and a half ago, so he knew he would not be surprising anyone. A little wreath of red berries decorated the flaking paint on Gary's apartment door. Liam waited outside for a minute, certain he was not at all up for the jolliness of the occasion. He had just begun to turn to leave when Gary opened the door and saw him standing there. With a hearty laugh, Gary threw his arms around Liam and dragged him inside the apartment.

"This one was trying to leave before he even arrived! I know this is no longer Central Park chic, but I still know how to throw a party!"

Gary immediately handed Liam a beer. In his nervousness, Liam swallowed the beer in two greedy swigs. Fast Trackers—mostly the young, cute, fast ones whom Gary notoriously adored—had congregated in trios and quartets across the 400-square-foot apartment. People sat on the futon bed, leaned up against the trash can in the kitchen, and perched on the little ledges of Gary's nightstand and bookcase. True, the place was jam-packed, but the crowded studio had proven itself a more graceful and festive party space than the cold, labyrinthine splendor of his old Fifth Avenue digs. Liam gave Gary a big kiss and then noticed Monroe dishing eggnog into a big serving bowl in the teeny kitchen.

Liam had not spoken to Monroe in a couple of weeks due to the crazy double issue that he had been tackling at the magazine—twice as much content as usual and three different editors taking vacations because of the holiday season. As Liam went over to lend Monroe a hand, his best friend shook his head testily and sashayed with the big glass bowl above his head across the studio to where Gary stood.

The two men danced around each other like awkward teenagers. This party clearly did serve as the stage for their coming-out publicly as a couple. Liam looked on and hoped that their romance would last. They had both so clearly earned this small chance at true happiness.

"Let's toast!" Gary said, grabbing some mugs of eggnog from Monroe and whisking Mitch and Zane and Liam off into a far corner for a group moment. The intensity of Gary's happiness startled Liam.

"To what?" asked Liam. "To *almost* winning, to *almost* finding love, to *almost* figuring out how to make life work?"

Liam did not know why he had blurted out anything. That was not the plan; he had promised himself on the walk over to the party that he would not get emotional. He tried to leave all his conflicted feelings about Didier on the cold December streets of New York City. Liam did not want to spoil Gary's big holiday party, but his emotions kept seesawing up and down. He hated that so little in life ever seemed to turn out right. The smashing defeat to the Urban Bobcats at the marathon. Tonight's fight with Didier in the wake of his spur-of-the-moment decision to skip the party, in what Liam had innately sensed was Didier's decision not to get into anything too deep too quickly. And if Liam really examined the situation in Didier's life—all the change that had gone on in the last few months alone—he could not really blame him. Didier deserved the free time to sow his wild oats and live an exuberant gay life in New York before settling down to the responsibilities of a boyfriend. But in a moment of agonizing self-flagellation, Liam could not help but wonder why it was that people so seldom got what they wanted.

"Toast to what? To the future? To something different down the line? To the possibility of greatness? To happiness?" Liam had started to well up, and people were looking at him stealthily, with a sad combination of judgment and pity.

"No, silly," said Gary. "I don't toast to what might be; I toast to what is. I want to toast to us. To this party. To surviving. You guys are my life, kid. We are what each of us will always have. And let me tell you *that* is worth more than you know. That is worth this whole fucking mug of eggnog—and all the booze in my liquor cabinet!"

They drank and talked and lit the Charlie Brown Christmas tree that rested on Gary's radiator. Someone had turned on the Yule Log and bars of "Have Yourself a Merry Little Christmas" wrapped their way through the room.

Noticing some wet snow floating through the black, bare trees in Gary's makeshift backyard, Liam slipped outside into the garden. He stood on the little square slab of cement that acted as a patio and quietly watched the first sign of the new season. The snow was weak but growing, struggling to become a truer version of itself, and Liam was so happy to bear witness. This was why he knew he would always live in New York. Seeing things change had become a part of his identity. He walked out across the dead garden grass and felt the newborn snowflakes turn to water on his skin. Liam lifted his head to the sky and spun in circles as a galaxy of white filled the night air. Gary shouted something indiscernible from inside, and Liam looked back in to see Monroe grabbing Gary and positioning him under a little sprig of mistletoe amid the crowded party. The night had begun to unfold, and people grasped desperately at whatever possibilities and prospects were within their reach. Liam wanted to watch the scene in quiet from the courtyard for a just a little while longer—to savor the moment. As he stuck out his tongue to taste the falling snow, a crop of Fast Trackers appeared at the window, pressing their noses intently against the glass and hollering at him to come back in and join the party.

THE MILES

Robert Lennon

ABOUT THIS GUIDE

The suggested questions are included
to enhance your group's reading
of Robert Lennon's *The Miles*.

DISCUSSION QUESTIONS

1. Liam admits to himself that he had felt lost prior to joining Fast Trackers and hopes the club will give him a sense of purpose. How is that sense of purpose defined—fitness, competitive focus, love, or something less tangible? Does joining the club get him there, and, if so, how? Do you get the sense, by the end of the book, that Liam has found what he is searching for?

2. Throughout *The Miles*, Liam intimates at what running has done for him and how it has changed the shape of his life. In what ways is running a metaphor for the journeys and the purpose that one seeks in life, and where does that journey lead Liam and the running club in this novel?

3. Monroe and Liam have a best friends' relationship that seems, at times, to border on flirtation and romantic love. As a result, Monroe has a natural jealousy over Liam's relationship to Fast Trackers. What does this jealousy say about their relationship, about the nature of gay male friendship, and about human nature, more generally?

4. When Liam brings Monroe into his family life, there appears to be a huge disconnect between what his family offers and what Liam feels in return. What tension is at play between Liam and his family, and what do religion, suburbia, and his upbringing symbolize to Liam? What does New York City represent to Liam, and what has city life offered him that is in contrast to all that came before?

5. What does the finish line represent in *The Miles*? Discuss the various people whom Liam clashes into at the literal finish lines that thread their way through this novel and what each of those instances represents. There is also the ending of the book, which is entitled "The Finish Line"—how has Liam changed from the first finish line in the book to this last one? In both the start and end of the book, Liam is on the outside looking in at the club. Discuss what has changed in terms of Liam as a character, the club as an entity, and the other main characters in the book.

6. The members at the "inner circle" of the club seem to belittle Gene and talk a lot behind his back. Liam reflects in the book that circles of friends need to have one of their members on the periphery as an outsider to poke fun at. Do you think this is, in fact, true? And if so, is it unique to gay male culture or a truth in any social grouping? Can making fun of friends help groups bond and bring people together and, if so, in what ways?

7. From the outset of the novel, Didier personifies the un-gettable object that Liam can't stop thinking about or pursuing. Why is it so important to Liam to chase someone who appears so unattainable? Does Liam ever, in fact, "get" Didier? What do you think transpired in their relationship, and do you think it changed Liam? If so, how?

8. Much of *The Miles* is concerned with effecting change in one's life and moving things forward—running miles, racing faster, finding love, becoming a stronger person. On a literal basis, Riser embodies that transformation most completely. Do you think that his story line is a cautionary tale of these impulses taken

to an extreme, or does he represent something different? Do you think that the members of Fast Trackers did all that good friends could do to help him?

9. Monroe and Gary both function, at different times and in different ways throughout the novel, as father figures to Liam. What does Liam get out of these relationships and what do Monroe and Gary get out of their respective friendships with Liam? How do the relationships differ from one another, and is it significant that these two men end up together? If so, why?

10. Fast-forward a year in time. Which of the relationships in the book do you think will be stronger, and which do you think may end? Focus specifically on Gary and Monroe; Monroe and Liam; and the "Four Musketeers" of Liam, Gary, Zane, and Mitch.